HIS SOUL TO KEEP

*A Frankie Dawson P.I. Mystery Thriller,
Book One*

Melinda Woodhall

Melinda Woodhall

Melinda Woodhall
Visit my website at www.melindawoodhall.com
Printed in the United States of America
First Printing: November 2022
Creative Magnolia

CHAPTER ONE

Josie Atkins leaned forward, straining to hear her father's voice, which was little more than a hoarse whisper. Blinking back hot tears as he clung to her trembling hand, she forced herself to look down into his emaciated face and dark, sunken eyes.

A year earlier, Dwight Atkins had been a brawny, handsome man who at thirty-eight years old had still been in the prime of his life.

But that had been before the smoker's cough he'd developed over the years had suddenly gotten worse.

Before he'd started losing weight and could no longer make it to the end of his usual morning jog or put in a full day's work without growing fatigued.

Cutting his two-pack-a-day habit back to just two cigarettes a day hadn't solved the problem.

By the time he'd gone to see Dr. Habersham, it had been too late. The lung cancer had taken hold and his prognosis had been bleak. Months of agonizing treatments hadn't managed to rid him of the cancer that had ravaged his body.

According to the doctor, it had been too little, too late.

"I'm sorry, honey..."

The raspy words rose from dry, cracked lips, and Josie reached for the cup of water on the bedside table.

"You don't have to say anything, Dad."

She held the straw to his mouth so he could take a sip as he lay limply on the narrow bed.

"Just rest," she said softly. "You can tell me whatever it is later. Once you're feeling better."

Struggling to clear his throat, Dwight shook his head.

"There might not be...a later," he managed, his voice stronger now. "I need you to know...I'm sorry. I haven't done right by you. You deserved better..."

His words trailed off as he sucked in a shallow breath.

Before he could speak again, Josie heard soft footsteps on the hardwood floor behind her.

She looked back to see her mother hovering in the doorway of what had once been Dwight's home office, but which now served as his sickroom, complete with a hospital bed and a table full of medications.

"Let your father get some sleep," Cheryl Atkins admonished, crossing the room to set a fresh pitcher of water on the table before turning to her daughter.

Reaching forward, she tucked a strand of dark blonde hair behind Josie's ear, studying the high cheekbones, pointed chin, and widow's peak that so closely resembled her own.

"Remember what Dr. Habersham said."

Josie's back stiffened as she stared into her mother's sad, blue eyes and heard the resignation in her voice.

So, she's giving up on Dad just like that?

Anger rushed in, constricting Josie's throat as the doctor's voice echoed inside her head.

"He could go at any time. Likely it'll only be a matter of days. Maybe a few weeks if he's lucky."

The verdict had been given in Dr. Habersham's usual, blunt manner. The older man had made no attempt to soften his devastating words.

"Let her stay."

Dwight's plea drew both sets of blue eyes back to the bed.

With a stiff nod, Cheryl stepped away but didn't leave the room. She stood poised as if ready to swoop in and intervene at the first sign of distress.

Gripping her hand even more tightly, Dwight pulled Josie closer, his eyes suddenly bright and intense.

"I'm proud of you, my girl," he said, his words labored. "I haven't told you near enough, but I am. You're about the only thing I've done that's good. The one thing I got right."

"Don't say that, Dad," Josie protested, unable to stop a tear from trickling down her cheek. "You've done lots of good things. You run your business, you're on the city council-"

He winced and shook his head.

"None of that...matters," he said in a halting voice. "I wish I'd known that when I was your age. It's too late for me...but not for you. You'll be a woman before you know it..."

His face twisted in pain.

"I wanted to be there...to see you grow up," he managed to choke out. "There are so many things I...want to tell you."

Cheryl stepped forward as a racking cough seized him.

"That's enough," she said, firmly pulling Josie back from the bed. "Go to your room and let your father rest."

A protest rose to Josie's lips, then died away as she saw the grimace on her father's pale face and noted the sweat beading on his forehead.

Reluctantly, she allowed herself to be pushed toward the door, not wanting to cause her father any more pain.

Once out in the hall, she hesitated at the bottom of the stairs, then stomped up to her room.

It didn't feel right to be leaving her father's side when he so obviously wanted her there.

Flopping onto her bed, she grabbed up her remote and switched on the television.

A reporter was standing outside the Barrel Creek Police Department speaking to the camera in a somber voice.

"Volunteers discovered more human bones along the banks of the Wolf River today as a new restoration project got underway-"

Josie muted the sound with an impatient jab of her thumb on the remote, unable to concentrate.

Normally, she would have been eager to hear all about the recovered bones and the growing speculation that a local serial killer had gone undetected for years.

Mysteries had always intrigued her.

When she'd been younger, Josie had read every Nancy Drew book on the shelves at the Barrel Creek Elementary School library, and lately, she'd started listening to true crime podcasts on her phone after lights out, staying up long after her mother thought she was asleep.

But even the possibility that a serial killer may be stalking her own little town couldn't distract Josie from the grief that gripped her at the thought of losing her father.

Lying motionless on her bed, she exhaled and closed her eyes. They shot open again as she heard the soft murmur of voices coming from her mother's room.

Confused, she stood and crept down the hall, then stopped outside her mother's bedroom door and peered inside.

The big room was dim, lit only by the moonlight streaming through the window, but she could see it was empty.

"I don't have much time..."

Josie jumped as a voice spoke from the shadows, then she relaxed with sudden understanding.

The voice was coming from what appeared to be a small white speaker on the bedside table.

Only it wasn't a speaker, it was a monitor. The type of monitor new parents used to listen out for their baby's cries.

Her mother had been using it to listen out for Dwight during the night. She must have left it on.

Looking back to make sure the hall was still empty, Josie closed the bedroom door and crossed the room.

The monitor's noise indicator light blinked on as she reached the bed.

"I need to make amends."

Her father's voice shook with resolve.

"*I can't go to my grave with Franny's death on my conscience. I need to speak to Frankie Dawson before it's too late.*"

Eyes widening, Josie sank onto the big double bed.

"*What are you saying, Dwight?*"

"*I'm saying Franny's death was no accident. She was murdered...just like those other girls. And I know who did it.*"

Too shocked to move, Josie stared at the monitor, holding her breath as she waited for her mother's response.

"*But Franny died of an overdose. She wasn't murdered.*"

Cheryl sounded incredulous. It was clear she thought Dwight must be hallucinating or making the whole thing up.

"*That's what he wanted everyone to believe. He set it all up.*"

"*Who? Who set it up? Who killed Franny?*"

Josie leaned forward, holding her breath as she waited for her father's reply, then quickly recoiled as a series of harsh, hacking coughs exploded through the monitor.

Her knee jarred the nightstand, sending the monitor tumbling to the carpeted floor where it fell face down, muffling her father's raspy words.

Dropping to her knees, she felt under the bed, pulling the monitor out too late to hear the name he'd spoken.

Cheryl was already shooting another question at him.

"*Why didn't you tell the police...or Frankie?*"

Doubt had entered her voice.

"*I was in too far. I didn't know who to trust...didn't know what he would do. And when the M.E. called it an accidental overdose, I had no way to prove it wasn't.*"

Dwight's words were growing harder to decipher.

7

"That's not all..."

He sucked in a noisy breath.

"Other girls have gone missing since then. I'm not sure, but I think...it could be their bones...along the Wolf River."

The effort to speak seemed to have drained Dwight's energy, leaving his voice thin and fragile.

Pushing herself to her feet, Josie felt her stomach twist at the thought of the human bones found along the riverbank.

"If you're telling the truth, we have to go to the police."

Cheryl's pronouncement was followed by an extended silence that worried Josie.

Had it all been too much for her father? Was he okay?

Then the monitor once again blinked to life, filling the room with a hoarse, whispered warning.

"You know it's too dangerous to involve...the police. I tried to tell the feds, but I don't think they believed me. You have to tell Frankie Dawson. He deserves to know...the truth."

As the monitor fell silent, Josie detected the soft rumble of an engine outside. Crossing to the window, she studied the shadows in the back yard.

A car door slammed somewhere out of view.

The sound was followed by a loud knock, and then the faint *tap, tap, tap* of footsteps on the hardwood floor as her mother hurried toward the front door.

Josie was halfway across the bedroom when her mother screamed. Reaching for the door, she heard the gunshot.

"You couldn't keep your mouth shut, could you, Dwight?"

The angry words carried up the stairs as Josie stepped

onto the landing and looked down into the foyer.

She stifled a scream at the sight of her mother sprawled across the floor, her head resting in a growing pool of blood.

"Why couldn't you just die and leave us all in peace?"

Panic bloomed in Josie's chest as she tried to make out her father's muffled response. Her throat began to close, making it hard for her to breathe.

Fighting back a wave of dizziness, she stumbled toward her bedroom, desperate to reach her phone.

I'll call 911. They'll send help. They'll send an ambulance.

A loud crash sounded below as Josie stepped into her room and looked around for her phone.

Hadn't she left it on her bed? Or had she left it downstairs?

Holding back a sob, she forced herself to think.

"You really think I'd let you ruin everything?" the man yelled. "You think I didn't know you were going to tell Frankie Dawson? That you were going to rat me out?"

Josie spotted her purse hanging from the back of her desk chair and lunged toward it. Her phone had to be in there.

Digging inside the small, black bag with a trembling hand, she managed to find the phone and carry it with her as she made her way back onto the landing.

Her numb fingers were already tapping out 9-1-1.

"It's a shame it had to end like this, after everything we've been through. But you gave me no choice."

The anger in the man's voice had begun to dissipate. When he spoke again, he sounded almost regretful.

"I'll have to try to make this look like a murder-suicide."

Josie's heart stopped at his next words.

"Where's your daughter?"

She pressed a hand to her mouth to stifle the sob rising in her throat and inched backward toward her mother's room.

"She's not here, and she doesn't know anything," her father gasped. "She's just...a little girl. Leave her out of this."

The man barked out an ugly laugh.

"She's old enough," he scoffed. "And real pretty, too. I couldn't help noticing the last time I saw her in town."

"Keep away from Josie, or–"

A sudden gunshot cut off Dwight's words.

"This is 9-1-1. What's your emergency?"

Josie looked down at the phone in her hand, her eyes wide with shock and disbelief as she listened to the heavy footsteps below. They were coming toward the stairs.

"Hello? You've reached 9-1-1. What's your emergency?"

Scrambling back into her mother's room, Josie dropped to the ground and rolled under the bed, still clutching the phone in her hand.

She peered out from her hiding place just as a pair of thick-soled, black boots came into view. They stopped in the doorway for a long beat before moving on down the hall.

"Is anyone there? Do you need an ambulance or the police?"

Josie ignored the voice and squeezed her eyes shut, recalling her father's warning.

"You know it's too dangerous to involve the police..."

Gripping the phone, she tapped *End Call*, not sure who she could trust, but knowing her dad had been right to be afraid.

Footsteps sounded again on the stairs, and Josie remained under the bed until she heard the car door slam again, and the engine rumble to life.

Crawling out of her hiding place, she hurried down the stairs, stopping first to check her mother's pulse with cold, shaking fingers, before moving into her father's old office.

As she approached the hospital bed, she saw the gun and the blood, and she began to scream.

CHAPTER TWO

Frankie Dawson drove north on I-55 toward Memphis, passing the exit to Graceland with an instinctive nod in the King's direction, his neck stiff, and his eyes heavy from twelve straight hours behind the wheel.

As the rain pelted down on the Mustang's windshield, Frankie kept his foot heavy on the gas, spurred on by the growing sense that time was running out.

Dwight Atkins was expecting him, and he couldn't afford to be late. His old friend didn't have much time left.

They'd both wasted too much time already running from the past and nursing old wounds. It was time to make amends while he still had the chance.

The idea of driving up to see Dwight had taken hold a few weeks before when his mother had called to check in on him for the first time since she'd moved up to Chesterville, Tennessee to help out with Granny Davis, who'd recently been diagnosed with Alzheimer's.

At first, Arlene Dawson had been eager to share the latest gossip from the Memphis suburb where Frankie had grown up, but then her enthusiasm had dimmed.

"You know I hate to be the bearer of bad news, but I have

it on the best authority that Dwight Atkins has *lung cancer.* The poor boy's been given only a few weeks to live."

Of course, Dwight was no longer a boy. He was close to forty years old. But he was still young, wasn't he? Only a few years older than Frankie. Definitely too young to die.

"Granny's prayer group added him to her list over the weekend. I tried to remind her what good friends you and Dwight used to be, but I don't think she remembered."

Frankie couldn't blame his grandmother. He hadn't mentioned Dwight to anyone for more than fifteen years.

Guilt over his long-standing intention to reconnect with Dwight had started to fester after the phone call.

It was another failure to add to his growing list. Just another *might-have-been* that never would be.

The realization had stung. Life was passing him by, and it seemed as if all the people he cared about were slipping away, too.

Then, out of the blue, Dwight had called.

"I need to speak to you, Frankie. There's something I need to tell you. And there's a favor I need to ask. But it has to be soon. Dr. Habersham says I don't have long."

Now, a few weeks on and a half-dozen calls and emails later, Frankie was on his way to see the man who'd been his best friend all through high school.

With luck, they'd get the chance to reconnect before it was too late. And, if he was honest, he had to admit he was also hoping the trip would help him clear his head.

The breakdown of his marriage had left him reeling, and with his two-year wedding anniversary quickly approaching, Frankie had been fighting the urge to start drinking again.

He was counting on the road trip to keep him sober.

That, and the support of his new partner.

Keeping the wheel steady, Frankie risked a glance toward the black Labrador retriever sleeping in the backseat.

The dog had been a last-ditch effort to save his marriage.

A thoughtless gesture really, considering everything that had happened between him and Peyton over the last six months, but Frankie had been desperate.

He hadn't realized just how desperate until she had slammed the door of their apartment in his face, with both Frankie and the confused dog on the outside.

It was then that Frankie had accepted that his marriage, and the perfect life he'd built with Peyton, might well and truly be over.

That night he'd driven the Lab back to the shelter, fully intending to return the dog before heading to the nearest bar to drown his sorrows.

Instead, he'd sat outside in the Mustang for close to an hour while the Lab had fidgeted in the backseat. Finally, he'd turned to meet the dog's puzzled eyes, studying the faint scar running down the side of his soft, furry face.

"That scar makes you look like a real badass, you know," he'd said, liking the way the Lab cocked his head as if listening carefully. "I bet you'd have some messed-up stories to tell if you could talk."

Of course, Frankie had plenty of his own scars collected over his years as a private detective, although the gunshot wounds and broken bones had all eventually healed.

He wished he could say the same about the rest of the damage he'd sustained. The kind that didn't leave a scar. At least not on the outside.

Something had told him the Lab could relate. Feeling slightly better, he'd turned and started the engine, instinctively heading toward Pete Barker's house.

His old partner had winced when he'd opened the door to see the two forlorn figures on his doorstep.

"She kicked you out?"

"Yeah, she dumped me. Big surprise, huh?"

Nodding to the Lab by Frankie's feet, Barker had raised a bushy eyebrow.

"Who's that?"

"My new partner," Frankie had shot back without missing a beat. "You retired on me, so I had to find some new talent."

Barker's eyebrow had risen even higher.

"A *dog's* your new partner?"

"This isn't just any dog."

Frankie had been instantly indignant.

"He's a goddamn prodigy, man," he'd sputtered. "A born genius. A canine Sherlock Holmes."

The name had hung in the air.

"Sherlock," he repeated softly, reaching down to scratch the dog's head. "Yeah...Sherlock H. Dawson. The newest partner at Dawson and Dawson Investigations."

Shaking his head, Barker had waved them inside with a shrug of his thick shoulders.

"Yeah, sure. Whatever you say. I'll tell Reggie to make up the bed in the guest room. She'll be happy to see you."

Frankie suspected that only Barker's unwavering support, and Sherlock's quiet, reassuring presence, had kept him from falling off the wagon that night.

And now, as he drove in the rain through Memphis, he was glad he hadn't had to make the long drive from southern Florida to eastern Tennessee all alone.

Speeding down I-69, he passed the exit toward downtown, picturing the neon lights along Beale Street even as he steered the Mustang north toward Chesterville.

He knew he should drive straight to the house Granny Davis had lived in for close to sixty years. Afterall, his mother and grandmother would be waiting.

But he was restless.

Maybe he'd stop by his uncle's bar first and grab a drink.

Nothing alcoholic, of course. Just something to quench the thirst that had settled into the back of his throat when Peyton had kicked him out, and which had never quite gone away.

The rain had stopped by the time he nosed the Mustang into one of many empty spaces outside Rowdy's Music Bar & Grill. Switching off the engine, Frankie studied the flashing neon sign.

Live Music Every Night!

He cracked the window, letting in a rush of damp April air, then opened the door and climbed out, leaving Sherlock staring at him sleepily from the backseat.

As he pushed his way through the front door, Frankie

wasn't surprised to see that the place was almost empty. It was Sunday night, after all, a night when most people were at home watching TV and dreading the workweek ahead.

A sudden image popped into his head. Peyton curled up on the sofa eating takeaway. A wave of longing and regret hit him squarely in the chest, making it hard for him to breathe.

Heading toward the bar, he nodded at the bartender, a handsome man in a skintight *Rowdy's Music Bar & Grill* t-shirt who was busy flirting with two young women in short skirts and cowboy boots.

"Hey, Jasper," he called out. "Long time, no see."

He hadn't expected the local heartthrob to still be working for his uncle. Maybe things hadn't changed that much in his hometown after all.

"Have you seen Rowdy tonight?"

The bartender flashed him a smile.

"Looks like you're in luck tonight, Frankie. I saw the boss stroll in about five minutes ago. He usually takes Sundays off. I'll go get him."

Frankie watched as Jasper disappeared into the back, followed by appreciative giggles from the women at the bar.

Moments later a big man in a long-sleeved denim shirt was standing at his elbow.

"Frankie, my boy! Where the hell have you been?"

Rowdy Dawson pulled Frankie in for a bear hug, his thick body twice the size of Frankie's skinny frame.

"Shame on you for not coming back sooner," the man roared, landing a cheerful punch on Frankie's shoulder.

Wincing, Frankie stepped out of his uncle's range.

"I bet your Ma and your Granny's glad to have you back home," Rowdy continued. "Colton will be sorry he missed you. You wouldn't even recognize that boy now. He's a real handsome fella. Takes after his old man."

"I bet he does," Frankie said, picturing his older cousin, who'd always been a little more handsome, a little taller, and a lot more muscular than he'd been. "I'll make sure to catch up with him while I'm in town."

Turning back to the bar, he motioned to Jasper. Ignoring all the tempting bottles around him, he ordered a club soda with lime, relieved when the bartender set the drink in front of him without comment.

"So, have you seen Dwight Atkins yet?" Rowdy asked, lowering his voice. "Your ma was in here the other night and told me you were coming to see him. I hear he's pretty sick."

Wondering why his mother felt the need to broadcast his business to the rest of the world, Frankie shook his head.

"No, I just got in, but I'm hoping to catch up with Dwight soon," Frankie said. "When I found out he was sick, I thought it was about time I paid him a visit."

"Well, you'd better hurry up."

The words came from a man sitting at the end of the bar.

Frankie turned, not sure the comment had been meant for him, but the man met his gaze and lifted his glass of beer in a sardonic salute, before taking a long slurp.

"I was out at the Atkins place earlier today," the man added after he'd wiped the foam from his upper lip. "I think it's fair to say he's not long for this world."

Meeting the man's cold eyes, Frankie frowned.

"And who are you? Some kind of psychic?"

The man produced a thin smile.

"I'm Gordon Habersham, Dwight's doctor."

The name rang a bell, but it took Frankie a full ten seconds to place the face. The man hadn't aged well in the last fifteen years, but he recognized the eyes.

Gordon Habersham had been a senior at Barrel Creek High when Frankie had started as a freshman. He was one of the rich kids who had always ignored him unless he happened to be with Dwight. Everyone, even the snobs, had liked Dwight.

"Didn't they teach you about doctor-patient privilege in med school, Doc?" Frankie asked, not sure why the man's self-satisfied tone had set his teeth on edge. "I doubt Dwight authorized you to update the whole bar here on his status."

Habersham's face tightened. He stood and set his glass down on the bar harder than was necessary, the frown marks on his forehead deepening.

As the bigger man stepped forward, Frankie's hands closed into fists. He tensed as Rowdy shifted beside him, suddenly reminded that he was in his uncle's bar and that he was supposed to be on his best behavior.

I didn't come home to start trouble with this asshole. I came here to make things right with Dwight.

But Habersham only dropped a twenty-dollar bill on the counter and brushed past him without another word.

19

Frankie turned to watch the doctor push through the door. He stopped to hold it open for a man pushing a trolley loaded with instrument cases and equipment.

"Hey, Diesel," Rowdy called out as the man rolled past them. "You setting up for Tara tonight?"

Sticking up a big thumb, the man nodded and began to load the equipment onto the stage.

"What about you?" Rowdy asked, slinging an arm over Frankie's thin shoulders. "You gonna stay for the show?"

Watching Diesel fiddle with a bulky amplifier, Frankie shook his head, sending his shaggy hair falling into his eyes.

"I think I'll take Dr. Bigmouth's advice," he said, making a sudden decision. "I'll go see Dwight while there's still time."

* * *

Frankie steered the Mustang north toward Barrel Creek, surprised he still remembered how to get to Dwight's house without any help from his phone's GPS.

Turning onto Ironstone Way, he drove to the end of the long, winding street before coming to a halt in front of the impressive two-story house.

He hadn't seen the place for fifteen years, but from what Frankie could see as he climbed out of the car, the house still looked the same.

"Come on, boy," he called out, opening the Mustang's back door for Sherlock. "Time to mend some fences."

The Lab jumped down onto the driveway, eager to stretch his legs while Frankie gazed around the darkened landscape.

"You know, the last time I was here, Franny was with me," he said, glancing down at the Labrador. "It was on the Fourth of July, and Dwight's parents had gotten these really cool fireworks."

His voice trailed off as he remembered Franny's joy when the fireworks had exploded into a million sparkling lights overhead, her eyes shining and her laugh ringing out like a happy child, although she'd just turned sixteen.

Glancing up toward the house, Frankie caught a flutter of movement in an upstairs window. A small, pale face was visible in the moonlight one minute and then gone the next.

Was that...Franny?

The question hovered in his mind, refusing to be dismissed as if it was completely reasonable to think his dead sister was waiting for him in the upstairs bedroom.

"I'm seeing ghosts, Sherlock. I must be going crazy."

He looked down, hoping for a little reassurance from his partner, but the dog was already halfway up the drive, his nose low to the ground and his thick tail wagging slowly back and forth.

"Hey, where are you going? Wait up!"

Squinting after Sherlock into the darkness, it suddenly struck Frankie that there were no lights on in the house.

Other than the fall of moonlight over the property, the place was dark. It appeared to be deserted.

Only, if Dwight is in there, shouldn't someone be with him?

The thought nagged at him as he walked toward the house, catching up to Sherlock on the porch.

As he lifted his hand to knock, Frankie hesitated.

The front door was ajar.

"Hello?" he called out. "Anyone home?"

When no one answered, he exhaled, frustrated with his impulsive decision to just drive over.

I should have known better. I should have called first.

As he turned to leave, a high-pitched bark stopped him.

"Quiet, Sherlock!"

But the Labrador wasn't listening. He'd already wriggled his snout through the crack in the door, pushing it open far enough for the moonlight to reveal a dark puddle of blood spreading across the hardwood floor.

"No!" Frankie yelled.

Reaching for the dog's collar, he pulled him away from the door, his heart thumping in his chest as Sherlock began to growl low in his throat.

"Sit...and stay!"

Hoping Sherlock would heed his commands for once, Frankie turned back to the door, pulled out his phone, and activated the flashlight.

He held it in front of him with a shaky hand as he leaned forward and peered inside the house.

A woman's body was sprawled on the floor. Although her long, blonde hair concealed most of her face, Frankie immediately knew who she was.

"Cheryl..."

The name stuck in his throat as he pushed open the door

and looked past the dead woman into the dark room beyond.

"Dwight?"

Wishing he'd thought to bring a weapon, Frankie looked around the porch, his eyes landing on a hand trowel sticking out of a flowerpot.

He grabbed it up and held it out in front of him as he stepped into the house, trying in vain to avoid the puddle of blood at his feet.

"Dwight, are you in here?" he called out, his voice rising in fear. "Come on, man...answer me!"

Shining the flashlight ahead of him, he forced his legs to move. Forced himself to follow a trail of bloody footprints leading down the hall, noting the cheerful star-shaped pattern on the sole of the shoe that had made them.

He stopped when he reached the room at the end and flipped on the overhead light.

Dwight Atkins lay across a narrow hospital bed, a bloody gunshot wound in his temple, a gun clutched in his hand.

Moving further into the room, Frankie stared down in horror at the man he'd once called his best friend.

"Why?" he gritted out. "Why didn't you wait for me?"

A noise from somewhere upstairs jerked Frankie's attention back to the dark house and the possible danger at hand. Two people were already dead.

If he wasn't careful, it could be three.

Realizing he was still clutching the trowel in one hand and his phone in the other, he used his thumb to tap in 9-1-1, then held the phone to his ear.

"This is 9-1-1. What's your emergency?"

Frankie spoke in a low whisper as he gave the operator the address on Ironstone Way.

"My friend and his wife are dead," he said. "They've both been shot, and the shooter may still be in the house."

"I'm sending officers to your location now, stay on the-"

Cutting off the operator's voice with a jab of his thumb, Frankie crossed back to the hall. He felt along the wall for a light switch without success, then turned the thin beam of light from his phone toward the stairs.

As he crept forward, something warm and solid brushed against his leg. He looked down to see two bright eyes staring up at him. With a start, he realized Sherlock had gotten tired of waiting for him outside.

Before he could muster a reprimand, Frankie heard a rustling sound from the second floor.

He reached for Sherlock's collar, but the Lab was already moving away, heading to the stairs, eager to investigate.

"Come back here, Sherlock!" Frankie hissed.

Hurrying up the stairs after the dog, he paused on the landing and looked down the darkened hall.

A sudden bark sounded from an open door near the end.

Frankie charged forward, then jerked to a stop.

A teenage girl was crawling out from under a big double bed as Sherlock snuffled excitedly nearby.

As the girl stood and faced Frankie in the moonlit room, he recognized the blue eyes framed by high cheek bones and a delicately pointed chin. She was the spitting image of her mother at the same age.

"You must be Dwight's little girl," Frankie said. "You must be Josie."

Dazed defiance filled her face as she studied him.

"Are you the man who killed my dad?" she asked numbly. "Did you come back to finish the job?"

Frankie shook his head.

"No...I was your dad's friend," he said softly. "Or at least, I used to be. I'm Frankie Dawson."

A look of recognition entered her eyes.

"My dad was waiting for you," she said. "He wanted to tell you about Franny. He wanted to tell you before..."

Her voice trailed away as the mournful wail of a siren sounded in the distance.

"What did he want to tell me?" Frankie asked, moving closer. "What did he say about Franny?"

"It doesn't matter," she murmured, looking toward the window with glazed eyes. "It's already too late."

CHAPTER THREE

etective Nell Kinsey turned the Ford Interceptor onto Ironstone Way where a patrol car was parked at an angle outside the Atkins place, its flashing lights illuminating the night with harsh splashes of red and blue.

Skidding to a stop behind a black Mustang, Kinsey surveyed the empty front porch, then looked at her partner.

"Where is everyone?"

Detective Sheldon Ranger shrugged his wide shoulders as if he wasn't concerned, but Kinsey suspected his cool demeanor was just an act. She watched with one eyebrow raised as he nervously scanned the area and then unbuckled his seatbelt.

"Only one way to find out," he replied curtly. "Let's go."

Kinsey nodded, checked her gun, then hesitated.

The 911 caller had said there'd been a shooter in the house. They could be walking into a dangerous situation, and she and Ranger had only been working together a few weeks.

She wasn't sure they were in sync yet. Couldn't be certain how he might react if things went south.

But her partner was already climbing out of the passenger's seat. Already stepping onto the dark driveway which lay beyond the reach of the flashing lights.

Knowing she had little choice, Kinsey swung open her door and followed him toward the porch, her hand resting on the leather holster buckled around her narrow waist.

They were halfway up the drive when a lanky man she didn't recognize stepped out of the shadows.

"Stop right there," she yelled, drawing her Glock. "Barrel Creek PD. Put your hands where I can see them."

The man froze in surprise, his brown hair falling forward over his eyes as he squinted into the flashing lights.

As he lifted both hands over his head, two uniformed BCPD officers appeared from the other side of the patrol car.

"It's okay, Detective, he's the guy who found the bodies."

Kinsey recognized Officer Will Jackson and his partner Kai Lang. Before she could respond, Ranger spoke up beside her.

"You're the one who called 911?"

The lanky man nodded but kept his hands in the air.

"Yeah, I'm Frankie Dawson," he said, his eyes on Kinsey's gun. "You mind putting that thing away? I mean, haven't enough people already been shot for one night?"

Realizing she was still holding her Glock in the ready position, Kinsey lowered the weapon.

"Sorry," she murmured, returning it to her holster.

Frankie dropped his hands, then pointed to the front door.

"They're in there," he said. "Names are Dwight and Cheryl Atkins...they've both been shot in the head."

Kinsey turned to Will Jackson, a ten-year veteran of the force. She'd heard rumors he'd been jockeying for the open detective position she'd recently filled.

"Have y'all secured the scene yet?" she asked, gesturing toward the house. "Anyone else inside?"

Jackson shook his head.

"Just the two bodies."

"There's the girl, as well," Lang said, turning to look over her shoulder, her dark eyes worried. "I think she's in shock."

She waved a small hand toward a teenage girl standing in the shadow of the big house. A black Labrador retriever sat at the girl's feet.

"That's Dwight's kid," Frankie said. "She was here when it happened. I asked her what she saw, but she's in no state to talk. She needs to rest first. She might even need to see a therapist or something, you know?"

Ranger stared at him for a long beat, then nodded.

"We'll be sure to take your advice into consideration once we get a chance to look inside, Mr. Dawson."

From the deadpan expression on his face, Kinsey didn't know if her new partner was being serious or sarcastic. But then, there was a lot she didn't know about him, yet.

"Y'all should go through the backdoor to avoid tracking through the blood," Jackson said. "It's a mess in there."

His words sent an uneasy shiver through Kinsey. As Ranger began moving toward the back of the house, she automatically fell into step behind him.

This was no time to get squeamish.

"No one leaves, and no one comes inside until we give the all-clear," she called to Officer Lang.

She threw an uneasy glance back at Frankie Dawson, and then at the despondent teen, unsure how to handle them.

Are they victims or witnesses? Maybe even suspects?

Turning to see Ranger's tall frame melt into the shadows along the side of the house, she hurried after him.

* * *

Officer Jackson had been right. Blood was everywhere.

A dark pool had spread out under the head of the first victim, a blonde woman in a blue track suit.

Sticky footprints led down the hall and into a back room where they found the second victim on a narrow hospital bed.

"You think that's the murder weapon?"

Ranger stood by the bed, his face pale and strained, staring at the gun clutched in the dead man's hand.

"I don't know," Kinsey said, averting her eyes from the grisly gunshot wound. "But even if it is, I don't think he's the one who pulled the trigger."

She looked up to meet Ranger's pale blue eyes.

"There's no blood on his feet," she explained, pointing toward the stiff, bare foot hanging off the bed. "I don't see how he could have shot the woman out there and then gotten back here on his own without getting blood on his feet."

Studying the tracks leading down the hall, she could make out a faint star-shaped pattern.

"You think that guy out there's involved?" she asked.

Ranger frowned.

"You mean Dawson? The guy who called it in?"

He seemed to consider the question.

"I guess it's possible he tried to set this up to look like a murder-suicide and then made the call acting like he found them," he said with a shrug. "Made a mess of it if he did. The CSI team will figure that out right away."

"So, we'll assume he's a suspect for now," Kinsey agreed, her eyes still on the bloody prints. "What about the girl?"

The question seemed to confuse him.

"What about her?" he asked.

"You think she could have done this?"

His eyes widened, then he shook his head.

"Why would she kill her own folks? And she's just a kid."

"She's fourteen," Kinsey said. "That's old enough to hold a gun. And old enough to rebel against her parents."

Seeing the doubt in his eyes, she relented.

"We'll consider her a victim for now," she said. "But I'm keeping an open mind. Someone came in and shot two people in cold blood but left the girl alive. We need to know why."

Ranger didn't argue the point. He remained quiet as they made their way through the rest of the house, checking the kitchen, garage, and downstairs rooms before heading upstairs to check all the bedrooms.

Kinsey even looked in the closets and under the beds, but there was no one in the house and nothing else out of place.

"Time to talk to the daughter," Kinsey said, standing at the top of the stairs. "I'm guessing her name's Josie."

When Ranger looked confused again, she nodded at the purple sticker affixed to one of the bedroom doors.

Josie's Room – Keep Out!

Hurrying downstairs, Kinsey exited through the backdoor, circling around to the side of the house with Ranger bringing up the rear.

Jackson and Lang had finished cordoning off the front of the house with yellow crime scene tape while Josie Atkins waited beside the police cruiser, shifting from foot to foot.

Frankie Dawson stood next to her.

"How long are you guys gonna keep her standing here?" he asked as soon as he caught sight of the detectives. "She's been through a lot. You need to call someone to-"

"We'll handle this, Mr. Dawson," Ranger said, coming up to stand in front of the lanky man. "Now, we need you to go wait next to your vehicle until we're ready to take your statement. Officer Jackson will escort you."

Half-expecting Frankie to put up an argument, Kinsey was relieved when he just sighed and moved toward the Mustang.

"Come on, Sherlock," he muttered, prompting the black Labrador to stand and trail after him.

Once both he and the dog were out of earshot, she looked at Josie, taking in the girl's slack face and dazed eyes.

"Josie? I'm Detective Kinsey, and this is my partner, Detective Ranger. We need to ask you a few questions."

The teenager's eyes flicked toward her but before she could continue, Ranger spoke up in a soft voice Kinsey had never heard him use before.

"I know this is difficult, Josie. And we're real sorry about your mom and dad," he said. "We'd like you to tell us what happened here tonight if you can. We need to know who did this to your parents."

For a long beat, the girl just stared at him, then she licked her lips and cleared her throat.

"I don't know what happened," she whispered. "I just came home, and they were...dead."

Wrapping both arms around her body, she shivered.

"Do you have any idea who might have done this?" Kinsey pushed. "Is there anyone who might have wanted to..."

But the teenager was already shaking her head.

"I said *I don't know.*"

Her voice quivered, and her eyes filled with tears.

Ranger reached out a big hand and awkwardly patted Josie's shoulder as Kinsey swallowed back her next question.

She caught Frankie watching them anxiously from across the driveway and turned away.

He'd obviously been right. The girl was in no shape to answer questions, and they weren't in the best place to conduct an interview.

"Let's get you down to the station," Ranger said, taking

Josie by the arm. "We can talk there...maybe even get you something to eat?"

Surprised by Ranger's gentle approach, Kinsey watched the big detective lead the teen toward the Interceptor, reminded again how little she knew about her partner.

They'd been working together for almost a month, but there was still something guarded about him. A barrier she hadn't yet managed to penetrate.

She knew she shouldn't be surprised that they hadn't instantly bonded. After all, other than both of them being newly promoted to Major Crimes, she and Ranger were about as different as they could be.

Kinsey had been raised in a quiet, middle-class family. Her father was a guidance counselor at the local high school and her mother worked as a pediatric nurse.

Both her parents had been surprised by her decision to major in criminal justice at college, and they'd followed her rise through the ranks of the Barrel Creek PD and her recent promotion to detective with growing concern.

The fact that she was the youngest detective in the department, not to mention the only Black female detective working in Major Crimes, had only heightened her parents' constant fear for her safety.

On the other hand, Ranger's father had been a local police detective. A well-known figure in town who'd worked in Major Crimes for decades before his tragic death in the line of duty.

Although Ranger rarely spoke about his father or his past, everyone knew that Detective Ike Ranger had been mere months away from retirement when he'd been shot and that his only son, still driving a patrol car at the time of his death, had made it his mission to follow in his father's footsteps.

Kinsey wondered what that kind of pressure must feel like. Maybe they did have something in common after all.

Perhaps we both have something to prove.

She looked toward the road as a van pulled up to the curb, relieved to see the Barrel Creek Medical Examiner's logo on the van door as it opened and a woman in scrubs climbed out.

"Good," Kinsey muttered under her breath. "Let's hope the M.E. can figure out what really happened here, cause right now, I don't have a clue."

CHAPTER FOUR

D r. Rosalie Quintero scraped her dark, shoulder-length hair into a low ponytail and pulled protective coveralls and booties over her blue scrubs. Sucking in a deep breath of fresh air, the Barrel Creek medical examiner steeled herself, and then stepped inside, carefully avoiding the large puddle of congealing blood on the floor.

Turning back to where Marty Prince stood on the porch holding his oversized bag of equipment, she grimaced.

"I knew I shouldn't have had that second glass of wine with dinner," she said, swallowing back a wave of nausea. "It looks like a bloodbath in here."

The forensic technician moved past her into the hall, pulling the hood of his coveralls over his close-cropped hair.

"Smells like the blood is pretty fresh, though," he said, wrinkling his nose. "And I'd say rigor mortis is setting in."

He pulled his camera out of his bag and began snapping pictures of the victim in situ as Rosalie crouched beside the body and used a gloved hand to brush a strand of hair back from her face.

"Cheryl Atkins," she said, looking up at Marty. "I went to

school with her and her husband at Barrel Creek High. They were a few years ahead of me."

Marty made a sympathetic noise, but Rosalie could see he wasn't really listening as he focused the camera on the grisly gunshot wound in the back of Cheryl's head.

"Would you say that's a muzzle stamp?" Marty asked.

Leaning over the dead woman's body, Rosalie studied the ragged entry wound, noting the soot and scorched skin.

"Yes, it looks like it," she agreed. "Which means the shooter was likely holding the gun against her head when he pulled the trigger."

She winced at the image of the barrel pressed against Cheryl's dark blonde hair as the gun fired, releasing gases into the subcutaneous tissue, causing the skin to split as the bullet slammed into the bone and tissue beneath it.

"The position of the wound..."

Marty hesitated, causing Rosalie to turn and look at him.

"What about it?"

But she suspected she knew what he was going to say.

"It's in the right occipital region," he said. "I guess it just reminds me of the holes in the skulls from the Wolf River."

She turned back to the body with a troubled frown.

"We've been spending too much time with those bones," she said, more for her own benefit than for Marty's. "We're making connections that probably aren't there."

Ever since the skeletal remains had been delivered to the medical examiner's office for evaluation, Rosalie had been immersed in the investigation, even calling in an outside expert in forensic anthropology to help her figure out who the victims were and how they'd died.

So far, about the only thing she was sure of was that the bones belonged to multiple homicide victims who all had bullet holes in the back of their skulls.

"And there's Vicky Vaughn's hoodie," Marty reminded her, apparently not ready to drop the subject.

Rosalie nodded. He was right.

Searchers had discovered a woman's hoodie caught on a branch near the spot where a cache of bones had been found.

A small wallet in the hoodie's pocket had belonged to Vicky Vaughn, and a bullet hole in the hood indicated the missing girl may have been shot.

"If Vicky had her hood pulled up, the wound would have been located in about that same spot," Marty said, pointing a gloved hand at Cheryl Atkins' head.

"Yes, I can see that," Rosalie said, feeling a headache coming on. "I've got eyes and a brain, too, you know."

She ignored Marty's injured expression.

"Now, let's get her temperature and find out how long she's been here. Don't forget, we've got another body waiting down the hall."

Marty huffed and opened his bag as Rosalie continued the examination. She'd soon concluded a rough time of death using the body temperature, air temperature, and the stage of rigor mortis.

"I'd say she's been dead for about two hours," she murmured as she stood and stretched her back.

"So, we're calling estimated time of death at 9:00 PM?" Marty asked as Rosalie looked down the hall.

"Yep, that sounds right," she said, her eyes following the trail of bloody footprints. "Now, let's see where our shooter went next. Stay to the side and take photos of all the prints. It looks like someone led a parade through here."

So much for not disturbing the scene.

Noting that multiple tracks had been left in the blood, she doubted the killer's prints could be isolated, but it would be worth a shot.

She moved down the hall, sticking close to the wall, then stopped outside the open door at the end.

A bright overhead light illuminated the makeshift hospital room, making it possible for Rosalie to see the state of the body on the bed in stark detail.

"What was wrong with the guy?" Marty asked from behind her. "I mean...what's with all the medicine?"

Rosalie crossed the room to look down at the bottles of medication lined up on the dresser and the bedpan propped on a chair. A pang of pity joined the nausea in her stomach as she noted the emaciated state of the body on the bed.

Dwight Atkins had clearly been a very sick man.

From the range of medication and equipment on the bedside table, she deduced the dead man had been suffering from late-stage lung cancer despite being relatively young.

Statistically, it was uncommon in people under forty, but she'd seen it enough times to know it happened more than people liked to think.

"Cancer," she said shortly. "Terminal, I'd say."

She doubted he could have stood on his own and made it into the hallway, much less been able to chase down his able-bodied wife and manage to fire a gun at point-blank range at the back of her head.

As Marty took photos of the bloody wound in Dwight's temple, and the gun clutched in the dead man's stiff hand, Rosalie tried to picture what had happened.

She was suddenly certain this wasn't the scene of a murder-suicide. No, it was clearly a double homicide.

Although someone has gone to the trouble of trying to stage it, even though they've done a poor job.

"We need to test his hand for gun residue," she said to Marty. "Although if someone had held the gun to his hand and forced him to shoot..."

The violent image stuck in her mind, and she shook her head to displace it. Who could have committed such a horrible crime?

And why kill a man who is already dying?

She thought of the gunshot wound in Cheryl's head, and the collection of bones in her cooler back at the medical examiner's office.

Was it all just a coincidence, or could Dwight and Cheryl Atkins have been victims of the so-called Wolf River Killer?

Just the name the press had given the unidentified serial killer made the hair on the back of her neck stand on end.

As a child, Rosalie had been wary of the wild, muddy river that wound its way through the area, refusing to swim in the murky, brown water even though her father had assured her it was perfectly safe, and that the off-putting hue was caused by harmless floating sediment from the river bottom.

But now that the recent efforts to restore the river had turned up a disturbing collection of human remains, her wariness had grown into something closer to fear.

It made her wonder if she was being irrational.

Am I letting the constant news coverage get to me?

"I'll go get the gurney," Marty said.

His face had grown as solemn and thoughtful as her own as he left her alone with the dead man.

Unsettled by the sudden silence, she made her way into the living room and looked out the wide front window, wondering if she should share her suspicions with the two detectives at the scene.

She studied Detective Ranger's strong, broad back with appreciative eyes, then turned her gaze to the tall, thin man he was questioning.

Something about the brown, shaggy hair and narrow, stubbled face looked familiar. Watching as he ran a nervous hand through his already disheveled hair, Rosalie suddenly remembered who he was, although it had been ages since she'd seen him.

When did Frankie Dawson get back in town?

The awkward teenager she'd known at Barrel Creek High had been Dwight Atkins' constant companion. A skinny, funny sidekick to the star football player and his friends.

She frowned, trying to remember the last time she'd seen him. She had the vague recollection that after graduating high school he had started working at Atkins Barrel Works for Dwight's father.

But then, he'd left town, although she wasn't sure why or where he'd ended up. It seemed so long ago now.

Looking back toward the hall, she pictured Dwight lying alone on the bed and felt a stone settle into her chest.

Once upon a time, he'd been a handsome, high school senior, and she'd been a lowly, invisible freshman, admiring him from afar as he'd strode through the halls.

She was suddenly glad she hadn't known then how it would end for him.

CHAPTER FIVE

Frankie held out both hands and waited patiently while a grim-faced crime scene investigator used double-sided adhesive tape to lift any potential gunshot residue that might remain on his skin or clothes.

He'd been a private investigator long enough to know they were hoping to find the tiny particles of lead, barium, and antimony that would indicate he'd recently fired a gun.

"Testing for residue at the scene prevents a suspect from washing it away," the investigator said, watching Frankie's face closely. "You didn't wash your hands while you were inside, did you?"

Shaking his head, Frankie tried to remember how close he'd gotten to Dwight and Cheryl.

Had he touched them? Could he somehow have been contaminated by the residue on their bodies?

Or Josie. Was I close to Josie?

The thought that the teenager might have been the one to pull the trigger wouldn't fully go away, no matter how many times he tried to dismiss it.

He remembered what Pete Barker had always told him.

Everyone's a suspect until they're eliminated.

The two Barrel Creek detectives running the scene obviously agreed with Barker, which must be why they were treating him like their number one suspect.

Rubbing his tired eyes, Frankie tried to calculate how long he'd been awake as Sherlock plopped down at his feet and opened his mouth in a wide yawn.

"You tired, too, pal?" Frankie asked, giving the Lab a rub.

The dog dropped his head on his paws in answer, and Frankie pulled a stick of gum from his pocket, pulled off the wrapper, and stuck it in his mouth.

As he began to chew, he turned to look toward the Interceptor, trying to catch sight of Josie.

Suddenly, Ranger appeared beside him, and a wide set of shoulders blocked his view. The detective's smooth, clean-shaven face was as hard and still as stone.

"Listen, man, I need to go," Frankie said, scratching at his chin. "I got people waiting for me and-"

"And this is a murder investigation," Ranger said. "We may have more questions for you."

Checking his watch, Frankie exhaled.

"It's getting late and my mom's waiting up for me," he said, keeping his voice calm. "So, I'm leaving now. You can either arrest me or get out of my way."

He braced himself for the big man's reaction, prepared to be shouted at or thrown up against the car. He'd experienced both reactions in the past when he'd found himself in similar situations.

But Ranger just continued staring at him with icy blue eyes that revealed no hint of anger or frustration.

After a long, awkward silence, Frankie sighed.

"I know your CSI tech didn't find any gunshot residue on me," he said. "Because I didn't shoot anyone. And I'm the one who called you guys, remember? Why would I rat myself out? That doesn't make sense."

"Just because there's no residue, doesn't mean you didn't pull the trigger. You could have been wearing gloves," Ranger replied. "You told me you're a private investigator, so you'd know not to leave forensic evidence."

Before Frankie could protest, the detective pointed down to his size-fourteen tennis shoes.

"And there's blood on your shoes."

A sense of déjà vu came over Frankie as he stared at Ranger's impassive face.

Haven't I been here before, telling a cop I'm innocent, and not being heard? Didn't I end up going to prison?

The memory of his unjust conviction hardened his voice.

"I told you *already*. I came here and found the door open. When I saw Cheryl like that, I knew Dwight could be in there, so I went inside. I wasn't worried about the blood as much as I was worried about Dwight."

"You said you haven't seen your friend for fifteen years," Ranger scoffed. "So why come here tonight? And why would you be willing to go inside if you thought the shooter could still be in there?"

Frankie shrugged.

"I was only thinking about Dwight," he said, meeting and holding Ranger's cold gaze. "I was worried I had arrived too late. I didn't want to let my friend down."

He forced his mouth to close before he could add the word *again* to the end of his sentence.

There was no need to get into the history of his relationship with Dwight and its sudden end. That didn't have anything to do with Dwight's murder. Did it?

Josie's words replayed in his mind.

"My dad was waiting for you. He wanted to tell you about Franny. He wanted to tell you before...

Realizing that Ranger was still watching him, Frankie shook his head to clear it.

"Ask the M.E. about the time of death," he demanded. "Dwight and Cheryl had to have been dead long before I got here. I was at Rowdy's Bar earlier. I have an alibi, as I told Detective Kinsey."

He looked toward Ranger's partner, who until now had stayed out of the combative exchange.

"I checked it out," Kinsey confirmed. "The bartender remembered him. Said he left there about nine-thirty."

Ranger glared at her, then called out to one of the evidence technicians who was loading a box into his van.

"Collect Mr. Dawson's shoes as evidence," he ordered.

He kept his eyes on Frankie's face.

"After that, you're free to go," he said. "At least for tonight. But don't go far, and don't even think about leaving town. We'll take a statement at the station tomorrow."

Frankie nodded, understanding that until they developed an actual lead, he would remain their number one suspect.

As the technician approached him, he saw Kinsey jog

over to the Interceptor and climb into the driver's seat.

"Where's she taking Josie?" he demanded.

"That's none of your concern. Just keep your distance from the poor girl," Ranger warned. "She's been through enough."

Managing to stop the angry response that filled his throat, Frankie kicked off his tennis shoes and handed them to the technician, who took them with gloved hands and dropped them into what looked like a brown paper grocery sack.

He stomped barefoot to the trunk of the Mustang and popped it open. Before he could dig through his little suitcase in search of the spare shoes he'd packed, his eyes fell on the pair of yellow flipflops he always kept in the trunk.

They'd been useful for the impulsive trips he and Peyton had often made to the beach. They hadn't been worn since she'd left him.

Slipping them on, he settled Sherlock into the backseat, then backed out of the driveway, tempted momentarily to head back to the highway and away from Memphis.

Instead, he steered the car toward Chesterville.

＊ ＊ ＊

Frankie pulled into the driveway of the wooden, two-story house his grandmother had lived in for as long as Frankie could remember. The kitchen lights were still on, shining through the homemade curtains in the window.

Turning off the Mustang's engine, Frankie remained in his seat, not sure he was ready to go inside and face his mother.

She would be full of questions that Frankie wasn't sure he was in the mood to answer.

But his hand moved to the handle at the thought of his grandmother's soft, smiling face. It was a face he hadn't seen in too many years. A face that had hovered over him during so much of his childhood. Always there for him through good times and bad.

Guilt roiled in his stomach as he calculated just how long it had been since he'd seen her.

I haven't bothered to visit in over fifteen years. Now I'm popping in to say hi...oh, and by the way, the police want to question me about a double murder?

Frankie stepped out onto the driveway and slammed the car door shut behind him.

He felt someone watching him and looked up at the small window over the kitchen, half expecting to see Franny's small face peering out as she'd done so many times in the past, but the window was dark and empty.

I'm sorry, Franny. I'm so goddamn sorry that I–

His thought was cut short by an indignant bark, and he looked back to see a black furry face in the window.

Opening the back door, he waited for Sherlock to jump out, then headed for the back porch, raising a bony fist to knock just as the kitchen door swung open.

Arlene Dawson stood in the doorway wearing a flowered house coat, her hair rolled up in pink curlers.

"Where have you been?" she demanded, reaching out to pull him inside. "Rowdy called and said you'd left the bar ages ago. I was about to call the police."

She looked down at his feet.

"And why are you wearing flipflops?"

Frankie ignored the flood of questions as he looked past her to the small, familiar figure standing by the sink.

His throat tightened as he crossed the little room and stared down into familiar brown eyes.

"Granny...it's me, Frankie."

Essie Davis nodded distractedly, patting his arm with one small hand.

"Of course, it's you," she said, her mouth lifting into a hesitant smile. "I knew you'd be back soon. I told Arlene you and your sister would be home in time for dinner, but..."

She looked around at the stove and frowned, her words trailing off at the sight of the empty burners.

"I'm not hungry, Granny," Frankie said, gently guiding her toward the kitchen table. "I'm just...tired."

Sinking into a straight-backed chair, he looked up at his mother, expecting her to lay into him, but she was kneeling beside Sherlock, scratching him behind one floppy ear.

"That's Sherlock," he said with a sigh. "My new partner."

Arlene laughed, her irritation at his late arrival forgotten as she ran a gentle finger down the scar on Sherlock's face, then stood and crossed to the refrigerator.

Rummaging through one of the drawers, she finally

pulled out a pack of sliced cheese.

"My poor little Pebbles used to love cheese," she said, holding out a slice in Sherlock's direction. "Of course, she'd eat just about anything I'd give her."

Relieved to have avoided his mother's wrath, at least for the time being, Frankie allowed himself to exhale.

Dropping his bony elbows on the table, he studied his grandmother's careworn face, wondering how much of her memory had been lost.

She didn't seem to remember that he'd been gone all these years, or that Franny had died. Frankie figured he should be glad their absence hadn't caused her grief.

Forgetfulness does have a few perks after all.

As a recovering alcoholic, he knew that to be true.

He'd often drunk himself into a state of forgetfulness while seeking relief from the pain of Franny's death.

And just remembering the sight of Dwight and Cheryl dead in the house on Ironstone Way made him crave a drink.

But now wasn't the time to slide back into that trap. He'd need to keep his wits about him if he was going to find out who killed Dwight.

"Okay, so, why were you late?" Arlene asked after she'd helped Granny up to bed. "I can see something's wrong."

"Dwight's dead, Ma," he said bluntly. "He and Cheryl were shot in the head. I found them when I went over there."

Gaping at him in disbelief, Arlene felt for the back of the chair across from him and lowered herself into it.

"You found Dwight and Cheryl?" she said slowly as if hoping she hadn't heard him correctly. "You went there tonight and...?"

He nodded and reached for her hand.

"They're both dead," he said. "And the cops are acting like I'm a suspect, even though I'm the one who called them."

"*You* called the cops?" she asked. "And now they think you killed Dwight and Cheryl? But why would you kill them?"

Frankie sighed.

"I wouldn't kill them, Ma. I *didn't* kill them. But try telling the Barrel Creek PD that. They don't have a clue as to who did it, so they decided I'm as good a chump as anybody."

"Why'd you have to go there, tonight?" Arlene asked, her voice rising with anxiety. "Now, it'll all start over again. The accusations. The false statements..."

Gripping her hands, Frankie shook his head, understanding her panic. He'd already been falsely accused, convicted, and subsequently exonerated of a crime once.

Why should she doubt it could happen again?

"No one's going to railroad me this time," he promised. "I'll find the bastard who killed them myself if I have to."

He thought of Detective Ranger's stony face. He couldn't afford to just sit back and wait for the Barrel Creek police to do the job. Not if he wanted to get justice for Dwight.

And then, there was Josie to think about.

"There's something else I should tell you," Frankie said,

leaning back in his chair. "I got an email from Dwight yesterday, just before I left Willow Bay."

He pulled out his phone, scrolled to the last email his friend had sent him and began to read out loud.

> *Frankie,*
> *I just saw Dr. Habersham, and he said I could go at any time, so I guess I'd better ask you for that favor I mentioned.*
>
> *There aren't many men I trust around here. Not anymore. So, I'm hoping you'll put the past aside and give a dying man some peace of mind.*
>
> *Once I'm gone, I want you to keep an eye on Cheryl and Josie. I hate to think of them on their own. Please, watch out for them and do what you can to keep them safe. I'm counting on you.*
>
> *Your old pal,*
> *Dwight*

Arlene's eyes widened as Frankie finished the letter.

"So, he wanted you to look after his family? Is Josie–"

"She's his daughter," he said. "She was in the house when I got there. I'm not sure what she saw, or if she..."

He hesitated, not liking where his mind was headed.

"I'm not sure she's going to be okay," he ended lamely, feeling guilty for his doubts about the orphaned girl.

Years ago, he'd been falsely accused of armed robbery and had ended up in a Florida prison, so he should know better than to accuse anyone without solid evidence to back him up.

As far as I know, Josie had no reason to want her folks dead. And if she didn't kill them, that means the real killer is still out there.

He suddenly had another thought.

And the bastard might go after Josie next.

Looking down at his phone, he reread the email, picturing Josie's dazed blue eyes in the moonlight, replaying what she'd said as her parents lay dead on the floor below.

My dad was waiting for you. He wanted to tell you about Franny.

What had Dwight wanted to tell him? What could his friend have known about his sister's death? He wasn't sure, but he intended to find out.

Getting to his feet, Frankie stifled a yawn, then called for Sherlock to follow him to the stairs.

"I need to talk to Josie," he said. "I need to make sure she's okay. But right now, I gotta get some sleep."

CHAPTER SIX

The Wolf River Killer turned the old Ford Bronco onto Monarch Avenue, never slowing as he passed the black Mustang outside the Davis house. He kept his head down, although he wasn't really worried he'd be recognized. Not when he was driving the old clunker he only used when he needed to remain incognito.

Circling the block, he made sure no one was watching, then slowed to a stop along the curb.

The old white house sat at the heart of Chesterville, a quiet Memphis suburb that had been incorporated before the Civil War. Despite its age, the town had somehow managed to hold on to its somewhat faded charm.

A shadow passed behind the kitchen window, sending the Wolf, as he liked to think of himself, accelerating forward.

He tapped his brakes as he reached the corner, then rolled through the stop sign, keeping one eye on the rearview mirror.

How much does Frankie Dawson know? Did Dwight rat me out about the barrels? Did he tell him about the bones in the river?

Franny Dawson's brother had left town just after the girl's sudden death had been declared an accidental overdose.

The Wolf snorted in disgust.

Frankie had never even questioned the findings of the Barrel Creek PD or the medical examiner.

The idiot accepted the story like all the other mindless sheep around here. None of them have a clue there's a wolf in the flock.

The possibility that after all these years the private investigator had come back to town just as Dwight had taken to his deathbed seemed an improbable coincidence.

More likely, Dwight had called his old friend home, hoping to cleanse his conscience and save his soul.

The thought sent a ripple of unease through the Wolf as he pulled onto the highway.

It doesn't matter why he's back...all that matters is he's a threat.

From what the Wolf had read over the years, the time Frankie had spent in Florida hadn't been wasted.

After earning his private investigator license, the man had helped bring down a slew of bad guys, including more than one serial killer.

He'd partnered not only with local police down in the Sunshine State but had also cooperated on multiple cases with the U.S. Marshals Service and the FBI.

Time to stop Mr. Hotshot P.I. before he gets any big ideas about making trouble closer to home.

Gripping the Bronco's steering wheel, the Wolf headed north, his anxiety rising as he neared the turn-off and caught sight of the dark water just past the muddy shore.

The Wolf River flowed over a hundred miles through

Tennessee as it made its way toward the Mississippi River near the northern end of Mud Island, carrying many of the Wolf's dark secrets in its murky depths.

He'd grown up with the river always at his back, and he'd often turned to its wild banks, seemingly so remote from the urban streets of Memphis, when he'd needed a place to hide evidence of his extracurricular activities.

Navigating the old SUV closer to the river, the Wolf pulled off the old one-lane road and parked under the flowering branches of a catalpa tree.

Undaunted by the darkness, he opened the door and stepped out, his boot sinking slightly into the mud at his feet.

Rustling noises sounded nearby, but he ignored them as he made his way through the underbrush toward the water.

Despite the river's name, he knew the only wolves in the area walked on two legs, although he'd encountered plenty of other predators over the years, including bobcats, foxes, and a few coyotes.

He'd even seen the occasional alligator hiding in the sloughs and cypress breaks nearer to downtown Memphis.

But none of the wildlife scared him.

Not with his trusty Glock at his waist and a little Ruger always at the ready in his ankle holster.

No, the wildlife had never been a concern.

It was the humans who were the real problem. The conservationists who organized endless campaigns to restore the habitat along the riverbank.

It had been their meddling that had led to the first bones

being discovered. Unsuspecting volunteers had gotten a nasty surprise as they'd collected debris and cleared out invasive plants.

Originally assuming they'd found animal bones, or perhaps ancient remains that had lain undiscovered for centuries, they'd called in the local medical examiner.

Dr. Rosalie Quintero had soon set them straight and opened a full-scale investigation. Last he'd heard, she'd even called in a forensic archeologist from out of state to help her examine the bones.

According to local reporters, all of whom had been drooling over the story for months, bones from three different women had already been identified.

The personal effects of a fourth woman whose body had yet to be recovered had also been found. The authorities were assuming she was dead, and the Wolf knew that, for once, they were right.

Vicky Vaughn had been his latest victim, and he figured her body would surface sooner or later, despite his best efforts to weigh her down.

Lifting his face to the sky, he looked toward the river, wondering if it was going to rain again, half expecting to be confronted on his way to the water's edge.

But the night remained his alone.

Taking a plastic storage bag from his pocket, he looked down at the dozen or so items inside. Several necklaces, a bangled bracelet, a few rings, and a plastic butterfly hairclip were twisted into a messy tangle.

A silver heart locket caught his eye. He reached into the

bag and pulled it out, studying the initials *F.D.* which had been engraved on the back.

The image of a skinny girl with limp brown hair and wide, accusing eyes flashed through his memory as he rubbed his thumb over the smooth metal.

The Wolf had kept the locket for over fifteen years, storing it with the other trophies he'd kept in a small safe in his bedroom closet.

But it had become too dangerous to keep the mementos any longer. With the open investigation into the remains found along the river and Frankie Dawson's unwelcome interference, he couldn't risk keeping the items.

Moving forward he hurled the locket into the air, losing sight of it as it fell into the dark water.

He reached into the bag again, pulling out the contents, studying each item before throwing it after the locket.

Just more trash for the volunteers to find.

He grunted in satisfaction when the bag was empty, then turned and made his way back to the Bronco.

CHAPTER SEVEN

Josie Atkins sat in the backseat of the Ford Interceptor gazing out the rain-streaked window with glazed, unseeing eyes. She took no notice of the other vehicles speeding past them or the dark forest of trees that lined the road as the last minutes of her parents' lives replayed over and over again in her mind.

She was unable to block the terrible gunshots echoing in her ears. Unable to block out the sound of her mother's scream or her father's weak voice as he'd spoken her name for the very last time.

He'd used his last breath to beg for her life.

Now she'd never see him again. Never get a chance to say a proper good-bye.

It just didn't make sense. First the cancer, and then the intruder with the angry voice and the gun.

What had her father done to deserve such a terrible fate?

The question brought back snippets of the conversation she'd overheard through the monitor just before the man with the gun had arrived.

"Franny's death was no accident. She was murdered...just like those other girls. And I know who did it."

She studied the back of Officer Kinsey's head as she recalled her mother's response.

"Why didn't you tell the police...or Frankie?"

Her father had claimed he'd been in too far. That he didn't know who to trust. His warning echoed in her mind.

"You know it's too dangerous to involve the police."

He hadn't had the strength or the time to explain why he'd been so afraid, but she'd heard the fear in his voice, and she knew without a doubt that she shouldn't trust them, either.

Leaning her forehead against the window, Josie closed her eyes, resisting the urge to give in to the grief and rage.

She couldn't let her emotions take over. She had to stay focused. If she couldn't count on the police, it would be up to her to find the man who'd killed her parents.

Her resolve to handle things on her own wavered only when she thought about her father's unexpected revelation.

"Other girls have gone missing since then. I'm not sure, but I think it could be their bones along the Wolf River."

Had her father really known who had killed Franny Dawson? Had it been the same man who'd left piles of bones along the riverbank to be discovered and collected?

Is the man who killed my parents the Wolf River Killer?

A wave of dizziness washed over her at the possibility that she'd been in the same house as a wanted serial killer. That she'd been only feet away and had heard his hateful voice.

"Where's your daughter?"

The memory sent a ripple of fear through her.

"Are you okay, Josie?"

Detective Kinsey was studying her in the rearview mirror.

"I don't think so," Josie said, shaking her head. "I need some air...now...or I'm going to be sick."

"Okay, hold on," Kinsey said, steering the Interceptor's right front wheel up onto the shoulder of the road.

Climbing out of the SUV, the detective circled around the Ford and opened the back door for Josie.

"Be careful when you step out," she said as the girl scrambled out of the backseat. "This is a busy street."

Josie nodded and hurried away from the road as cars whizzed by, spraying up rainwater and mud.

She stopped under a streetlight and retched, letting her dark hair fall forward over her face.

"Are you okay?"

Kinsey appeared beside her looking worried.

"I need some water," Josie said, turning away as her stomach heaved up the last of her dinner.

"I have a bottle in the car," Kinsey said. "Wait here."

She turned and jogged back toward the Interceptor. When she reached the road, Josie took her chance.

Darting forward at top speed, she headed toward the edge of a forested area dotted with tall purple flowers she recognized as ironweed.

As she ran past, she thought about her mother's habit of naming the wildflowers they saw on their trail hikes. Hot tears sprang to her eyes as she realized her mother would never see ironweed, buckeye, or bluebells again.

"Josie!"

Kinsey called out just as she plunged under a dark canopy of trees that blocked the light from the street and the traffic and obscured the patches of moonlight filtering through the clouds in the night sky.

Reaching into her pocket, Josie remembered too late that the crime scene techs had collected her phone along with the rest of the electronics in the house as evidence.

She choked back a frustrated sob as she realized she would be forced to make her way through the dark forest without any light or map to guide her.

"Just follow the sound of traffic and stay close to the road," she whispered to herself, forcing her legs to keep moving. "It's safer out here than in the police station."

No matter what happened, she couldn't let them take her to jail. Not when she wasn't sure who was on her side, and who might be there waiting for her.

CHAPTER EIGHT

F rankie woke with a start, momentarily disoriented to find himself in the attic bedroom he'd slept in whenever he had visited his Granny's house on Monarch Avenue as a child. Arlene Dawson had usually taken her two children to her mother's house whenever she and Frankie's father had a fight, and he felt as if half his childhood had been spent in the little room.

Lifting his head, he saw Sherlock curled up on the end of the bed, fast asleep. It had been a late night for both of them.

He let his head fall back onto the pillow and stared at the ceiling, listening to the sounds from the kitchen downstairs.

He'd thought that going home to Memphis would help him escape the pain that seemed to live inside him now, filling his thin chest with a constant, lonely ache.

But he'd been wrong. If anything, being eight hundred miles away from the woman he loved made their separation seem more real. More final.

He'd been living in denial for the last six surreal months, which had been as foggy and disorienting as a bad dream.

It seemed impossible that his marriage could really be over, just like that. Especially after the first eighteen months had been so idyllic.

As newlyweds, he and Peyton had been blissfully happy, grateful to have found each other, and relieved to have made it through the complicated, turbulent start to their relationship.

Everything had seemed perfect until he received the call.

Somehow that one call had changed everything.

"Frankie?"

His mother's knock at the bedroom door pulled Frankie's thoughts back into the room and prompted Sherlock to raise his sleepy head.

"Come down and have some breakfast," Arlene called.

He listened to the creak of the stairs as she made her way back down to the kitchen, then sat up and looked at Sherlock.

The dog had jumped off the bed at the sound of Arlene's voice. He yawned, stretched his back legs, and gave his whole body a vigorous shake as if shaking off a nightmare.

Frankie suddenly wondered if dogs dreamed the same way humans did. If so, he imagined Sherlock's sleep the previous night must have been full of blood and dead bodies.

He stood and pulled on baggy jeans and a long-sleeved button-up shirt, then slipped on the watch Peyton had given him for his last birthday.

Hunching over to avoid bumping his head on the low ceiling, he checked the little mirror over the dresser, ran a hand through his shaggy brown hair, and rubbed at the dark stubble on his chin, deciding a shave would have to wait.

With Sherlock on his heels, he made his way downstairs and into the kitchen where his mother was cooking breakfast.

"Morning, Ma."

He sank into a chair at the worn wooden table and looked out the window, smiling as he caught sight of Granny Davis sitting in the little rose garden that had always been her pride and joy.

When he looked back down, he saw that Arlene had shoveled two greasy eggs onto his plate.

She added a slice of toast slathered with butter.

"You trying to kill me, Ma?"

He stared down at the plate unable to muster an appetite.

"This is a heart attack just waiting to happen."

Arlene ignored him as she poured steaming black coffee into his mug and added a long splash of cream.

"You're too skinny," she said as she slid into a chair across from him. "You need to eat more."

"Pardon me for not being hungry," he shot back. "Having your wife leave you and finding your ex-best friend dead will do that to you, you know?"

Picking up the toast, he took a bite and started to chew, ignoring the churning feeling in his gut.

"So, you finally gonna tell me what happened between you and Peyton?" Arlene asked, raising her thin, penciled-on eyebrows. "You guys seemed so happy..."

She kept her eyes on his face as she took a small sip of her unsweetened coffee and nibbled on a slice of dry toast.

"It's complicated," Frankie said.

He forked half an egg into his mouth and took his time chewing, not sure he could actually speak the words that needed to be said, hoping the greasy bite wasn't going to come back up.

"Something happened...something bad."

He stared down at the creamy liquid swirling in his mug.

"After that Peyton just...changed her mind. She didn't want to be married anymore. At least, not to me."

His mother's eyes narrowed, and Frankie imagined she was already plotting her revenge on the woman who'd rejected her only son.

"It's not her fault," Frankie said with a sigh. "And for once, it's not my fault, either. It's just...bad luck."

Shoving his plate away, he stood and called to Sherlock.

"Let's go for a walk, buddy," he said. "I'll show you the neighborhood."

It took him a while to remember that the detectives had confiscated his tennis shoes, and to dig out the only other shoes he'd packed.

He slid his feet into the stiff leather loafers that Peyton had helped him pick out and which, although they'd ended up causing a painful blister to form on his big toe, he couldn't bear to replace.

As he led Sherlock down the driveway and onto Monarch Avenue, Frankie realized the Chesterville neighborhood felt more like home to him than anywhere else, even though he'd never officially lived there.

His mother and father had moved around a lot, trying to find a place they could afford to call home. The last house they'd lived in together had been a rental out in Barrel Creek.

That's where Frankie had met Dwight Atkins, a local rich kid who had walked the halls of Barrel Creek High School like he'd owned the place.

But for reasons still unknown to Frankie, Dwight had taken the gangly, awkward new kid under his wing, and had even talked his father into giving Frankie a part-time job at the family business, Atkins Barrel Works.

They'd become close friends. In Frankie's mind, best friends. But after graduation, things had changed. Dwight had changed.

Frankie stopped at the corner, lost in thought as Sherlock lifted his leg next to the stop sign.

"Mr. Dawson?"

He turned to see a pair of pale blue eyes staring at him from the passenger's side window of a black SUV.

The vehicle was unmarked, but Frankie recognized it as a Ford Interceptor. A vehicle designed for law enforcement. It was the same vehicle he'd seen at Dwight Atkins' house the night before.

Detective Kinsey was driving while her partner rode shotgun. It was clear from Ranger's stony expression that he still considered Frankie the BCPD's number one suspect.

"Like I said last night, we need you to come down to the station with us and give a statement," Ranger said.

His eyes dropped to Sherlock.

"You got someone who can look after your dog?"

Frankie was about to protest, then thought better of it, not wanting Sherlock to be taken to the pound if the local yahoos did end up arresting him despite their lack of evidence.

"My grandmother's house is up the road," he said, pointing toward Monarch Avenue. "I'll take him there and drive my own car down to the station. I know where it is."

He didn't wait for their approval, just started walking, glad when Sherlock made it all the way back to the house without needing to stop again to do his business.

"Watch Sherlock for me while I go down to the Barrel Creek PD, will you, Ma?" he asked as he opened the back door and hustled Sherlock inside. "They want to talk to me."

Arlene put a hand to her throat, instantly alarmed, but Frankie didn't give her a chance to ask questions.

"You stay here and hold down the fort," he told Sherlock, giving the dog a quick scratch on the head. "I'll be back before you know it."

Spinning on the heel of his loafer, he turned and walked out to the Mustang, his mind frantically replaying the events from the night before as he sped toward Barrel Creek.

Someone had killed Dwight and Cheryl in cold blood, and if he didn't figure out who was responsible, he could end up taking the blame.

CHAPTER NINE

Detective Sheldon Ranger paced outside the Barrel Creek police station as he and Kinsey waited for Frankie Dawson to arrive. They'd had no luck locating Josie Atkins after she'd run off the night before and he worried that Chief Shipley might boot them off the case if he found out they'd already managed to lose a key witness to the double murder.

"You didn't see which way she went?" Ranger asked for what had to be the tenth time.

"No," Kinsey snapped. "I told you, she pretended to be sick and then took off into the forest. It was dark...I didn't have a chance."

Scanning the agitated crowd that had gathered outside the station after news of Dwight and Cheryl Atkins' death had gotten out, he shook his head, wondering what they were hoping to see.

His eyes narrowed as he spotted a thin, wiry man with straggly blonde hair pushing his way through the crowd.

"Why the hell is Dusty Fontaine covering a murder?" he muttered as the man pulled out a camera and started taking pictures. "Isn't he the Gazette's *entertainment reporter?*"

Kinsey just shrugged her shoulders, her mouth set in a tight straight line.

Ranger figured she was still feeling defensive over losing the only witness to a double murder that had ended up on the front page of every newspaper in the state.

Not that the growing hysteria was her fault.

The atmosphere in town had already been tense. Everyone knew that human bones had been pulled out of the Wolf River. Then Vicky Vaughn's jacket and wallet had been discovered on the riverbank.

The aspiring singer had gone missing on her way from Nashville to Memphis for a gig two months earlier, and she was now presumed dead.

So, it wasn't exactly a surprise that a double murder involving one of the town's most prominent families would prompt a throng of scared and angry residents to descend on the police station demanding answers.

"There he is," Kinsey said, nodding toward a black Mustang pulling into the crowded parking lot. "I was starting to think he might have left town."

Ranger didn't tell her he hadn't been too worried.

Innocent men didn't usually go on the run. And Frankie Dawson was innocent, at least of Dwight and Cheryl Atkins' murders.

Maybe Kinsey hadn't figured it out yet, but she would soon enough. She was sharp, and she didn't miss much.

In the meantime, he needed to find out why Frankie had really come home, and what he knew about his sister's death.

Was it possible that, like Dwight, the P.I. had suspected there could be a connection between Franny's death and the other girls who had gone missing or turned up dead?

Watching as Frankie climbed out of his car, Ranger waited by the entrance as the lanky man began to push his way through the crowd.

He planned to use Frankie's current status as a suspect to get answers to all his questions, but he'd have to be careful not to arouse Kinsey's suspicions.

He couldn't have his new partner running to Chief Shipley with her concerns just when things were heating up.

Just as Frankie reached the steps, Dusty Fontaine stepped in front of Ranger with his camera at the ready.

"Detective, I'm sure you're probably busy running the investigation into the murders of Dwight and Cheryl Atkins," the reporter said. "But I'd like to ask you some questions about the bones found in the Wolf River."

Ranger frowned down at the little man, hoping the angry scowl might be enough to scare him away.

But the reporter seemed unfazed.

"As I'm sure you know, there have been a string of missing women going back years in this area, several of them were seen at the same local bar just prior to disappearing," he said. "Has the BCPD investigated a possible connection between these women and the bones found in the river?"

"I assure you, we're looking into all viable leads and connections," Ranger said, eager to get rid of the man. "But

I can't give you any information that might jeopardize the investigation. Now, if you'll excuse me."

Glancing past the reporter, he saw Frankie standing on the bottom step wearing a puzzled frown.

"Right this way, Mr. Dawson," Ranger called, keeping his expression neutral as he motioned for Frankie to follow him into the station.

"Have you found Vicky Vaughn's body yet?" the reporter called after them in a petulant voice. "Have any of the bones from the river been identified, detective?"

Ranger looked back in relief as the door swung shut, cutting off Dusty Fontaine's barrage of questions.

It looked as if the reporter had made a connection he hadn't counted on.

* * *

Ranger closed the door to the interview room and hurried down the hall toward his office, making a detour by Shipley's office to verify the chief was safely inside.

He knew he shouldn't leave Kinsey and Frankie alone for long, but he needed to make a quick call.

Stepping into his office, he closed the door and locked it, then pulled out his phone and tapped on a saved number.

A gruff voice answered the call on the second ring.

"Dusty Fontaine with the *Gazette* was asking questions about Vicky Vaughn and the Wolf River bones," Ranger said. "He asked if we were investigating a possible connection between the victims and a local bar. I'm guessing he meant

Rowdy's."

There was a brief pause on the other end of the call.

"Okay, so we may have a problem. I'll look into it. Anything else?"

Lowering his voice, Ranger glanced back toward the door, making sure he was still alone.

"I'm about to go in and question Frankie Dawson. I'll find out why he was at Dwight's house and how much he knows."

"And the girl? Have you talked to Josie Atkins?"

Ranger felt his face flush. He'd made a big mistake there. He should have taken the teenager to the station himself. He shouldn't have trusted Kinsey with such an important task.

"She ran off before I could question her," Ranger admitted. "But we're looking for her, and–"

"You need to bring her in before anyone else gets to her. You need to be the one to question her."

Hearing footsteps in the hall, Ranger tapped on *End Call* just as Kinsey pushed open the door.

"We're waiting. Are you coming?"

"Yep, I'm right behind you.

Jumping up, he followed her back down the hall to where Frankie sat at a small wooden table in the interview room.

Ranger sat across from him but remained quiet as he studied the narrow face, stubbled jaw, and tired eyes.

It was obvious the P.I. hadn't gotten much sleep the night before, but he didn't seem particularly nervous, and he didn't appear to be in a hurry.

As they stared at each other across the table, Frankie reached into his shirt pocket and pulled out a stick of gum.

Peeling off the foil wrapper, he stuck the gum in his mouth and began to chew slowly, his eyes never leaving Ranger's.

"I've done my research on you," Ranger said. "I see you served time down in Florida for armed robbery, and-"

"And I was exonerated," Frankie said. "I'm sure you saw that, too, if you looked hard enough."

Ranger cocked an eyebrow.

"You must have had a pretty good lawyer to get you off on that one," he said. "Or friends in high places."

"I did have a good lawyer," Frankie agreed. "But I also had something you don't seem to care much about...the truth."

He leaned back and crossed his arms over his thin chest.

"I was innocent," he said. "That should be enough to keep a man out of prison, but I found out the hard way that it isn't always that simple."

Kinsey shifted in her seat, obviously getting impatient with the line of questioning.

"This isn't getting us anywhere," she said. "We need to discuss what happened last night. Now, let's start from the beginning, Mr. Dawson."

She ignored Ranger's stare as she looked down at a folder open in front of her. He could see she'd prepared a pageful of handwritten notes and questions

"You told us that you hadn't seen Dwight Atkins in fifteen years," she said, checking her notes. "So why go to his house last night...after all that time?"

"He was dying of cancer," Frankie said. "He wanted to see me. He asked to talk to me. And I wanted to say good-bye."

Cocking her head, she frowned.

"What I don't understand is why he had *to die* to get you to talk to him," she said. "Whatever happened to make the two of you fall out must have been pretty bad."

Frankie nodded, but Kinsey didn't give him a chance to explain before she continued.

"Was it bad enough to make you want to kill him? Did you decide to go over there and do the deed yourself before the cancer ruined your chance to take revenge?"

A flush of anger reddened Frankie's face.

"I went there to patch things up," he said. "I wanted to make things right. Dwight had been my best friend, before..."

"Before what, Mr. Dawson?" Kinsey asked.

Her voice had softened.

"Call me Frankie," he said. "I hate that *Mr. Dawson* crap."

Kinsey cleared her throat.

"Okay, Frankie. What happened between you and Dwight? What happened that ruined your friendship?"

"Franny died."

The two words hung in the air between them.

"Franny?"

"My little sister," Frankie said. "She died of an accidental overdose fifteen years ago."

Chewing hard on his gum, he dropped his eyes to the

table.

"Dwight never showed up at her funeral," he said in a low voice. "It pissed me off. When I split town a few days later, I didn't bother telling him where I was going. We never spoke again. At least, not until a few weeks ago."

"And his cancer diagnosis was the only thing that prompted him to get in touch?" Kinsey asked. "Did he say there was anything else bothering him?"

Frankie shrugged, but he didn't lift his eyes.

"Isn't dying of cancer bad enough?" he asked.

The words were intended to be flippant, but Ranger heard the pain in Frankie's voice and knew the P.I. hadn't taken his friend's death lightly.

"Did you blame Dwight for your sister's death, Frankie?"

Kinsey asked the question almost gently, and Ranger turned to look at her, wondering what she was thinking.

"I blamed myself," Frankie said in a hoarse whisper. "I've been blaming myself every day for fifteen years."

The answer obviously wasn't the one Kinsey had been expecting, and she paused to look down at her folder as if searching for the next question.

"Why blame yourself, Frankie?" Ranger asked. "Were you the one who gave your sister the drugs?"

Frankie's head jerked up, his eyes suddenly blazing.

"No, I didn't give her the drugs," he said. "Her so-called friends were probably the ones who gave her the smack."

"Smack? You mean heroin?"

When Frankie didn't answer, Ranger leaned forward.

"Which friends gave her the drugs, Frankie?"

He tensed as he waited for the P.I. to respond, unsure how much he knew and how much he would be willing to tell.

"Her best friend," Frankie said in a bitter voice. "A girl named Lacey Emerson. Her and this guy she hung out with. A real loser named Booker Boudreaux. The guy was a low-level drug dealer. Real scum of the earth in my opinion."

Kinsey's eyes widened at the name.

"Lacey Emerson?" she said. "Isn't she in Larksville?"

"Yeah, she is," Frankie said. "After Franny died, she went off the rails. I hear she's doing twenty-five years for murder, and I can't say that I'm sorry."

Ranger frowned, trying to decide if Frankie was being straight with them. If he was, then the man didn't suspect his sister's death was anything but an accident.

"Okay, let's move on," Kinsey said, moving down to the next note on the page. "You said you arrived at the house, found the bodies, called 911, and then discovered that Josie was upstairs hiding. Is that right?"

"Yeah, that's about right," Frankie agreed.

"So, what did Josie say to you when you saw her?"

Frankie hesitated as if trying to remember, and Ranger saw his jaw clench and both hands tighten into fists in his lap as if the memory was painful.

"She asked if I was the man who killed her parents," he finally said. "When I told her my name, she said her dad had been waiting for me. That he wanted to tell me...something."

Leaning forward, Ranger frowned.

"Did she say what it was? Do you think someone could have been threatening him?"

Frankie shrugged as Kinsey wrote something in her folder.

"We had talked and emailed a few times before I decided to drive up. He said he had something important to tell me but that he'd rather do it in person."

"But he didn't tell you what it was?" Ranger asked, unable to mask the tension in his voice.

Feeling Kinsey's eyes on him, he forced himself to relax back into his chair.

"Well, he did tell me one thing," Frankie said. "He sent me an email telling me to watch out for his daughter once he was gone. He asked me to make sure she was alright."

Ranger studied the P.I.'s thin, downturned face.

"Was that it?" he demanded. "Was that all he said?"

Frankie nodded grimly, then looked toward Kinsey.

"We done here?" he asked. "Can I go now?"

She cocked an eyebrow.

"How do you know we're not going to arrest you?" she asked, sounding more curious than confrontational. "You *were* found at the scene of a murder last night."

"I've already been railroaded for armed robbery once and managed to clear my name," Frankie said. "I'm pretty sure if you try to pin a bogus murder charge on me I can do it again. One way or the other, the truth always comes out."

He leaned back in his chair.

"But going to prison isn't what's worrying me right now," he said, turning to lock eyes with Ranger. "I'm more worried about finding the shooter who killed Dwight and Cheryl."

"That's not up to you," Ranger said, feeling his back stiffen. "That's our job."

Frankie rolled his eyes.

"That's just it...that's the problem. If the Barrel Creek PD can't find the guy, it means I'll have to. But first, I need to talk to Josie and–"

"Josie's missing," Kinsey blurted.

Ranger motioned for her to be quiet, but she ignored him.

"She ran off last night before we could bring her to the station," she admitted. "We haven't been able to locate her."

Frankie's eyes widened.

"I've got to go find her," he said, jumping up from the chair. "Dwight asked me to take care of his daughter. It was the last request he made. I don't plan on letting him down."

As he headed toward the door, Ranger grabbed his arm.

"You're still a person of interest in a double murder," he reminded him. "You need to keep out of our investigation."

But Frankie wasn't listening, he shook off Ranger's hand and strode to the door, disappearing into the hall before either of the detectives could stop him.

"You don't think he's our guy, do you?" Kinsey asked once they were alone. "If you did, you wouldn't have let him leave. So, why bother bringing him in?"

"No, I don't think Frankie's our killer," he agreed. "But I wanted to know if he had any idea who was in that house last night, or who killed his friend."

"And?"

Kinsey raised her eyebrows as she waited for his answer.

"And I don't think he does," Ranger said. "Not yet."

He cocked his head at the door.

"You ready to go update the chief?"

Her face fell at the prospect, but she followed him down the hall to the police chief's office, where Otto Shipley sat at his desk, which was neatly organized and recently polished.

He was still a handsome man despite being sixty years old. His salt and pepper hair remained thick, and his body appeared to be toned and fit under his jacket.

"We just finished interviewing Frankie Dawson," Ranger said once Shipley waved them inside. "He's the man who discovered the bodies out at the Atkins place."

Shipley propped his elbows on the desk and leaned forward, clearly hoping for good news.

"Does he look good for the murders?"

Kinsey shook her head before Ranger could reply.

"It doesn't look like he's our shooter," she said. "But of course, we'll keep an open mind."

A sullen expression fell over Shipley's face.

"So, what are you going to do to bring in a suspect? The public and press are out there wanting somebody's head, and it isn't going to be mine."

"I'm going to start by going over to the medical examiner's office," Kinsey said, seemingly unperturbed by Shipley's irritation. "Hopefully, the M.E. can give us more to go on."

Once they'd left the chief's office, she looked at Ranger.

"Are you coming with me?"

"No, I think I'll go back out to the Atkins place and walk the scene in the daylight," he said. "The CSI team is still out there so I can get an update at the same time. And who knows, maybe I'll find something they missed."

CHAPTER TEN

Rosalie Quintero adjusted her white coveralls and tucked a wayward strand of dark hair under her blue, disposable cap. Pulling down the protective shield to cover her face, she slid her hands into a second pair of gloves, then leaned over the autopsy table and tugged down the white sheet covering Cheryl Atkins' body.

She surveyed the stiff, discolored remains of the woman she'd known since high school. One of the golden few who'd been on the cheerleading squad and the homecoming court, Cheryl had been part of the popular crowd that Rosalie had admired and envied from afar.

Now, all these years later, she lay on a metal dissecting table in Rosalie's autopsy suite, her seemingly gilded life cut short by the half-inch cylinder of lead lodged in her brain.

Next to Cheryl, under a stiff white sheet on a matching metal table, was Dwight Atkins, who would be autopsied immediately after his wife.

"This gives new meaning to the vow *until death do us part*," Marty said as he set a tray of dissecting tools beside Rosalie. "You think this qualifies as romantic or macabre?"

Ignoring Marty's question, Rosalie pressed the *ON* button on the small voice-activated recorder mounted beside the table and began to speak.

"Our first decedent is a white female measuring sixty-five inches and weighing one hundred thirty-three pounds," she said. "External appearance is consistent with the victim's age, which is known to be thirty-eight years."

Rosalie continued to describe her findings and observations in a soft, measured voice while Marty used the camera to document the process, taking photos from every conceivable angle for later reference.

Working her way up from Cheryl's stiff feet, she noted that there were no visible injuries or abrasions on the body. A soft knock sounded at the door as she reached the head, and she turned to see Detective Nell Kinsey.

The detective stepped into the room and immediately wrinkled her nose at the sickly-sweet smell of death which filled the autopsy suite.

Her eyes flicked to the metal table, then slid away at the sight of the grisly gunshot wound in Cheryl's head.

"How's it going?" she asked. "Have you had any luck recovering the bullets?"

"Not yet, but we're working on it," Rosalie said, nodding at two empty containers waiting on the tray. "I was just getting to that step now if you want to stay."

She returned her attention to the body on the table and again began to dictate into the recorder.

"Decedent has a penetrating gunshot wound to the right occipital scalp and perforation of the occipital bone with fractures," she said, studying the wound.

Selecting a long pair of stainless-steel tweezers, she bent over Cheryl's head and prodded the wound, picking out bits of bone fragments.

Finally, she straightened up and reached for a scalpel, making long, quick cuts in the skin over Cheryl's skull before pulling back two large flaps of skin to expose the bone.

Kinsey winced and turned away as Rosalie picked up the handheld oscillating bone saw and began to make an incision around the skull cap.

Once the top of the skull had been removed, she concentrated on mapping the trajectory of the bullet and removing the spent shell.

"The bullet trajectory is rightward and slightly forward," Rosalie dictated. "One spent bullet has been recovered from the right petrous temporal bone."

She motioned for Marty to turn off the recorder.

"You can look now, Detective Kinsey," she finally said, holding up the tweezers to display a battered cylinder of lead.

Dropping what remained of the bullet into one of the empty collection containers, she turned to look at the second body in the room.

As she pulled down the sheet, Rosalie's stomach knotted in sympathy at the sight of Dwight's emaciated body.

With a sigh, she clicked on the recorder and began to repeat the whole process.

"Our second decedent is a white male measuring

seventy-four inches and weighing one hundred fifty-eight pounds," she said. "External appearance shows signs of significant deterioration consistent with the victim's known diagnosis of advanced stage small cell lung cancer."

Working quickly, she performed the exterior examination and then moved upward, repeating the necessary steps to remove the skull cap and extract the bullet lodged in the dead man's head.

Rosalie's shoulders and back had begun to ache by the time she dropped the second spent bullet into the remaining collection container, which Marty held up triumphantly for Kinsey to see.

"Both of them are intact," he said, sounding pleased. "You should be able to run them through the ballistics fingerprint database to see if there's a match. Maybe bullets fired from the same gun have been recovered in another scene."

Holding the containers side by side, he studied the bullets, ignoring Kinsey's outstretched hand.

"I'm actually a bit of a forensics geek," he said absently. "Tool markings happen to be an interest of mine. If you let me take this to the lab I can look under the microscope."

Kinsey shook her head and held up a brown paper evidence bag she'd brought with her.

"I'm sending this off to the state crime lab," she said. "They'll enter it into the national database for me."

He frowned and squinted at the little lead cylinders.

"Won't that take too long?" he protested as he handed over the containers. "From what I see there, it looks like two different types of ammo. Which may mean the shooter used two different guns."

Kinsey raised both eyebrows.

"If the bullets are from two different guns, that definitely puts the nail in the coffin on the murder-suicide theory since we only found one gun at the scene."

Rosalie nodded.

"And it's clear from our initial examination of Dwight's body at the crime scene that he had no gun powder residue on his hands to indicate he'd fired a weapon, and no blood on his feet or legs to make us think he'd walked back down the hall after shooting his wife."

"So, we've got a murderer on the loose in Barrel Creek," Marty said, sounding somewhat excited. "I mean...in addition to the Wolf River Killer."

"I'm not so sure about that," Rosalie said. "If you look at the wound in Cheryl Atkins' head, and the bullet marks on the skulls we found in the river and the bullet hole in Vicky Vaughn's hoodie..."

Kinsey's eyes widened.

"Are you saying what I think you're saying?"

Rosalie glanced at Marty to gauge his reaction, worried she was opening a can of worms by telling Detective Kinsey her theory before she was sure.

Leaving Marty to collect the needed fluids and tissue samples from both bodies for toxicology testing, Rosalie led Kinsey to the exit.

"So, you really think the Wolf River Killer could have killed Dwight and Cheryl Atkins?" the detective asked.

She didn't wait for an answer.

"I mean, it's possible they'd seen something. Maybe witnessed the killer dumping bones in the river, or..."

Rosalie wasn't sure if Kinsey was speaking to her or to herself as her face grew more animated.

"It's just a theory," Rosalie cautioned her as they walked out toward Kinsey's SUV. "We need to be careful who we tell until we know more. If the public hears that the Wolf River Killer may be shooting people dead in their homes, we could start a panic."

"Of course," Kinsey agreed as she opened the door and slid into the driver's seat. "I'll share this information on a need-to-know basis only. Just my chief and my partner for now."

She rolled down her window and handed Rosalie her business card.

"If you think of anything else, call me right away," Kinsey said. "And if you happen to see Josie Atkins, let me know. We can't find her and I'm starting to get worried."

As Rosalie watched the detective drive away, a voice spoke up behind her.

"So, you think a serial killer shot Dwight?"

She spun around to see Frankie Dawson sitting in a black Mustang a few parking spaces away.

A furry black face poked out of the open back window.

"You weren't supposed to hear that conversation," Rosalie said, blushing a bright shade of pink.

"Then you shouldn't be having it out in public," he countered. "And speaking of the public..."

He climbed out of the Mustang.

"You plan to keep this information from the people around here? Don't they have a right to know?"

Rosalie folded her arms over her chest.

"No need to scare people unless we know we're right," she said. "I don't like to cry wolf, if you know what I mean."

Frankie scratched at the stubble on his chin.

"And what about Josie?" he asked. "What if this wolf goes after Dwight's daughter next? She's already missing. She could be in danger."

Rosalie opened her mouth, then closed it again, not sure she had a rebuttal to his argument.

"What is it you want, Mr. Dawson?" she asked, suddenly flustered. "Why are you here?"

"As I said, Josie Atkins is missing. I'm trying to find her. I thought she might have come here."

He hooked a thumb toward the medical examiner's office.

"It may be a longshot, but I thought she would have wanted to see her folks. You know, to find out what's going to happen to them. They're all she had from what I can tell."

"I'm sorry, but I haven't seen her," Rosalie said, pushing away the unwelcome questions that sprang to mind.

Did the teenager run away, or was she taken like the others? Will they find her bones in the Wolf River next?

"And it'll be some time before we release her parents' bodies," she added. "I'm assuming Dwight's parents-"

"Both his folks are dead," Frankie said bluntly. "I'm not sure about Cheryl's family, but for now, I'd say it's best to assume Josie is their next of kin."

"And what about Josie?" Rosalie asked. "Who's her next of kin? Who's responsible for her?"

Frankie's eyes narrowed.

"I am," he said. "Dwight asked *me* to take care of her. So, if you see her, make sure you call me first."

CHAPTER ELEVEN

Frankie climbed back into the Mustang and sped away from the medical examiner's office, unsure where to look for Josie next. Leaving the windows open, he followed Sherlock's example and lifted his face to the morning sky, sucking in the cool, fresh air and letting the wind blow his hair around his face.

One thing was for sure. He wouldn't be holding his breath waiting for Rosalie Quintero's call. The M.E. came across as a strict rule follower.

If she heard from Josie or found solid evidence proving that Dwight and Cheryl had been killed by the Wolf River Killer, she wouldn't be tapping his name on her speed dial.

No, she would share sensitive or confidential information on an open case only with the police.

Unfortunately, Frankie doubted the Barrel Police PD would know what to do with it.

He'd gotten the feeling that Detectives Ranger and Kinsey had their own agendas, although he couldn't yet figure out what either one of them was really after.

But as he turned the mustang onto Barrel Creek Trail, he decided if he wanted to know who had killed his friend, and why Josie had run away from the police, he'd have to take the investigation into his own hands.

Now, if I was a fourteen-year-old girl trying to stay under the radar, where would I go? Where would I feel safe?

The night before, he'd seen the crime scene techs taking her phone and computer out of the house, so she wouldn't have been able to contact her friends easily.

She was on foot and alone, so she's probably still nearby.

Making a sudden decision, Frankie executed a quick U-turn and headed back to the turn-off for Atkins Barrel Works.

The weathered wooden building appeared to be abandoned as he pulled into the lot. Parking the Mustang in front of the long, low structure, he saw a hand-written sign hanging on the front door.

Closed Today Due to Emergency!

He studied the careful, looping handwriting and the exclamation mark after the words.

Although it was possible that some well-meaning manager had decided to shut the place down for the day after finding out about Dwight and Cheryl, he figured he knew who had hung up the sign.

The place had been in the Atkins family for generations, and now there was only Josie left to carry on. From what Frankie knew, it was the only barrel plant still open in a town that had been named for the local industry back in the 1800s.

The question of who would run the place now and if it would close down like the others would have to wait.

Pulling on the door, he confirmed it was locked.

He crossed to the dusty window beside it, attempting to look inside, then hesitated as he heard a faint bark.

"Sherlock?"

The dog had been in the car, but he'd left the windows open. Looking around, he saw that the Labrador was gone.

Frankie decided that the bark must have come from the side of the big building.

Jogging around the big wooden structure, his stiff leather loafer rubbing painfully against his blistered toe, his mind flashed back to the years he'd spent as a teenager and young man working at the old place.

The sweet vanilla scent of charred oak hung in the air as he rounded the corner just in time to see Sherlock disappear through an open window.

"No, Sherlock!" Frankie called too late.

He hurried to the window and peered inside.

"Sherlock? Come here, boy!"

Hearing no responding movement or sound from the Labrador, Frankie cursed under his breath.

"You'd have thought someone would have trained that mutt how to follow basic commands," he muttered as he hoisted a skinny leg up and over the windowsill.

Minutes later he was standing inside a cool, dimly lit warehouse where an army of barrels had been stacked three-high on long wooden racks.

Frankie walked among the rows, calling softly for Sherlock, breathing in the sharp, sweet scent of the wood with nostalgia so deep it made his chest ache.

So many hours, days, and weeks had been spent in the old place with Dwight. So many years had flown by since.

Making his way through the warehouse, he saw Sherlock standing just inside the main workshop looking up.

The dog barked once and wagged his tail.

Frankie followed the dog's gaze to the small loft above the workshop floor and smiled, remembering the many afternoons he and Dwight had climbed up to the cozy space during their breaks to pass a bottle of whiskey back and forth.

He crossed to the steep staircase tucked against the wall and carefully began to climb. He paused at the top and looked down at the dog below.

"Stay!" he ordered Sherlock in a low whisper, then stepped up and onto the loft's creaky, wooden floor.

Moving further into the small, warm space, he stopped and looked down at a small figure curled up on the floor.

Josie lay on her side, fast asleep, her fist curled up beside her face. The scene summoned memories of Franny falling asleep on Granny's sofa while watching TV, and Frankie's throat tightened with pain at the thought of all he'd lost.

A sharp bark from below caused Josie to stir. Her eyes blinked open to see Frankie standing over her and she sat up with a gasp.

"Whoa there," Frankie said, lifting both hands in the air. "You're okay. I'm not here to hurt you. I just wanted to make sure you were alright. Everybody's been pretty worried."

Shrinking back against the wall, Josie stared up at him.

She opened her mouth to say something, then hesitated at the sound of claws scrabbling against wood.

Both Frankie and Josie looked toward the stairs as Sherlock's head appeared in the stairwell.

"I told you to stay, Sherlock," Frankie said, shaking his head as the dog crossed the narrow floor to stand beside him.

He turned to Josie, who was watching the Labrador closely, her blue eyes wide.

"Don't worry, he might not know how to listen, but he won't hurt you. Go ahead, pet him if you want."

She hesitated, then scooted toward Sherlock.

Kneeling next to him, she gently ran her finger down the scar on his face.

"How'd he get the scar?" she asked in a croaky voice that hinted she'd spent much of the night crying.

"I'm not sure," Frankie admitted. "But it makes him look tough, doesn't it? Like he should be in a dog gang or something, right?"

Cocking her head, Josie studied it, then nodded and produced a reluctant smile.

"Yeah, I guess it does."

When her smile faded, Frankie lowered himself to the floor, sitting across from Josie and Sherlock with his back propped against the wooden wall.

"Look, I know you're probably in shock about your folks," he said. "You're gonna be sad for a while. Maybe a long time. But that doesn't mean you won't smile sometimes, too."

When she didn't respond, he continued.

"I lost someone, too, so I kinda know how it feels."

He reached into his pocket and pulled out two sticks of gum. When he offered one to Josie, she took it.

"My little sister Franny died a long time ago, but it still makes me sad. I still miss her. It can take a while to-"

He stopped when he saw Josie staring at him with a startled, almost frightened expression.

"What's wrong?" he asked. "Did I say something?"

"Your sister was Franny?" she asked in a small voice.

A seed of apprehension took root in Frankie's stomach as he nodded.

"Yes, but she died...back before you were born."

He thought back to the previous night and frowned.

"You said something last night," he reminded her. "You said your dad wanted to tell me something about Franny. What was it?"

Josie dropped her eyes and bit her lip.

"My dad was really sick," she said, her words barely audible. "Dr. Habersham had told him he could die at any minute, so he was trying to...say his goodbyes, I guess."

A low simmer of anger rolled over Frankie as he remembered the callous man at the bar.

"I overheard my dad telling my mom about your sister."

She hesitated as if trying to build up her courage.

"He said Franny's death wasn't an accident," she finally whispered. "He said she was murdered just like those other girls, and that he knew who killed her."

Gaping at her, Frankie tried to make sense of Josie's

words. Franny had been *murdered?* Like the other girls?

"Are you sure that's what your father said?" he asked, his lips suddenly stiff and numb with shock. "He said she was murdered like the other girls?"

Josie nodded

"Who?" he demanded. "Who killed Franny?"

"I don't know," Josie said, her voice cracking in fear as she looked into Frankie's enraged eyes. "I couldn't hear what he said. I couldn't hear..."

Turning to Sherlock, she hugged the dog to her, burying her face in his soft, black coat as if seeking his protection.

"I'm sorry," Frankie said, shaking his head, trying to clear the fog of anger. "It's not you I'm mad at. But I've got to find out what happened. I've got to report this to the police."

He started to jump up, but she reached out a hand and grabbed his shirt sleeve.

"You can't go to the police!" she cried out. "My dad didn't go to the police because he said they couldn't be trusted. He was scared of them. Look what happened to him."

Seeing the panic in her wide blue eyes, he sat back down.

Had that been why Dwight had asked him to watch out for Cheryl and Josie? Had he thought the people who should be protecting them might actually hurt them?

He pictured Sheldon Ranger. The man was definitely hiding something. What would he do to keep it hidden?

"Okay, I won't go to the cops," Frankie heard himself say. "At least, not yet. Not until I figure out what's really going on around here."

Josie raised both eyebrows.

"You believe me?"

"Yes," Frankie said in a hard voice. "I believe if your father was scared, he had a good reason. I know for a fact that even cops can be crooked."

"You do?"

She sounded surprised.

"Yep, I do," he said with a sigh. "Corrupt cops down in Florida charged me with an armed robbery I had nothing to do with. I ended up spending time in prison. If I hadn't found a lawyer to help get me out, I might still be there now."

Her eyes grew even wider.

"You were in prison?"

She scooted backward.

"Hold on, I was innocent," he reminded her. "And that was a long time ago. I'm a private detective now. I work with cops all the time. I've even worked on cases with the FBI a few times to track down some pretty bad characters."

Cocking her head, she seemed to consider Frankie's words.

"If you did all that...can you find the man who killed my mom and dad?" she asked, her eyes suddenly bright with unshed tears. "I think he might try to kill me next."

Frankie thought about the bloody scene at the Atkins place, and about the bones along the river.

There was no way he could leave the girl in Barrel Creek while a madman was on the loose. Not if he planned to honor Dwight's last request. And not if he planned on finding out what had really happened to Franny.

"You know, your dad asked me to look out for you before he died," he said. "I never got a chance to tell him I would, but I'm telling you. I won't leave here until I find the man who killed your mom and dad."

Or the man who killed Franny.

He swallowed back a lump in his throat.

"I won't leave until I know you're safe."

She studied him with a doubtful expression.

"If you're a private investigator, don't you have to go home and work on your cases?" she asked. "Won't your family be waiting for you?"

Frankie slowly shook his head.

"There's no one waiting for me back in Florida," he said, trying to hide the pain the words caused him. "And for now, the only case I'm working on is right here in Barrel Creek."

CHAPTER TWELVE

eyton Bell ignored the incessant buzzing of the phone in her pocket as she parked her bike in the rack. Pulling off her helmet, she ran a hand through her dark pixie cut, then headed up the stairs to her apartment. Once inside, she reluctantly dug out the little device and looked down at the display. Her stomach twisted when she saw two missed calls from Arlene Dawson.

She hadn't spoken to her mother-in-law since the break-up, but she imagined Frankie had been forced to tell her about their split now that he was back in Tennessee.

She's probably calling to give me a piece of her mind.

Tempted to stick the phone back in her pocket, she sighed and tapped on the display, then held the phone to her ear, bracing herself as the voicemail began to play.

"Peyton honey, this is Arlene. I know you and Frankie are having some trouble, and I'm not one to interfere, but I thought you should know what's going on up here, just in case things escalate. Maybe Frankie's already called you, or maybe you've seen it on the news, but please, when you get this, call me back."

Peyton stared down at the phone, a frown forming between her troubled amber eyes.

Arlene had sounded stressed. Almost panicked.

And what did she mean when she'd said things could escalate?

Dropping the phone back in her pocket, Peyton moved out to the balcony and looked down at the Willow River below.

How many times had she and Frankie stood in that same spot together talking about their future and making plans?

Back then it had seemed like destiny. As if all the struggles and pain they'd been through had led them to each other.

Resting a hand on her stomach, Peyton felt the familiar pang of loss and regret, followed by the usual surge of anger.

She'd been foolish to believe in happily ever after. Those kinds of fairytales didn't come true for people like her.

That much was now clear.

But Frankie...he still had a chance. Without her, he could move on and have the future and the family he deserved.

She thought of Arlene's message again, replaying it in her mind, then moved back into the apartment, her concern growing.

What trouble is Frankie in that I would have seen it on the news?

Sinking into the chair in front of her laptop, she navigated to the *Memphis Gazette* website, not sure what she was expecting to see.

Her eyes widened as she read the top headline.

Police Question Suspect in Barrel Creek Double Murder!

The accompanying article detailed a gruesome double

murder at the house of a prominent business owner in Barrel Creek, Tennessee. Dwight Atkins and his wife, Cheryl, had been shot dead in their home on Sunday evening. The bodies had been discovered by a man who had called 911.

The Barrel Creek police department had issued a statement claiming that they had interviewed a person of interest in the investigation but hadn't provided the press with a name yet.

The article's author, a reporter using the byline Dusty Fontaine, went on to claim that anonymous sources within the department had confirmed that the man who'd called 911 was in fact a suspect in the killings.

Peyton read the article again, then pulled her phone out of her pocket. She navigated to the last text Frankie had sent.

Sorry, but I gotta reschedule the thing with the lawyers on Monday. Driving home to see my buddy Dwight in Barrel Creek. He's real sick. P.S. Not too late to change your mind.

Leaning back in her chair, she exhaled loudly.

He'd sent the text less than forty-eight hours ago, but somehow he'd already managed to become the prime suspect in a double murder eight hundred miles away.

Perhaps, considering that they'd originally met when she'd arrested him for an armed robbery he hadn't committed, and considering how frequently Frankie had managed to attract the undue attention of law enforcement since then, she shouldn't be surprised.

She'd been a detective in Memphis earlier in her career,

before she'd moved back to Willow Bay, and before she'd left Major Crimes to become an instructor in the Willow Bay Police Academy.

She knew better than most that the public would be pressuring the local police to find the killer, and she could imagine the assigned detectives would be looking for a quick way to silence the criticism and buy themselves time.

Frankie, with his complicated history and knack for getting into sticky situations, would be a natural target.

But he'd have to get himself out of this predicament on his own. It was no longer her concern. She'd made her choice and now, no matter how hard it was, she had to live with it.

Closing down the browser, she squeezed her eyes shut, trying to block out the memories that flooded through her, telling herself she had to stay strong.

She stood and walked slowly to the kitchen, planning to have just one drink. Just a small glass to take the edge off her anxiety. Just enough to dull the lonely ache in her chest. The ache that never seemed to go away.

The bottle of whiskey was new, its metal screw-top lid still firmly in place, and when she picked it up, it felt luxuriously full and heavy in her hand.

This would take away every last thought in my head if I let it.

All the memories, all the worries, all the pain could be gone in an hour, along with half the bottle and what was left of her tenuous will power.

Opening the nearest cabinet, she shoved the bottle inside and slammed the door shut, knowing she couldn't take the risk, no matter how much she craved the relief.

If I drink, I'll lose control. And if I lose control, I'll call him.

No, if she was truly going to help Frankie, she had to stay sober. Stay in control. She had to let him go.

CHAPTER THIRTEEN

Sherlock looked up as Frankie moved toward the stairs, then snuggled closer to Josie, who sat beside him on the floor, her back propped against the old wooden wall, her slim legs sprawled out in front of her, her small hand resting on his back.

"Come on, Sherlock," Frankie called. "Let's go."

Reluctantly getting to his feet, the Labrador sniffed at Josie's outstretched legs, then produced an uneasy whine.

The girl's tennis shoes still smelled of blood. The scent conjured an image in Sherlock's head. An image of the dark house where he had found the bodies of the man and woman.

Sherlock thought of it as the Death House. It reminded him of the place he'd stayed before he'd been taken to the shelter.

The bad place where he'd gotten his scar.

Not wanting to leave the girl alone and unprotected in the strange place, Sherlock turned and barked at Frankie.

Couldn't the man sense her fear?

"Quiet, Sherlock! Now, let's go."

Giving a final sniff to the offending shoes, the dog moved

across the room and descended the stairs behind Frankie.

The scent of blood in the air was soon replaced by another odor. There were mice in the building, he had picked up their scent as soon as he'd arrived, and he could hear them scurrying in the walls.

He sniffed again as he followed Frankie back the way they'd come, first through the workshop and then through the warehouse full of barrels, and relaxed when he didn't detect the scent of other humans nearby.

That was good, he decided.

The girl was much safer with mice as her companions than with men. Sherlock had learned that lesson when he'd received his scar.

Following Frankie back to the Mustang, he took up his usual position in the backseat and waited patiently for Frankie to roll down the window so that he could stick his snout outside.

The fresh air would get rid of the blood scent that seemed to linger in his nose even though the wooden building was already growing smaller behind them.

As the car pulled onto the highway, he stuck his head out, allowing his ears to flap back in the wind as he squinted against the rush of air against his face.

By the time the car stopped, he was feeling sleepy and ready for an afternoon nap, but Frankie was already opening the door and motioning for him to get out.

Looking up at the big building in front of him, Sherlock recoiled at the blare of music streaming through the door.

He waited for Frankie to snap on his leash, taking in the

heady scents coming from the kitchen, and the sweaty odor of two men passing by on the sidewalk.

As he trotted behind Frankie into the noisy building, he tensed and lifted his head, then began moving forward, anxiously sniffing along the floor, pulling Frankie after him.

He smelled blood in the building. The same blood that had been on the girl's shoes. Someone had tracked it inside.

Looking back at Frankie, Sherlock let out an excited bark.

"No dogs inside," a man behind the bar called, pointing toward a side door. "But he can hang out on the porch."

Sherlock gave the bartender a doleful stare, then allowed Frankie to tug him toward the door.

Luckily, the music wasn't as loud on the porch, giving Sherlock's ears a break, and the smell of the blood was fainter, although not entirely gone.

Frankie led him to a small round-top table outside and looped his leash over the back of a chair. He turned and went inside but was back moments later with a bowl of water.

Digging a dog treat out of his pocket, Frankie looked down at him with the stern expression Sherlock had come to recognize.

That expression meant he was about to get a treat as long as he stayed still and didn't break eye contact.

"Stay here and keep watch," Frankie said, holding up the treat. "I'll be back as soon as I've had a chance to catch up with my cousin. Shouldn't be long."

Sherlock woofed down the treat and licked his jowls, then

stared after Frankie as he made his way through the porch door, which was propped open with a plastic doorstop.

A woman with fiery red hair stood on the stage inside. She looked a little like the woman who'd taken care of Sherlock at the shelter. The woman who'd helped bandage his scar.

That woman had been a bit older, but she'd had the same pretty red hair, and her voice had been soft and soothing, like the woman on stage.

Keeping his eyes on Frankie, who now stood at the bar, Sherlock noticed a man in the crowd.

The man appeared to be watching Frankie with a cold, furtive expression that raised the fur on the back of Sherlock's neck.

No longer sleepy, the dog growled low in his throat and sat up straight, watching Frankie with dark, worried eyes, ignoring the loud music bombarding his sensitive ears, and the dizzying array of smells that couldn't quite mask the scent of blood.

He couldn't let his guard down. He needed to stay alert.

Death was in the building.

CHAPTER FOURTEEN

Frankie approached the bar and ordered a soda and lime from Jasper, swallowing back his craving for a whiskey sour. He knew it probably wasn't a good idea for a recovering alcoholic to hang out at a bar, especially after just learning that his sister's death hadn't been a tragic accident after all, but he'd promised to catch up with his cousin, and he didn't want to let his Uncle Rowdy down.

Scanning the room, he saw Gordon Habersham seated at a two-top table by the stage and quickly turned back to the bar before the doctor could catch sight of him.

But he didn't have to worry, the man's eyes were glued to Tara Wilder, who was setting up for the night's show.

The pretty, young singer was laughing with the roadie named Diesel, who seemed to be taking more time than was strictly needed to adjust her microphone.

"What are you doing standing here on your own?" Rowdy bellowed, causing all eyes to turn in his direction as he made his way across the room. "I've invited a few friends along. Thought we could turn this into a welcome home party."

He grabbed Frankie's arm, pulling him toward a table on

the opposite side of the stage.

"Come on, we're over here, Colton's dying to see you," Rowdy called over his beefy shoulder. "And your Ma's here, too. Thought it was only right to ask her to come as well."

Looking past the big man, Frankie was surprised to see his mother at the table, dressed up in a ruby red sweater and seated next to a man Frankie recognized as Bill Brewster, an old friend of his father's.

"You can sit here, Frankie," Bill said, moving down to make room for him next to Arlene.

He wondered why the man had been sitting so close to his mother, then frowned as Arlene flashed the man a coy smile.

They can't really be an item...can they?

Of course, he should be happy to think his mother might be dating again after she'd spent so many years alone.

Just because I'm a loser when it comes to relationships, doesn't mean Ma shouldn't give it a try.

A big man with spiky blonde hair and a wide smile stood up and held out a hand.

"Colton!"

Frankie turned to his cousin, instinctively straightening his spine as he pulled him in for a hug.

"Have you grown taller?" he asked as he pulled away.

"I don't know about that, but I weigh twice as much," Colton boasted, flexing a muscular arm. "Although you're still as skinny as ever. Doesn't your wife feed you?"

Before Frankie could respond, Tara Wilder stepped down from the stage, offering a welcome interruption.

"Aren't men supposed to be able to feed *themselves* nowadays, Colton Dawson?" she drawled. "Or can't you figure out how to turn on the stove?"

Colton blushed and kept his eyes on the singer as she brushed past him on her way to the bar.

"Can I have a cherry coke please, Jasper?" she said, producing a smile that lit up her sea-green eyes.

"It'd be my pleasure," the bartender replied, giving Tara his trademark wink. "One cherry coke coming up!"

"You gonna let Jasper flirt with your girlfriend like that?" Arlene asked when Colton had returned to her side.

She emphasized her question by jabbing a sharp elbow into his ribs, causing his face to flush scarlet.

"Tara's not my girlfriend," he protested, then added under his breath, "but I sure wish she was. Just like every other man in here."

"Well, you can't blame them. That girl sings like an angel," Arlene said with a sigh. "Makes me think of Patsy Cline whenever I hear her, don't you think, Bill?"

She looked past Frankie, but her potential new boyfriend hadn't been listening. His attention was focused on the television, which was turned to the news.

"Can't anyone think about anything but those bones?" Arlene complained, pointing to the reporter on the widescreen TV. "I'm getting sick and tired of hearing about the Wolf River Killer."

"I'll ask Jasper to turn the channel," Frankie said.

He rose quickly, stopping off to make his request to the bartender, before heading out to the porch to get some fresh air and check on Sherlock

He scratched the dog's head, then used his loafer to kick away a cigarette butt that had been discarded on the ground.

"Sorry about that," a soft voice said behind him. "That's mine I bet. I should have put that in the trash."

Frankie looked up to see Tara Wilder, who was pulling a pack of cigarettes out of her pocket.

"I usually have better manners, but Diesel was fussing at me to hurry up and test the mic earlier and, well...there's not an ashtray out here."

She held the pack toward Frankie, but he shook his head.

"Thanks, but I don't smoke," he said. "Not anymore."

"Well then, you're smarter than me," Tara teased.

Lighting the cigarette, she took a long drag.

"I keep telling myself I'm going to quit."

"You should listen to yourself. Those things will kill you," he said, thinking of Dwight as he pulled a piece of gum from his pocket. "Try one of these instead. It helps me when I have a craving. Which is just about every day. Sometimes twice."

Tara looked startled and then laughed.

The tinkling sound made Sherlock's ears perk up and the Lab looked up at the singer with adoring eyes.

"Cute dog," she said, bending to scratch Sherlock between the ears. "He must be a real comfort to you."

Frankie heard something wistful in her voice.

"I've got the amp set up if you're ready for a run-through."

Diesel stood in the doorway.

The man's face was inscrutable. He kept his eyes on Frankie a beat too long as if he was sizing him up.

Tara gave Sherlock a final pat, then turned and followed Diesel back into the bar.

Looking after her through the open door, Frankie saw his mother laughing with Colton and Bill.

Arlene caught Frankie's eyes and smiled.

He was suddenly glad to see she was out socializing instead of sitting on her sofa and living vicariously through reality television as she had done in Florida.

Maybe moving home had been what she needed all along.

Maybe she never should have left.

Maybe neither of us should have left.

The thought lingered as Frankie sucked down two glasses of soda. He had just ordered his third when Tara finally started her first set.

Arlene had been right. She did sound like an angel, and Frankie leaned back and let himself enjoy the first few upbeat songs that got all the boots under the table tapping the floor.

But when the intro to *If I Die Young* started up, Frankie abruptly stood and looked at the familiar upturned faces around the table.

"I gotta go," he said, backing away. "I'm tired and...anyway, thanks for this. I'll see you back home, Ma."

Turning on his heel, he nodded at Tara as he passed the stage, but the singer's eyes were closed, and she had her head thrown back as she belted out the lyrics about a life cut short.

The sweet smooth voice followed Frankie out to the porch, each line of the ballad delivering a stab of regret and pain as he grabbed Sherlock's leash and led him to the Mustang.

* * *

The Mustang's tires turned left out of Rowdy's parking lot, taking Frankie and Sherlock away from the lights of the city. They didn't slow down until the gates of Old Dominion Cemetery came into view.

Frankie brought the car to a stop outside an ornate stone mausoleum and surveyed the neatly manicured lawn, which was shaded by an impressive collection of oak trees and filled with row after row of white gravestones.

He hadn't been back to the cemetery since Franny's funeral, although he knew his Granny had visited often after her death to leave fresh flowers on the grave.

And once Granny Davis had gotten too old to make the twenty-minute drive over from Chesterville, she'd arranged for a rotation of the ladies from her prayer group to stop by at least once a month.

Of course, now that Arlene had moved home, she would be expected to take over the task and make sure there would be no absence of fresh flowers for little Franny Davis.

Without searching, Frankie's eyes immediately turned to the winding stone path that led to his sister's grave.

He'd been following that same path in his dreams for the

last fifteen years as his sleeping mind had forced him to relive the worst day of his life again and again.

Now, standing by Franny's grave, he read the epitaph on her gravestone with sad, dry eyes.

Our Sweet Girl
Francis Susan Dawson
Beloved Daughter and Sister

His heart squeezed as he realized his sister had spent as many years in the ground as she had spent walking the earth.

Could it really have been fifteen years?

The day of her funeral he'd stood in the same spot he was standing in now, his skinny arm wrapped around his mother's shaking shoulders as she had sagged against him, supported on the other side by a stoic Granny Davis.

Frankie closed his eyes, reliving the grief and guilt that had overwhelmed him as he'd surveyed the pitifully small group of mourners who had gathered.

His father had been gone for years by then, and they hadn't been able to track him down in time to make the service. Instead, Rowdy had stood stiffly in Henry Dawson's place, one big arm gripped tightly around his cousin Colton's shaking shoulders.

Anger had quickly risen in Frankie's chest when he noted Lacey Emerson's absence. His sister's supposed best friend was nowhere to be seen, nor was Lacey's drug-dealing boyfriend, Booker Boudreaux.

The two wild teens had led Franny astray. It was likely their fault she was dead, and yet they hadn't even bothered to pay their respects.

His eyes had searched the faces of the remaining attendees in vain for his own best friend, but Dwight Atkins had also been a no-show.

If he hadn't been in so much pain, Frankie might have let it pass. He might have put Dwight's absence down to a mix-up of time or location. But he was filled with too much self-recrimination to give anyone else a pass.

If I'd handled things better...if I'd never gone to find Dwight that afternoon, the rest of my life could have been so different.

Shaking his head, Frankie forced the useless thoughts away. Regrets, no matter how strong, couldn't turn back the clock. He placed two fingers on his lips, then touched them gently to the gravestone.

"I miss you, Franny Sue," he said, smiling at the sound of the childhood name he'd always teased her with. "But I'm home now. And I'm going to find out what happened to you if it's the last thing I ever do."

CHAPTER FIFTEEN

The Wolf got out of his old black Bronco and crept closer to the wrought-iron fence, ducking into the shadow of an oak tree as he watched Frankie Dawson lean over and place two fingers on his sister's grave.

His cold, calculating eyes remained fixed on the lanky figure until Frankie had driven away in his Mustang.

Realizing he'd been holding his breath, he exhaled and moved toward Old Dominion Cemetery's open gate, wanting to slip inside before it was closed and locked for the night.

The pressure had been growing inside him again, rising and pulsing as it always did before a kill.

But this time he was feeling unusually anxious, perhaps sensing that the net around him was tightening as more and more of the bodies and bones he'd discarded over the years were being discovered.

Following the same winding path Frankie had walked only moments before, the Wolf found himself standing in front of a gravestone he'd never seen.

The bodies of most of his victims had been thrown into the river or buried in the darkest part of the forest where few people dared to go.

Rarely did he get a chance to visit their graves or reminisce about their deaths. But Franny Dawson had been different from the start. She'd been an unintended casualty.

What the military might call collateral damage.

Staring down at the grave, his mind rewound the last fifteen years, returning to the chaotic night that had ended with Franny's death.

The workshop was nestled in the small clearing of a forest that bordered a remote, overgrown section of the Wolf River.

His grandfather had left it to him in his will, and the Wolf had kept his ownership of the property to himself, rarely inviting anyone out to see his secret hideaway.

Visitors would ask too many questions.

Of course, any of his legitimate acquaintances knew where he lived, and the lowlifes he associated with as part of his smuggling operation knew how to find him if needed.

But not at his workshop. That was meant to be private.

So, when Booker Boudreaux appeared in the workshop doorway, the Wolf hadn't been expecting him.

"What the hell are you doing here, Booker?" he demanded. "How'd you even find this place?"

"I followed you after you left Rowdy's the other night," the younger man said with a cocky confidence the Wolf didn't like. "I saw you leave with Georgia Treadwell."

A nasty smile spread across Booker's face.

"You know who I mean, right? The hot blonde who was trying to get a gig at the club? The one who went missing?"

"Missing?" the Wolf scoffed. "That girl was so high when I

dropped her off, she was practically flying. She's probably holed up with some dealer back in Nashville right now."

Booker shrugged.

"That may be," he said, flashing a wiseass grin. "Should we see what the Memphis PD thinks about that idea?"

The Wolf frowned, unable to hold in the question he knew Booker wanted him to ask.

"Why the Memphis PD?"

The smile widened on Booker's face.

"That's where her mother filed a missing person report," he said. "She put up flyers all over town, too. So, I'm thinking I may go and give a statement. Let them know the last place I saw Georgia."

He paused for effect.

"Which was in your truck."

"Why would you do that?" the Wolf asked as he stuck his hand in his pocket, settling his fingers over the little Ruger inside. "I doubt they'd listen to a small-time drug dealer with a big-time smack habit anyway."

The smile slid off Booker's face.

"Oh, they'll listen alright," he said. "I'll make sure of that. Unless you're ready to pay up. It'll cost to keep me quiet."

"Fine, how much do you want?"

The question seemed to startle his would-be blackmailer.

"In fact, let me see what I've got in my wallet, and we can just settle this right now," the Wolf said with a shrug. "It's over there on my workbench if you want to grab it."

Booker hesitated, then turned toward the bench, but before he had taken a full step, the Ruger made contact with the back of his head.

"Try something stupid and your brains will end up on the floor."

Before Booker could react, the Wolf shoved him toward the door, forcing him to the battered Toyota parked outside.

"Whose piece of shit is this?" he asked, pushing Booker toward the trunk.

"It's my girlfriend's," Booker stuttered. "It's Lacey's."

Opening the trunk with one hand, the Wolf ordered the now-shaking drug dealer to get in, knocking the hard metal of the gun against his head to hurry him up.

"What are you going to-"

The sudden crack of the gunshot echoed in the air, scattering a flock of birds in a nearby tree.

Booker lurched forward, blood and brain tissue splattering around him, then slumped headfirst into the trunk.

Shoving the rest of his body inside, the Wolf slammed the trunk closed and ran around to the driver's side of the Toyota.

He saw the blood on his hand just as he went to open the door.

Running back inside his workshop, he washed off the blood the best he could, pulled on a clean pair of work gloves, then jumped into the car.

As he drove the Toyota back to Booker's apartment, careful to stay under the speed limit the whole way and to stop fully at every stop sign, he cursed himself yet again for impulsively killing Georgia Treadwell without thinking of the consequences.

Of course, it hadn't been his fault that the aspiring singer had been so beautiful. And that she'd been willing to do whatever he asked in exchange for the drugs.

But when he'd been unable to take what was offered, the embarrassment and the frustration had been unbearable.

Her pitying eyes, hungry for the white powder in the little bag he'd handed her, had ignited his rage.

As she'd turned to leave, he'd acted before he'd known what he was doing, sticking the small barrel of his little Ruger against the back of her head, and pulling the trigger with a wolf-like growl, setting off a satisfying explosion that had rocked him to his core.

It had been a careless act considering he'd been seen leaving Rowdy's Bar with the girl, and now he might pay for his foolishness with his freedom.

But if he could make it to the drug dealer's apartment unseen and leave the car parked at the complex with the body inside, the police might assume the young man had been a victim of a drug deal gone wrong, or that a domestic quarrel had gotten out of hand.

There would be no search. No bothersome questions.

Only when he parked the Toyota in an empty space beside the dumpster did the Wolf allow himself to exhale.

"What are you doing in Lacey's car?"

Franny Dawson stood beside the open car window. She leaned over, looking past him toward the passenger's seat, a slight frown forming between her curious brown eyes.

"What am I doing here?" he repeated stupidly as he thought of the Ruger he'd left by the sink in his workshop. "I should ask what you're doing here."

"I'm waiting for Lacey," she said, rolling her eyes.

The Wolf tried to think fast.

"Well, you shouldn't be hanging around with a girl like that," he said, glancing in the rearview mirror to see if they were being observed. "Booker's gotten in some trouble, so I offered to drop off Lacey's car so it wouldn't be towed."

The curious expression on Franny's face turned to worry, but he didn't give her a chance to ask any questions.

"Let me drop off the keys inside and then I'll make sure you get home safely. Come on, you shouldn't stand out here on your own."

Pulling the keys from the ignition, he stepped out of the car and headed toward the building, silently formulating a plan as he went.

Franny had already seen him in the car. Even if he disposed of Booker's dead body, his blood and brains were all over the trunk. There would be a search. An investigation.

The girl was sure to say that she'd seen him in the car. And he would spend the rest of his life in prison.

He couldn't let that happen. He couldn't let her live long enough to talk. But he would have to do something fast before he was seen.

He'd gotten halfway across the lot when he looked back.

"You coming?" he asked, trying to summon a smile.

"I guess," Franny said, sounding hesitant.

Walking past him to the door of a ground-floor apartment, she waited while he fumbled with the keys. Once he figured out which key opened the door, he let her inside and stepped in after her.

Before she could switch on the light, he had his arm around her throat and was squeezing with all his might.

Franny's legs kicked out behind her, but she was wearing lightweight tennis shoes that made little impact.

Within minutes she had slumped forward in his arms.

Letting her limp body fall to the floor, he quickly removed the shoelaces from her tennis shoes and bound her arms and legs, then began to search the house.

It didn't take long for him to find several bags of white powder stuffed under the sofa, along with all the necessary paraphernalia to carry out his plan.

Opening one of the bags, he spilled a small mound of white powder onto the coffee table, then added a little more. Using a spoon and a lighter, he melted the heroin into liquid and filled the entire syringe.

As Franny's eyes began to flutter open, he jabbed the needle into the soft flesh of her arm. She winced and stared down at her arm then up at the Wolf in disbelieving horror.

"My brother knows I'm here," she gasped out. "Frankie will come for me. He'll find you and he'll...he'll..."

Her words died away as her eyes drooped shut.

Exhaling in relief, the Wolf dragged Franny's lifeless body down the hall. He untied her hands and legs, then arranged her on the bathroom floor, satisfied that her death would be deemed an accidental overdose.

As he turned and crossed through the living room, he spotted a silver locket lying on the rug by the front door.

He picked it up, saw the initials FD engraved on the back, and dropped it into his pocket.

The parking lot was deserted and quiet when he stepped outside and locked the door behind him. Making his way along the alley to the main road, he crossed the street just in time to jump on a city bus heading west.

He made it all the way back to his house before he allowed himself to think about Booker's body in the trunk.

"They'll just think it was a drug deal gone wrong," he muttered to himself as he tucked the locket into his box of souvenirs. "They'll never trace it back to me."

And, as he stood over Franny's grave all these years later, the Wolf realized they never had.

Her cause of death had been documented as an accidental heroin overdose, and it had taken over a week for the smell in the trunk of Lacey's car to attract attention.

By then, Booker's body had been too badly decomposed for the M.E. to discern an exact time of death, and it had been relatively easy for the Wolf to use his contacts inside the Barrel Creek Police Department to point the investigation in Lacey Emerson's direction.

The impulsive, drug-addicted girl had been quickly convicted and sentenced to twenty-five years at Larksville Correctional Facility for the murder of her boyfriend.

It had all seemed to work out just fine in the end.

Or so he'd thought before things had started unraveling.

First, the interfering tree-huggers had decided to restore the Wolf River, uncovering his stash of bones.

Then Dwight had been diagnosed with a fatal illness, prompting his pathetic attempt to clear his conscience before he met his maker.

And now Frankie Dawson coming home to investigate his sister's death? That just might be the final blow that would take him down once and for all.

Retracing his steps back to the Bronco, the Wolf reassured himself that he had everything under control.

After all, he'd handled Booker, Franny, and Lacey without anyone ever finding out the role he'd played. He could handle Frankie Dawson as well, so long as he didn't make any more foolish mistakes.

He'd already gotten rid of his souvenirs. There was no more evidence to connect him to the bones they'd found and the bodies he'd dumped. No evidence to prove he was the Wolf River Killer.

But perhaps I should delay my plans for tonight. Just to be safe.

Was he tempting fate by trying to take another victim so soon? The Wolf clenched his fists, feeling the urge growing inside him. He needed a way to stop the craving, and as far as he knew, there was only one way to do that.

Another girl would have to die.

CHAPTER SIXTEEN

Tara Wilder pushed open the door and dropped her guitar case on the wooden floor. She had been using the renovated barn as a makeshift apartment and music studio for the last few weeks and was beginning to feel at home. The place had retained a faint aroma of hay, livestock, and manure that reminded her of her family's barn back in Waynesboro.

As she shrugged off her leather jacket and hung it on the rack, she sensed a sudden, furtive movement behind her.

Spinning around with a gasp, she scanned the dimly lit room, her wide green eyes searching for the source of the noise, half-expecting someone to jump out of the shadows.

The place appeared to be empty.

"All that talk about bones has got me skittish as a newborn colt," she murmured, reaching for the light switch.

Just then something soft brushed against her leg.

Letting out a scream, she jumped back to see Dolly, the calico barn cat recoil, and then scurry under the sofa.

"You nearly scared me to death," Tara gasped as Dolly reappeared. "How'd you get in here, anyway?"

The cat belonged to her landlord and had free run of the property, including the barn, but usually preferred to roam outside at night.

Pulling off her boots, Tara wiggled her toes, regretting her decision to turn down the rides offered by more than one potential suitor in favor of walking home on her own.

I should have let Colton give me a ride. He's a sweetheart, and he's easy on the eyes, too. So, what's my problem?

She knew she should jump at the chance to date a man like Colton. After all, he was Rowdy Dawson's son, and Rowdy owned the only bar currently giving her steady work.

But no matter how many times she'd tried to talk herself into starting up something with the overtly eager man, she just couldn't go through with it.

It wouldn't be fair to him. Not when she was stupidly and whole-heartedly in love with someone else.

She looked down to meet Dolly's wide, golden eyes.

"As the song says, the heart wants what the heart wants. Or was it Emily Dickenson? Well, whoever said it, it's true."

The cat blinked up at her in what Tara took to be silent agreement as she began to massage her aching feet.

It didn't matter that Colton offered her the possibility of a stable relationship with a respectable man. Her heart had been snared by someone else.

And that someone wasn't in the market for anything more serious than a casual fling. He'd made that much clear.

No, Jasper Gantry wasn't a one-woman man, and she was a fool for letting him get under her skin in the first place.

But, at least I didn't let him into my bed.

And she was determined to make sure it stayed that way.

In fact, it was probably best not to mix business with pleasure at all. Best not to date anyone at Rowdy's. That would only lead to complications and hard feelings.

She'd made that mistake before. Like the time she'd broken up with a promoter in Nashville and all her gigs there had suddenly been canceled.

No, it wasn't a good idea to date Colton or Jasper.

Or any of the other men sniffing around after my shows.

Deciding to take a bath in the old cast-iron clawfoot tub that dominated the bathroom, she turned the faucet on full blast, allowing the water to heat up as it filled the tub.

Before she could climb in, Dolly padded to the door and looked back at her with wide golden eyes before issuing a plaintive *meow.*

"Have you got a cute Tomcat out there waiting for you?" Tara asked as she opened the door.

Dolly didn't reply as she slipped out into the darkness, and Tara turned back toward the bath with a smile.

Her fingers were already unfastening the top button of her shirt when she heard the soft sound of an engine.

Frowning, she went to the window and peered out, but could see only darkness.

She was about to move away when she saw movement among the trees that lined the dirt driveway leading to the barn. Straining to see past the shadows, she decided it must just be the wind blowing the leaves around.

Perhaps the sound wasn't an engine, but just–

Her thought was cut short by a strong hand grabbing a fistful of her fiery red hair.

"Too good for the likes of me, are you, Tara?" a deep voice growled in her ear. "We'll just see about that."

The intruder lifted a gun in front of her face. It was a Glock, the same kind of gun her father had taught her how to shoot with back in Waynesboro.

"Stay quiet, or I'll put a bullet in that pretty little head of yours," he said. "Now, we're going to walk outside and get in my car. Don't try anything stupid."

Still gripping her by the hair, he forced her toward the back door. The wood around the lock had been broken, and she felt shards of splintered wood under her bare feet as he pushed her outside.

A black Bronco was waiting close to the barn, its engine running and its back door open. She couldn't let him put her in the car. Not if she ever wanted to be seen alive again.

Tara waited, knowing he'd have to loosen his hold on her hair if he planned to shove her inside. That would be her only opportunity to make her move.

As soon as he released his grip, she twisted around and grabbed his hand, yanking it toward her and biting down on his arm with savage determination. She didn't let go until the world around her exploded and went dark.

CHAPTER SEVENTEEN

Franny called out from the darkness, her familiar voice far away but coming closer. Straining to hear what she was saying, Frankie sat up and looked around the attic room, his tired, bleary eyes searching the morning shadows for any sign of his little sister.

"Franny?"

His voice was a strangled whisper in the quiet room, waking Sherlock, who shifted at the foot of the bed.

Squeezing his eyes shut, Frankie concentrated on Franny's voice, trying hard to remember the dream as it began to fade.

What was she saying? What was Franny trying to tell me?

But it was too late. The words, and Franny, were gone.

Frankie sighed and rubbed the sleep from his eyes, then leaned over and checked the time on his phone.

He'd made it to dawn, despite much tossing and turning.

It wasn't hard to figure out what had been bothering him. The visit to Franny's grave the day before had unsettled him, and he'd been further stressed after returning to Atkins Barrel Works to find the loft empty and Josie gone.

And those were only the latest problems.

Even if he found Josie, he still had to figure out who had killed her parents. And who'd killed Franny. Not to mention who'd been dumping women into the Wolf River.

Wishing that Peyton was there to give him advice, Frankie got dressed and quietly descended the stairs after Sherlock, hoping not to wake up his mother.

He went out the back door to find Granny Davis sitting in her rose garden.

"You're up early," he said with a start.

She shrugged and patted the bench.

"I like the sunrise," she said matter-of-factly, sounding like her old self. "Sit down and enjoy it with me."

Frankie crossed the lawn and sank down next to her. He felt her small hand tuck itself into the crook of his arm.

"I'm glad you're finally home."

She looked up at the crimson sky above them.

"I knew you'd come back."

"You did?" Frankie asked.

"Of course," she said with a knowing smile. "Eventually, when things get tough, we all want to go home."

He nodded and squeezed her hand, realizing the answer was simple, just as Granny had said.

Josie would want to go home.

And if she's not there now, she'll go there eventually.

Frankie waited until Granny Davis had gone inside, then led Sherlock to the Mustang and headed for Ironstone Way.

Yellow crime scene tape blocked off most of the driveway and the porch, although there were no vehicles parked outside, and no one appeared to be guarding the place.

Pulling the Mustang along the curb, Frankie took his Glock from the glove compartment and checked the chamber.

It had been a while since he'd used the weapon, but with everything going on in Barrel Creek lately, he figured he might need it, especially if the man who'd killed Dwight and Cheryl decided to return to the scene of the crime.

He got out of the car and snapped a leash on Sherlock, not wanting the Lab to lead him on another chase.

As Frankie approached the big house, he surveyed the empty upstairs windows, remembering the pale, scared face he'd seen the last time he'd been there.

He'd thought for just a moment it had been Franny looking out, but it had been Josie's face, he knew that now.

Bypassing the front porch, he walked around the house to the back patio and tried the kitchen door. The knob turned easily in his hand.

"Hello?" he called out as he stuck his head inside the silent, empty kitchen. "Anyone here?"

When no one answered, he stepped inside and waited for Sherlock to follow, then closed the door behind him.

His loafers made a soft *tap, tap, tap* on the marble floor as he crossed to the hall.

"Josie?"

Only silence greeted him as he moved to the bottom of the stairs and looked up at the landing.

"Josie, if you're here, it's just me, Frankie Dawson."

Still no sound or movement from anywhere in the house.

"Sherlock's with me!" he added, trying to sound cheerful. "He'd like to see you and make sure you're okay."

Deciding to check out Josie's room first, Frankie made his way up the stairs and stopped outside the open door with the purple sticker.

Josie's Room – Keep Out!

The room was disheveled as if it had been rifled by burglars, and Frankie assumed the crime scene team and investigators had been through all of her possessions.

He made a point to look in her closet and under her bed, but Josie wasn't hiding in her room.

Remembering where he had found her the last time he was in the house, Frankie turned and went down the hall to her parent's room. He stepped through the open door and gaped at the mess the investigators had left behind.

The bedspread had been pulled off the bed and was lying in a heap on the floor beside what looked to be the entire contents of the dresser.

All the drawers had been removed and were haphazardly stacked in the corner. All the pictures had been taken off their hooks and had been carelessly thrown to the floor.

He looked around at the mess with a frown. Had the cops really left it like this? Or had someone else come inside to search the place?

Search doesn't cut it. They've ransacked it.

The idea stayed with him as he moved to the closet and surveyed the piles of clothes, shoes, and purses that had been thrown on the floor.

It seemed whoever searched the house hadn't found what

they were looking for. Their mounting frustration showed in the mess they'd left behind.

Frankie was just about to turn and leave the room when he had a vague memory of being in the closet once before.

He'd come home with Dwight one day after school and had followed him up the stairs. But instead of going to his own room, Dwight had quietly motioned for Frankie to follow him into his parent's room.

Leading him into the closet, Dwight had grabbed hold of a coat hook on the far wall and pulled down. Instantly a panel in the wall popped open revealing a secret compartment inside.

"This is where my mother keeps her good jewelry," Dwight had whispered. "And my dad always has a few rolls of bills in here. He'll never miss a few."

Frankie had protested that they'd get caught, but Dwight peeled two fifties off one of the rolls and they'd gone to the mall to buy the basketball shoes Dwight had been eyeing.

Deciding it was worth a try, Frankie stepped forward, grabbed the coat hook, and pulled. The panel sprang open just as it had for Dwight.

His pulse quickened as he looked inside. He wasn't sure if he could believe his eyes.

The secret compartment was stuffed full.

Thick bundles of one-hundred-dollar bills had been crammed in next to a shoe box and a folder full of documents. The folder rested on a gallon-size plastic storage bag filled with white powder.

Frankie froze in place

What the hell has Dwight been up to?

Sherlock growled at his feet, then barked toward the bedroom door, but Frankie held on to his leash, still staring into the secret compartment, trying to come to terms with what it all might mean.

A creak on the stairs finally got his attention.

Someone was in the house.

Heart racing, Frankie pushed the panel closed and spun around just as quiet footsteps reached the bedroom.

"Come out, Mr. Dawson," a deep voice called out. "I'm armed, so keep your hands where I can see them."

Lifting his hands over his head, Frankie stepped out of the closet. Detective Sheldon Ranger stood in the middle of the bedroom, his Glock pointed at Frankie's chest.

"I thought our killer might return to the scene looking for the girl," he said. "And here you are."

Frankie kept his eyes on the gun in Ranger's hand as Sherlock continued to growl.

"Josie's not here. And neither is the bastard who killed her parents. So, you can go ahead and put that gun down."

Ranger made no move to lower his weapon.

"Mr. Dawson, I need you to come down to the station. You can come willingly, or I can arrest you for vandalism and trespassing at a crime scene. Your choice."

Lowering his hands, Frankie shrugged.

"Calm down, man. No need for threats," he said, trying not to look at the coat hook. "I'll come, no big deal. But my dog comes with me."

CHAPTER EIGHTEEN

Kinsey held open the door to the Barrel Creek Police Station and waited for Ranger to usher Frankie and Sherlock inside. As they started down the hall to the interview room, Chief Shipley came around the corner. His forehead creased into a deep frown as he drew near.

"I need to talk to you two," he barked. "Put Mr. Dawson in the interview room and then meet me in my office."

He brushed past them and was already halfway down the hall when Kinsey heard him call over his shoulder.

"And get that dog out of here!"

Staring after the chief's wide shoulders and thick thatch of graying hair, she sighed and turned to Frankie.

"If he goes, I go," he said, nodding to Sherlock.

Before she or Ranger had a chance to respond, he lifted a hand as if to stop them.

"You can skip the whole *we're going to throw you in a cell* act. We all know I'm not the shooter, so save your breath."

Ranger's back stiffened as Kinsey suppressed a smile.

"I was going to say that the dog can stay with you in here," she said, pushing the door open and motioning him toward a wooden table in the middle of the room. "Take a seat. Detective Ranger and I will be back shortly."

She smiled down at Sherlock, then closed the door behind her before Ranger could object.

"After you," she said, gesturing toward Shipley's office.

She suspected she already knew what the chief had to say. The man was predictable if nothing else.

"Let's get this over with."

Minutes later she was standing beside Ranger listening to Shipley rant about his unfair treatment in the press, just as she'd expected.

"We need to get the public and the reporters off our backs," Shipley admonished. "This is getting out of hand. I've had calls from every member of the city council as well as the mayor. They're all asking what we're doing to find the Wolf River Killer. They need something solid to tell their constituents."

He sucked in a deep breath.

"I expect you two to find something to give them, pronto."

Turning to Ranger, he lowered his voice, adopting an intimate, paternal tone that didn't match his cold eyes.

"Son, I'm counting on *you* to make your father proud."

There was an awkward pause as if he was waiting for Ranger to respond. When he didn't, Shipley sat back in his chair with a dissatisfied huff.

"What about Frankie Dawson?" he asked, turning to Kinsey. "Are we ready to charge him? What do we have?"

"Charge him?"

She arched a smooth eyebrow.

"The only charge we could make stick right now would be trespassing at a crime scene," she said, careful to keep her mounting frustration out of her voice. "We don't have sufficient evidence for anything else."

Shipley seemed to consider the idea, then shook his head.

"That's not going to satisfy the mayor or the press. We need a murder charge to make this go away," he said, slapping both palms on the table. "You get in there and question him. See what you can get out of him. See if you can get enough to charge him. Or better yet, see if you can get him to confess."

Kinsey gaped at him.

"Sir, we don't think Frankie Dawson is our shooter."

Her words didn't seem to register.

Shipley got to his feet and pulled on his suit jacket.

"Just do your job and put the pressure on him," he said, walking to the door. "And keep me updated. I want to know as soon as you're ready to take this to the district attorney."

She watched him leave, then turned to Ranger.

"Should we have told him the Atkins murders may be the work of the Wolf River Killer?"

Shaking his head, Ranger got to his feet.

"Shipley just wants this case closed and off his plate as soon as possible," he said. "Unless we have an actual suspect we can name and charge with the murders, he won't give a damn that there's a link."

Kinsey figured her partner was probably right.

As she followed him back into the interview room, she also figured that questioning Frankie Dawson again was going to be a total waste of time.

They needed to be out questioning Dwight and Cheryl's friends and neighbors. They needed to find out who may have been holding a grudge. Who had something to lose or to gain by their deaths?

Stopping just inside the interview room door, she saw Kai Lang kneeling beside Sherlock, her sleek black ponytail hanging over her shoulder as she stroked his soft coat.

The pretty, young officer had brought in a bowl of water for the Labrador and was talking to the dog in a high-pitched playful voice that contrasted with her somber blue police uniform.

"Who's a thirsty dog? You're a thirsty dog, aren't you?"

Kinsey suppressed a smile as she caught the disgruntled expression on Ranger's face.

"Officer Lang, can you leave us now, please?" he asked stiffly. "We need to interview the subject."

Lang quickly stood and left the room as he and Kinsey sat in the metal folding chairs across the table from Frankie.

"Okay, Mr. Dawson, what-"

"I said to stop with the act. No more *Mr. Dawson*. Call me Frankie. And sitting here is wasting my time, so just tell me what you want to know. Or is this just a fishing expedition?"

Drumming his long fingers on the top of the table, Frankie met Ranger's eyes in what appeared to Kinsey to be a staring contest.

"What were you doing at the Atkins place, Frankie?" Kinsey asked quietly, trying to break the tension. "What were you hoping to find?"

Frankie flicked his eyes to hers. After a long beat, he allowed his shoulders to relax.

"I was looking for Josie," he said. "I went back to the house because I was worried for her. She's just lost both her mom and her dad, and now she's alone out there. I want to help the poor kid. Is that a crime?"

Kinsey studied his thin, stubbly face.

She believed he had been looking for the girl, and that he did want to help her. But he was also hiding something.

"Why did Josie run off? Why is she hiding from the police?" she suddenly asked, lowering her voice, and leaning forward. "Do you know what's really going on? Is there something you can tell us about Josie?"

A flicker in Frankie's eyes told her she was on the right track. He knew something about the girl that he wasn't willing to share.

"Listen, Frankie. We want to help Josie, too," she said.

"Then how about you start by finding her parents' killer," Frankie shot back. "What are you doing about that besides sitting here questioning a guy you know for a fact didn't pull the damn trigger."

Ranger stood and banged his fist on the table.

"We don't know who shot that couple," he said, his voice tight with anger. "And until we do, you are still considered to be a person of interest."

He exhaled loudly and sank back into his chair.

"Now, all we know for sure is that it wasn't a murder-suicide and that two guns were used, one of which is still missing. But we have no solid evidence as to who actually pulled the trigger."

Kinsey watched the emotions play over Frankie's face.

His defensive anger seemed to dissipate at Ranger's frank admission that they were no further along in finding Dwight's killer than he was.

She caught a flash of something that looked like fear in his eyes. Whether it was for himself or for Josie, she wasn't sure.

"We do have a tentative theory..."

Glancing toward Ranger, she saw his look of warning but decided they had nothing to lose.

"You see, we have reason to believe that the man who shot Dwight and Cheryl could be the Wolf River Killer."

She paused, expecting some sort of reaction, but Frankie didn't appear to be surprised by the revelation.

He just returned her stare, scratching softly at the stubble on his chin, as if waiting for her to continue.

"You already knew?"

Ranger's question exploded into the room.

"How'd you find out?"

He turned accusing blue eyes toward Kinsey, but she held up her hands in denial.

"I'm a private investigator," Frankie reminded him. "It's my job to find things out. Just like I'm going to find out who killed my friend and his wife, with or without your help."

A knock on the interview room door saved him from the angry response that had formed on Ranger's lips.

Officer Lang appeared in the doorway.

She was no longer smiling.

"Sorry to interrupt, but there's been a call," she said in a hushed voice. "Another body's been found."

"Where?" Kinsey demanded.

But she already knew what Lang was going to say.

"In the Wolf River. Some people were canoeing and.."

Her words were drowned out by the scrape of the chair as Frankie jumped to his feet.

"Have they identified the body?" he asked. "Do they know who it is?"

The fear in his voice told Kinsey that he must be thinking the same thing she was.

Could it be Josie? Could the body in the river belong to Josie?

* * *

The Interceptor bumped down an uneven dirt road, surrounded on both sides by a dense forest of red maple, tupelo, and bald cypress trees, before finally emerging onto a patchy expanse of grass and weeds along the Wolf River.

Kinsey parked behind a Barrel Creek PD patrol car and stepped out into the fresh April morning, noting the circling birds in the sky just downriver.

Walking toward the riverbank, she surveyed the murky brown water, which seemed still and stagnant, but which she knew would ultimately flow past Memphis toward Mud Island and the Mississippi River.

"We turned too soon," Ranger said, holding his handheld

radio as he came up behind her. "The body's further downstream. We can walk along the riverbank there."

He pointed to a muddy path leading into the trees.

"You're kidding right?" Kinsey said, looking at the thick undergrowth, thinking about snakes.

But Ranger was already striding forward, his eyes searching the riverbank ahead for signs of the responding officers and the body they were there to investigate.

Slowly making her way along the edge of the river after him, Kinsey again looked up at the sky, realizing they were heading toward the circling birds.

"Damn vultures," she murmured under her breath as she caught sight of their wide black wings and small red heads.

She began to walk faster as she saw Officer Jackson waiting for them on the riverbank. Ranger turned and waved to her, motioning for her to hurry up.

Hurrying forward, she slipped on the muddy ground and stumbled toward the water, her stomach lurching in sudden panic. Pinwheeling her arms, she regained her balance just in time to stop herself from going into the river, managing to suppress the scream that had risen in her throat.

Cheeks hot with embarrassment, she caught up to Ranger just as Jackson gestured toward the water.

"Two women in a canoe were passing by here a few hours ago. They saw something caught in those cattails."

Kinsey's eyes followed his hand, searching the water.

"I don't see anything," she said.

"Oh, she's not out there anymore," Jackson said. "Once they saw it was a woman, they dragged her up on the dock."

He turned to point to an old wooden dock beside the water.

"She's down there under that tarp."

The officer hitched up his belt and holster and frowned.

"The problem is, there's a parking spot just past the dock. A few reporters have already arrived. Must have been listening to the police radio. More will be coming soon, I bet."

Kinsey nodded, knowing the word would spread fast.

"We've got to cordon off the area as soon as possible."

"I've already told the responding officers," Jackson said. "They're putting up the tape now. And Lang should be here any minute. She'll help them secure the perimeter."

A startled yelp sounded from behind them.

Kinsey spun around to see Frankie Dawson trailing behind them on the muddy path. He'd gone down on one knee, and she assumed he'd slipped at the same spot where she'd almost fallen into the water.

"He must have followed us over here," she said, turning to Ranger, but her partner wasn't listening, and he hadn't noticed Frankie.

Instead, he was stomping purposefully toward the dock, his face a stony grimace, his fists clenched by his side.

Racing after him, Kinsey saw the target of his anger.

Dusty Fontaine from the *Memphis Gazette* was aiming his camera at two women huddled near the dock, a battered canoe at their feet.

They appeared to be ignoring the reporter as he snapped

their photo, then turned his attention to the tarp, which had blown back to reveal a pale white face surrounded by a sodden tangle of fiery red hair.

"How could you do this?" Dusty yelled as Ranger stormed up. "How could you let another one die?"

"Mr. Fontaine, you need to back away, now!" Ranger said.

But it was clear that the sight of the man's obvious distress had drained away some of the detective's outrage.

"She was a singer."

Kinsey turned to see Frankie standing behind her.

He looked pale and shaken.

"I saw her sing a set at Rowdy's just last night," he said. "Her name was Tara Wilder."

Kinsey nodded, wondering how Chief Shipley was going to take another victim being added to the count.

Especially a pretty young victim with a fanbase.

"Call the medical examiner," she said in Ranger's direction as she moved forward to adjust the tarp and cover the dead woman's face. "Tell her she's got another body to collect at the Wolf River."

CHAPTER NINETEEN

Pulling open the wide, stainless-steel drawer, Rosalie stared down at the collection of grayish-white bones inside. Reaching out a gloved hand, she carefully picked up a skull and studied it with a thoughtful expression.

"They all have a small-caliber entrance gunshot wound to the right side of the occipital bone," she said, handing the skull to the petite woman beside her.

Dr. Uma Chandra cocked her head, a delicate line forming between her warm, brown eyes as she considered the hole in the bone and the fracture lines radiating out from it.

So far, the forensic anthropologist had examined three of the skulls discovered during the restoration project along the Wolf River and had quickly concluded that they had all belonged to female homicide victims.

She'd determined that two of the skulls had belonged to girls in their late teens, while the other belonged to a woman in her early twenties.

"I have to say I've never worked on such an interesting case," Uma said. "The fatal wounds are remarkably similar in each skull, and the weathering of the bone is consistent."

Rosalie motioned to the rest of the bones in the drawer.

"Well, there's a lot more work to be done," she said with a sigh. "I hope you find the other bones just as interesting."

Uma laughed and handed the skull back to Rosalie, who carefully returned it to the drawer.

She was grateful that her former college roommate, now a respected expert in the forensics field, had offered to help her examine all the skeletal remains that had been collected.

It wouldn't be an easy task to identify each one of the assorted bones and determine how long they'd been lying in and around the Wolf River.

But that information was vital. It could help the police discover who had dumped them in the water. And if they could help the police find the culprit, they could hopefully prevent more bones from turning up in the future.

As she slid the drawer shut, Rosalie felt her phone vibrate in the pocket of her lab coat. She winced when she saw the number on the display.

"Detective Kinsey, I'm sorry I haven't gotten the autopsy report over to you, yet," she said, thinking of the paperwork stacked up on her desk. "But I promise, this afternoon I'll-"

"No, that's not why I'm calling," Kinsey quickly interrupted. "It's just...there's been another homicide. I need you to come down to the Wolf River."

Rosalie's heart dropped.

Gripping the phone to her ear, she heard a loud, plaintive bird call out in the background.

"Please hurry," Kinsey said. "The press is already here, and the vultures...the *real* vultures, are circling as we speak."

Ending the call, Rosalie dropped the phone back into the pocket of her lab coat and turned to Uma.

"Marty and I need to go down to the river to pick up a body," she said with a grimace. "You want to come along?"

Uma nodded eagerly.

"I never turn down a chance to get out of the lab and work in the field," she said, flashing a blindingly white smile. "Especially in springtime. It's a beautiful day out there."

But her smile dimmed when they pulled up to the scene in the big white medical examiner's van to find an unruly crowd of reporters and onlookers.

"Are there usually so many people at your crime scenes?" she asked, staring around in dismay. "Aren't the police afraid they'll contaminate the evidence?"

Rosalie didn't get a chance to answer as someone rapped loudly on the van's window.

"Pull up to the dock," a uniformed officer yelled, moving aside a long strip of yellow crime scene tape, and pointing toward the river. "Detective Kinsey is waiting for you."

Minutes later Rosalie, Uma, and Marty were standing with Kinsey on the rickety dock in their protective coveralls, staring down at the recovered body of a young woman with pale skin and bright red hair.

She was barefoot, wearing only faded jeans and a baby-blue, long-sleeved, button-up shirt. There was also a faint ring of bruising around her slender throat.

Marty pulled out his camera and began taking pictures as Rosalie crouched down beside the dead woman and used a gloved hand to turn her head gently to the side.

"Rigor mortis has set in," she said quietly, looking up at Uma, who stared down at the body with keen interest.

"And the back of her head?" Uma asked.

Bending forward, Rosalie confirmed what she'd already suspected. She met Uma's eyes and nodded.

"She's been shot. Just like the others."

Uma sighed and shook her head.

"What a terrible shame," she murmured. "Such a young, beautiful woman. Do they know who she is, yet?"

"We had a visual ID by several people who knew her," Kinsey said. "And we found this in her back pocket."

The detective held out a plastic evidence bag with a damp piece of paper inside. Rosalie could see it was a check from Rowdy's Music Bar and Grill.

The ink was smeared, but the handwritten words were still legible. It had been made out to Tara Wilder in the amount of three hundred dollars.

"Apparently, she was a singer down at Rowdy's," Kinsey said. "And she was last seen leaving the bar late last night."

"Okay, that gives us a start on calculating time of death then," Rosalie said. "And we can pretty much guarantee what the cause and manner of death are right now."

Looking past the detective, she caught sight of a reporter aiming a camera in their direction.

"We'd better get a tent set-up to shield her from the

crowd while we complete the examination."

Her words sent Marty jogging back to the van.

"It shouldn't take long since this isn't the primary crime scene. She was obviously killed elsewhere and dumped."

Kinsey nodded.

"We're trying to find out where she's been staying."

As Marty returned with the tent, Uma knelt next to the body, then pointed at Tara Wilder's slightly open mouth.

"Is that what I think it is?" she asked, leaning closer.

Rosalie leaned forward for a better look and felt her pulse jump. A bloody chunk of skin tissue appeared to be stuck between Tara's front teeth.

"Take a picture of this, Marty," she said. "I think she may have bitten her attacker."

She glanced back at Kinsey with a grim smile.

"This could mean we'll get DNA."

Hope surged through her at the thought. They just might catch the Wolf River Killer after all.

Determined to get back to the lab and collect the sample from Tara's mouth for DNA testing as soon as possible, Rosalie completed the examination in record time and helped Marty load her body into the van.

Pulling up to her office twenty-minutes later, she rushed inside the building, eager to get into the autopsy suite.

She came to a standstill when she saw the small figure huddled on a chair in the lobby.

Josie Atkins had been waiting for her.

The girl looked as if she hadn't slept in days.

"I want to see my parents," she said with a catch in her

throat. "I want to tell them good-bye."

CHAPTER TWENTY

Frankie wandered through the crowd of police officers, reporters, and stunned onlookers who were still gathered along the riverbank even though they'd seen the medical examiner load Tara Wilder's body into a van twenty minutes earlier and take her away.

Studying the faces around him, he suspected the Wolf River Killer might be in the crowd, wanting to revel in the fear he'd caused with his latest kill, or maybe trying to find out what the police were doing to catch him.

I need to find him. I need to stop him from doing this again.

The sight of Tara Wilder's pale, lifeless face had shaken Frankie to his core, reminding him that the man responsible could go after anyone, at any time.

No one's safe in this town until he's been taken down.

The thought circled his mind as he walked back toward the path leading along the river.

He needed to get back to the Mustang, where he'd left Sherlock sleeping with the windows cracked.

Frankie hadn't expected to be gone long, but it had been over an hour. The dog might have woken up and would need to stretch his legs and take care of business.

He stopped in mid-stride as a man stepped in front of him.

The man was thin and wiry with small eyes, a sharp nose, and longish hair that appeared to be thinning on top. He wore a leather jacket, tight jeans, and a pair of pointy-toed boots with thick two-inch heels.

"You're Frankie Dawson, aren't you?" he asked as if making an accusation. "I'm Dusty Fontaine, a reporter for the Memphis Gazette, and I–"

"I know who you are," Frankie cut in. "You're the one who's been writing all those articles about the missing girls," he said. "And you're also in my way."

As he tried to brush past him, the reporter held out a hand.

"This isn't about the girls," he said. "This is about Dwight and Cheryl Atkins."

Frankie paused and frowned down at him.

"What about them?"

"I understand you were the one who found their bodies and called 911," Dusty said. "Can you tell me what your relationship with the victims was?"

Shaking his head, Frankie pushed past him onto the path and began to walk along the river's edge.

He turned at the crunch of footsteps on the mud and gravel behind him and saw that Dusty was giving chase.

"Why were you at the Atkins house on Sunday evening?" the reporter called out, breathing hard as he tried to keep up with Frankie's much longer legs. "What did you see while you were there?"

As Frankie turned again to see if Dusty was still behind him, the persistent reporter whipped out a camera and snapped a photo, catching the moment he instinctively lifted a hand to shield his face.

Relieved to see the Mustang parked where he'd left it with Sherlock safely inside, Frankie reached for the handle.

"Is it true you've been in prison?" Dusty prodded.

Opening the back door for Sherlock, Frankie sucked in a deep breath, then spun around to face Dusty.

"I'll tell you what's *true*," he said, pointing a skinny finger in the reporter's face. "What's *true* is that it's none of your goddamn business where I've been."

He exhaled loudly, as the shock and stress that had been building inside him the last few days finally boiled over.

"What's *true*, is that you're trying to make a buck and a name for yourself by writing about a sick, twisted killer. But that just gives him the attention he craves. That just makes him feel important."

Trapped beside the car as he waited for Sherlock to finish his business, Frankie shook his head in disgust.

"What's *true*, is that you're egging on a psychopath," he said. "So, you can stop pretending like you're on some kind of crusade to stop him."

Seeing that the Labrador was ready to go, Frankie gave the reporter a final piece of advice.

"Now, I suggest you stay away from me in the future, or I guarantee, you'll wish you had."

The reporter stepped back and lifted his camera, which Frankie now realized had probably been recording all along.

"Threats and insults won't stop me, Mr. Dawson. I'll only stop when the Wolf River Killer is dead or behind bars."

Frankie opened the door for Sherlock and waited for the dog to jump inside before sliding into the driver's seat.

As he sped out of the parking lot, he looked in his rearview mirror and saw Dusty holding up his camera, recording his hasty departure.

"I guess I told him, didn't I, Sherlock?" he said, glancing in the backseat. "Real smooth, huh?"

But the dog wasn't listening.

He'd stuck his head out the window and was staring back at the receding river as they drove away.

Berating himself for letting the reporter get under his skin, Frankie headed the Mustang toward Chesterville.

His phone rang before he'd made it to the highway.

At first, he didn't recognize the number, or the woman's voice on the other end.

"Mr. Dawson? This is Rosalie Quintero, the Barrel Creek medical examiner. I have Josie Atkins here, and she's asking for you. Do you think you could come down to my office?"

* * *

Frankie's eyes watered as soon as he stepped into the building. The acrid scent of decay and disinfectant clogged the air, causing his stomach to turn.

"I'm here to see Dr. Quintero," he said to the woman behind the reception desk. "She called me earlier and–"

"This way, Mr. Dawson."

Rosalie Quintero stood at an open door leading into the back. Her dark hair was coiled into a loose bun at the nape of her neck, and she wore royal blue scrubs.

"I really should be in the autopsy suite right now, but I've got Josie in my office," she explained as Frankie followed her down the hall. "I told her the police have been looking for her, but she threatened to run away if I called them. I wasn't sure what to do, and then she asked for you."

Stopping outside a closed door, Rosalie hesitated.

"I've already notified the Barrel Creek PD that she's here," she said quietly. "Hopefully, you can convince her not to run off again before they arrive."

The medical examiner looked up at Frankie as if expecting a response, but he only nodded, eager to see the girl and make sure she was alright. As the door swung open, Josie glanced up in alarm, then relaxed when she saw Frankie standing in the hall behind Rosalie.

"Where've you been?" he asked, relieved to see the teen. "I've been looking for you."

She shrugged and dropped her eyes to the floor.

"I came here to see my mom and dad."

"And I explained that we're not prepared just yet," Rosalie said gently. "We need time to get her parents ready for a viewing if she wants to see them."

Expecting Josie to protest, Frankie was relieved when she just nodded her head, as if she understood.

"Dr. Quintero said I can come back on Thursday. I was

thinking I could stay with you until then."

She sneaked at peek at his face, then cocked her head and frowned at the empty corridor behind him.

"Is Sherlock with you?" she asked hopefully.

"I dropped him off at my Granny's house," Frankie said. "I didn't think Dr. Quintero would appreciate me bringing a dog into her office."

Frankie lowered his voice into a conspiratorial whisper.

"And I didn't think Sherlock would appreciate the smell in here," he added, earning a nod of agreement from Josie. "But maybe I can take you over to see him. You could hang out with my Granny while we figure things out. She'll like you."

He glanced at Rosalie in time to see her shoulders stiffen.

"I'll need to let the authorities know where you are."

She gave Josie a stern look.

"Apparently, they need to ask you some questions..."

Her voice trailed off as a stubborn expression fell over Josie's face. When the medical examiner spoke again, she sounded resigned.

"I guess I could tell the detectives you've gone with Mr. Dawson to meet his grandmother and get some rest."

A knock followed her words. The door opened and a young man wearing green scrubs stuck his head in the door.

"Sorry to interrupt, but there's a Detective Kinsey here for you, Rosalie. She said you called her about a witness?"

"Thanks, Marty. Please ask her to wait just a minute."

But Nell Kinsey was already stepping around the forensic technician, her eyes lighting up as she saw Josie.

"Thank goodness you're alright," she said, sounding genuinely relieved. "I thought we'd lost you for good."

Catching sight of Frankie, she blinked in surprise.

"What are *you* doing here?" she asked.

"Watching out for her," Frankie replied, sounding more confident than he felt. "As I told you before, Josie's father asked me to take care of her if anything bad happened to him. I'd say getting murdered qualifies."

Kinsey raised a skeptical eyebrow.

"I think we need to let Rosalie get back to her autopsy," she said. "The three of us can go to the station and sort everything out down there."

"I'm not going anywhere with you."

Josie stood and backed away, her eyes instantly filling with tears as Frankie stepped between the teen and the detective.

"Listen, the girl's tired and she's traumatized," he said, his eyes beseeching Kinsey. "Let me take her back to my Granny's house. She can rest up and get some sleep. Tomorrow, when she's feeling better, I'll bring her down to the station and she can answer your questions."

Kinsey hesitated, then to his surprise, she nodded.

"Okay," she said. "It wouldn't do much good to force her to come in if she's not prepared to talk. And we've got our hands full with the new scene down by the river."

She pinned her eyes on Josie.

"I hope you'll be ready to tell me everything you can remember tomorrow," she said solemnly. "We want to catch whoever killed your parents, but we need your help."

Stepping back into the hall, Kinsey met Frankie's eyes.

"I'll call you tomorrow to set up a time for you to bring her down," she said. "Make sure you answer your phone."

And with that, she was gone.

"Okay, Josie," Frankie said, waving a hand toward the door. "Looks like we're going to Granny's house."

CHAPTER TWENTY-ONE

Josie followed Frankie out to his black Mustang and settled into the passenger's seat next to him. As he pulled onto Hastings Highway, she buckled her seatbelt and kept her eyes trained on the increasingly unfamiliar terrain flashing by outside the window.

Although she'd grown up on the outskirts of Memphis, she hadn't spent much time outside of Barrel Creek, and she'd rarely ventured into the suburbs that surrounded the city.

She'd never thought too much about it before, but she'd had a lot of time on her own during the last few days to think, and she'd decided that her parents must have been trying to protect her from something all along.

Or maybe they were protecting me from someone.

Remembering the cold, faceless voice of the man who had shot her parents, she shivered. The man would have surely killed her, too, if he'd found her under the bed.

Wrapping her thin arms around herself, she stared out the window, assuring herself she was safe.

She was with Frankie. A man her father had trusted.

And from everything she'd learned about him in the last

twenty-four hours, she thought he might be the only one capable of finding her parents' killer.

"So, where'd you go?" Frankie asked. "When I got back to the loft, you were gone. Where were you?"

"I got scared," she said. "Men came into the warehouse after it got dark. I heard them talking. They were moving barrels around."

Her chest tightened as she remembered the sound of their deep, loud voices in the warehouse below her.

"They didn't come up to the loft, but when they left, I thought I'd better leave, too, while I had the chance. Just in case they came back."

Frankie frowned.

"Men moving the barrels after dark? That's weird."

She nodded in agreement.

"After that, I went back to my house," she said. "I thought if the police were gone, I could get some of my stuff, maybe even sleep in my room."

Her throat constricted and her eyes watered as she pictured the mess she'd found in the house.

"But someone had been there," she said. "They messed everything up and threw things around. I couldn't stay..."

Faltering on the words, she looked out the window until she managed to swallow back her tears.

"Anyway, I walked into town. Everything was closed, even the library, but I saw someone inside. A woman was rolling around a cart with all this cleaning stuff. When she left to carry some things out to her car, I kind of snuck in."

"You *kind of* snuck in?"

Frankie glanced over at her with wide eyes.

"So, you broke into the library and stayed there?"

She nodded, thinking she wouldn't mind living at the Barrel Creek Public Library, as long as they started stocking their vending machines with better food.

"I used the computers to play games and look up some stuff," she said. "I even read a book."

Josie decided not to tell Frankie the book was called *Self-Defense: A Teen Girl's Guide*, or that she'd also spent a full hour googling his past and reading about the cases he'd solved on the library's computers.

From what she could tell, he'd helped a lot of people, and had tracked down some pretty scary criminals, including a few serial killers.

"I stayed at the library as long as I could," she said. "But once it opened, the librarian started giving me weird looks, so I thought I'd better leave. That's when I decided to go to see my parents."

Her stomach suddenly twisted at the prospect of seeing her mother and father again.

But she knew she needed to see them one more time. Just to know it had all been real. To prove to herself she hadn't imagined or hallucinated that whole terrible night.

And she needed to say good-bye.

"Here we are," Frankie said, sounding relieved.

Turning the Mustang onto Monarch Avenue, he pulled into the driveway of a wooden, two-story house.

"Not as fancy as your place," he teased. "But it's been a second home to me since I was a kid."

Josie stared up at the weathered porch and the flowerboxes in the windows with approval.

Something about the place seemed familiar and safe, although she wasn't sure what it was. She definitely had never been to Chesterville before, much less to the modest white house on Monarch Avenue.

Following Frankie around to the back door, she hovered behind him as he rapped twice then walked into the kitchen, where Sherlock waited by the door, his tail wagging.

As Josie gave the dog a hug, she looked around the room.

A small woman with snow-white hair sat at the table, her head bent over a square of white linen, her knotted fingers embroidering a design on the fabric with pale pink thread.

"Granny? We've got a visitor," Frankie said, motioning for Josie to step forward. "She's Dwight Atkins' girl, and she's going to stay with us for a while if that's okay with you."

The woman looked up with a faint frown.

When she saw Josie standing beside Frankie, her small face lifted into a happy smile.

"Franny, I was wondering where you were."

Getting slowly to her feet, the woman crossed the room.

Josie froze in place as she lifted a soft hand to caress her cheek, her brown eyes gleaming.

"Granny, this is *Josie Atkins*," Frankie said, his voice soft and patient. "She's Dwight Atkins' daughter."

"It's nice to meet you, Mrs. Davis," Josie said, thinking

of the manners her mother had taught her.

The woman shook her head.

"Call me Granny, child. That's what you always call me."

She turned and went back to her chair, picking up her embroidery with a sigh.

"And make me some tea, dear. I'm feeling parched."

Glancing over at Frankie for help, Josie saw him point at a kettle on the stovetop.

"You do know how to boil water, don't you?" he asked with a smile. "Even I know that."

Josie nodded and crossed to the stove, feeling instantly at home in the small, cozy kitchen as she poured fresh water into the kettle and pulled a teabag from a box on the counter.

Later, after the tea had been brewed and Josie had eaten a peanut butter sandwich and gulped down two glasses of milk, Frankie showed her to a small room upstairs.

"This was Franny's room whenever we visited, which was a lot," he said, crossing to the window and opening the curtains. "Some of her stuff is still here. I'm not sure what all she left. Maybe some clothes..."

He pulled open a dresser drawer and looked inside.

Slowly, he lifted out a shiny, purple wallet, staring at it with sad, somber eyes.

"Purple was her favorite color," he said, opening the wallet and looking inside. "Yours, too, right?"

Josie narrowed her eyes.

"How'd you know?"

"I saw the sticker on your bedroom door," he said. "I'm

a P.I., remember? I have to notice these things."

As he flipped the wallet closed, a row of photos fell out. The kind taken by the photo booths in the mall.

Leaning over, Josie picked up the pictures.

"That's Franny," Frankie said, pointing to a thin girl with straight brown hair and big brown eyes. "And those were her so-called friends, Lacey Emerson and Booker Boudreaux."

His voice hardened as he said the names.

Josie stared down at the teenagers in the photos.

They were a little older than she was, but they looked like regular kids. The kind she passed in the halls every day at Barrel Creek High.

"What happened to them?" she asked in a small voice. "What happened to Franny?"

The question hung in the air as Frankie pulled a piece of gum from his pocket.

"You want a piece?"

Josie shook her head as Frankie peeled off the wrapper and stuck the gum in his mouth.

"Franny was a great kid. I mean, really smart and funny," he said. "And she loved school. She was always making good grades no matter how many times Ma dragged us to a new house and a new school district."

He rubbed at the stubble on his chin and sighed.

"Then we moved to Barrel Creek, and when she started high school, she started hanging around Lacey Emerson."

From the way Frankie said the name, Josie figured the girl must have done something terrible. She held her breath as she waited for him to continue.

"Lacey was always getting Franny to sneak out and do things she shouldn't do," Frankie said. "And her boyfriend, Booker Boudreaux, was bad news."

He gritted his teeth as if the memory still made him angry.

"The guy was a small-time drug dealer. A real loser. But Lacey was hooked, and Franny started hanging around with the two of them, going out at all hours. I told her they were trouble. I tried to stop her. I'd nag her...follow her. But she said Lacey was her best friend. She wouldn't listen."

He sucked in a deep breath and looked toward the window with a faraway expression.

"Then one night, Franny was found in Booker's apartment. She'd died all alone on the bathroom floor. The medical examiner called it an accidental overdose."

Josie's stomach twisted into a tight knot as she recalled her parents' final conversation.

"Franny's death was no accident. She was murdered...just like those other girls. And I know who did it."

"But Franny died of an overdose. She wasn't murdered."

"That's what he wanted everyone to believe. He set it all up."

"Who? Who set it up? Who killed Franny?"

If only she'd been able to hear her father's response. Then she'd be able to tell Frankie what had really happened. And she would know who had killed her parents.

"But it wasn't an accident," Josie said softly. "The man made it look that way to hide what he'd done."

Frankie nodded.

"I didn't know that then. I thought I'd let her down. That she'd gotten involved with drugs and lowlifes and..."

He ran a distracted hand through his hair.

"I thought Booker had gotten what he deserved. I heard his body was found in the trunk of Lacey's car a week after Franny died," he said. "He'd been shot in the head. The police claimed Lacey killed him during a drug-fueled argument. I figured it was karma."

"You think she really killed him?" Josie asked.

She studied Lacey's face in the photo, wondering what it would be like to spend half of your life in prison.

"She's serving a 25-year sentence at Larksville...but I don't know," Frankie said. "It's possible it was all a lie. Just like what they told me about Franny's death. I guess, after all this time, there's no way to know what really happened."

Looking down at a photo of Franny with her arm around Lacey's shoulders, Josie wasn't so sure.

"If anyone knows the truth about Franny's death, I think it would be her best friend," she said. "I think you need to talk to Lacey Emerson."

The idea seemed to appeal to Frankie.

He nodded.

"Yeah...maybe I should," he said as his phone buzzed in his pocket.

His face tightened as he looked down at the display.

"What's wrong?" Josie asked.

"Nothing," he said, dropping his phone into his pocket. "Just my wife's lawyer trying to reschedule a meeting."

Josie blinked.

"You have a wife?" she asked.

"Yeah, I have one," he confirmed. "Or, at least, I used to."

CHAPTER TWENTY-TWO

Peyton had woken early that morning, unable to dispel the worry that had wormed its way into her mind after she'd listened to Arlene's pleading message the day before. Jumping out of bed, she had immediately checked the *Memphis Gazette*, dreading what she might see.

She'd been relieved to find no update on the search for Dwight and Cheryl Atkins' killer, and no mention of Frankie. Maybe it had all blown over.

But now, as she sat in Dr. Ellicott's waiting room, she checked the site again, then immediately wished she hadn't.

Wolf River Killer Strikes Again as Body Found in Barrel Creek!

Scanning the story under the headline, she saw that a young singer named Tara Wilder had been seen walking away from Rowdy's Music Bar and Grill after a performance. Her body had been discovered in the Wolf River the next morning.

A photo of two women huddled in front of a canoe accompanied the story, along with a dozen other photos of the crime scene. The same kind of scene Peyton had been called to many times during her years in law enforcement.

As she scrolled through the images, she saw the victim's

body being wheeled toward a medical examiner's van on a gurney, then inhaled sharply at the sight of Frankie's tall, lanky figure standing in the crowd.

Moving her eyes down the page, she noticed another article below the main headline.

Man Questioned in Double Murder Threatens Gazette Reporter.

This time, Frankie's angry face was front and center in the photo. An accusing finger pointed at the camera.

She grimaced at the first line of the story.

Florida P.I., Frankie Dawson, who has been named a person of interest in the murders of Dwight and Cheryl Atkins by the Barrel Creek PD, was seen at the scene of the latest murder along the Wolf River threatening Gazette reporter Dusty Fontaine.

After skimming through the rest of the article, Peyton closed out the news site and tapped on her email inbox, holding her breath as she waited to see if her contact at the Memphis PD had responded.

Her heart skipped a beat as she saw the reply. Tapping to open the message, she read it with growing concern.

> *Hey Peyton, good to hear from you – it's been a while. You've been missed around here for sure. As for your questions about the Barrel Creek P.D., I've heard rumors for years about corruption. Some say it goes up to the highest level, but so far, nothing's been proven as far as I know. With all the bodies turning up in their jurisdiction, I'd be surprised if the feds don't get involved soon. My advice: stay well away from*

Barrel Creek...

She jumped as an impatient voice called her name, closing the email without reading the rest of it.

"Dr. Ellicott can see you now."

Slinging her purse over her shoulder, Peyton stood and followed the nurse into the back, quickly stepping on the scale without any interest in the numbers it showed.

The nurse led her to a small room, giving her curt instructions to remove her clothes and put on a paper gown.

She was sitting on the cold examination table with her hands folded limply in her lap when Dr. Ellicott came in.

The doctor looked through Peyton's chart, then sighed.

"It's been six months now since the loss," she said, regarding Peyton with warm, empathetic eyes. "Have you and your husband tried the support group I mentioned?"

Peyton shook her head.

"My husband and I are no longer together," she said, swallowing hard, managing to keep her voice steady. "But, I still have the information you gave me, so I might try the support group on my own. Once I feel up to it."

Concern filled the doctor's face.

"I know how excited you both were," she said hesitantly. "And the loss of a pregnancy, and the knowledge that future conception isn't possible, can be traumatic. Most people need time to process their grief. And counseling can-"

"I'm in a hurry, Doctor," Peyton said, keeping her eyes on her hands in her lap. "If we can get to the exam, I'd appreciate it."

Seeing the tight set to Peyton's jaw, Dr. Ellicott nodded and called to the nurse, but her eyes remained troubled as she completed the exam and told Peyton to get dressed.

Before leaving the room, she looked back.

"Forgive me for saying this, but I hope you won't make any rash decisions right away. Sometimes time and healing give you a different perspective."

Peyton nodded stiffly, not trusting herself to reply.

Riding her bicycle back home, she allowed herself a quick cry, drying her eyes as she walked upstairs to the apartment.

I did what needed to be done. I set Frankie free.

By ending their marriage, she had given him the chance to start a new life before it was too late to have the children and family he so badly wanted.

How could she live with herself if she let him give up the one thing he wanted more than anything else? Hadn't he already lost too much of his life to bad luck and misfortune?

She thought of his father abandoning the family when Frankie had still been a teenager, passing on a legacy of alcohol abuse and addiction. And his little sister's death had filled him with guilt and regret that had never gone away.

Then of course there had been his arrest and conviction for a crime he hadn't committed, an injustice in which she herself had played a part.

When they'd found out they were going to have a child, she'd never seen him so happy. He'd confessed he'd always wanted to be a father. The memory of his happy tears that day still broke her heart.

But their happiness had been short-lived, soon replaced with the unbearable pain of losing their unborn daughter.

When they'd been told Peyton could never conceive again, she'd felt her whole world drop out from underneath her.

She would never be a mother, and Frankie would never have a chance to be a father. Of course, he had argued that they could always adopt, but she'd known better.

What agency would allow two alcoholics to take home a child?

She'd had to accept that the only way Frankie could have the life he'd always wanted, was without her.

And now it seemed as if he was throwing his chance for that life away by risking both his safety and his freedom.

If he's locked up or killed, it will all have been for nothing.

Spurred on by the depressing thought, Peyton dug out her phone and scrolled through her contacts, then tapped on a number she hadn't called in years.

She just hoped it wasn't already too late.

CHAPTER TWENTY-THREE

Frankie came downstairs to see Josie sitting beside Granny Davis on the sofa, with Sherlock resting at her feet. The teenager didn't seem to mind that the elderly woman called her Franny, and she had instantly bonded with Sherlock, who didn't want to leave her side.

Grabbing his jacket and car keys, Frankie headed toward the door, calling out for his mother to hurry up.

"You sure you're going to be okay here with Granny Davis while we go to the fundraiser?" Arlene asked as she slipped on a jacket and picked up her purse. "You can always call us if you need anything, and we'll come straight home."

Josie nodded and squeezed Sherlock tighter as Frankie ushered his mother out to the car.

They were headed to Rowdy's, where his uncle was holding an impromptu memorial fundraiser for Tara Wilder's family, to help cover her funeral expenses.

"I just can't believe this has happened," Arlene said, as they drove west toward the city. "That girl was the sweetest thing. What reason could anyone have to kill her?"

"There is no good reason, Ma," Frankie said. "I learned

that lesson a long time ago. Some people are just born bad. It's like they don't have a soul the way normal people do."

He tried to imagine the anger and hate it must take to put a gun to the head of an innocent woman and pull the trigger.

"Sometimes, I think people like that must be motivated by hate the same way normal people are motivated by love. It can make them do stupid, senseless things."

An image of Peyton flashed through his mind.

What would I do to win her back? How far would I go?

He left the question unanswered as he turned the Mustang onto Flintlock Drive and pulled into Rowdy's parking lot.

The place looked busy, with people standing outside the door and on the side porch as he helped Arlene out of the car.

As they walked inside, his mother saw Bill Brewster standing by the bar and made a beeline for him.

She ordered a whiskey sour from Jasper and took a seat on the barstool next to Bill as Frankie walked to the stage and stuck a hundred-dollar bill in the overflowing collection cup.

He turned to see Rowdy coming up behind him.

"This is a sad day," his uncle said, forgoing his usual bear hug and slap on the back. "A mighty sad day for us all."

Frankie nodded as he looked around, noting the long line of sad faces waiting to get a drink at the bar.

"Everybody's looking to drown their sorrows tonight,"

Jasper said when he stopped to take Frankie's order. "And I can't say that I blame them. Tara was a very special girl."

"She was too damn good for this place," Colton said over Frankie's shoulder, his voice slurred and his breath stinking of whisky. "I don't know why she even bothered with us. With her voice, she should have been a goddamn star."

He leaned forward and lost his balance, bumping into the glass of soda and lime Jasper had just placed in front of Frankie on the bar.

The cold liquid splashed onto Frankie and dripped to the floor. As Colton tried to regain his balance, his foot landed in the slippery liquid and he fell backward, knocking into the people behind him like a bowling ball knocking down pins.

Just before he hit the floor, two big hands reached out and grabbed him under the arms.

"Help me get him back on his feet," Diesel muttered to Frankie, who was still wiping the soda water from his jacket.

Stepping forward, Frankie took hold of Colton's left arm while Diesel kept hold of his right arm.

They struggled to keep the muscular man on his feet as he swayed and sagged under the effects of the whiskey.

"Where should we put him?" Diesel asked Rowdy. "He's getting kind of heavy."

"Bring him in the back," Rowdy said, leading them toward the kitchen while Jasper tried to make a path in the crowd.

Once they'd laid Colton out on a couch in the

management office, Frankie started to head back to the front when Diesel put out a hand to stop him.

"I saw you talking to Tara the other night."

He kept his voice low.

"What was she saying to you?" he asked. "Did she say if anyone had been bothering her? Did she seem scared?"

Frankie frowned, not sure why the big man was asking, but tried to think back to his conversation with the singer.

"No, she didn't mention anything to me," he said. "She just wanted a smoke, so I guess maybe she was stressed. But the only person she talked about was you."

Diesel raised his dark eyebrows.

"Me? What did she say about me?"

"She said you were rushing her...something like that."

The man nodded.

"Yeah, I guess I could get a little impatient," he said, looking glum. "She was a good kid. I was just trying to help."

Before Frankie could turn away, Diesel cocked his head and frowned, as if he'd just thought of something.

"Are you the guy who found Dwight Atkins and his wife?"

The question took Frankie by surprise.

"Why are you asking?"

"Just wondering," he said. "It's a terrible thing that happened. I mean, a couple being killed in their house. And their poor daughter. Do you know what's happened to her?"

Frankie shook his head.

"No, I have no idea," he said, crossing his arms over his

chest. "Why do you want to know about their daughter?"

"I'm worried about her," Diesel said. "A lot of bad things have been going on around here. I'd hate for something bad to happen to her, too."

The words sounded too much like a warning for Frankie's liking. He was about to ask what the man was talking about, when Arlene and Bill appeared at the door, drinks in hand.

"Is Colton okay?" she asked.

"Yeah, he just needs to sleep it off," Frankie assured her. "I'll be back out there in a minute."

She nodded and closed the door.

When Frankie turned back to finish his conversation with Diesel, the man was gone.

* * *

The next morning, Frankie headed out to Larksville first thing, intent on taking Josie's advice. He would talk to Lacey Emerson and find out what she knew about Franny's death.

Of course, she might have been too drugged out and messed up to remember anything. And it had been fifteen years, which was a long time.

But then, she'd had a lot of free time to think.

He arrived at Larksville Women's Detention Center just before noon, staring up in awe at the silver razor-wire fence and blocky concrete building as he steered the Mustang through the heavy security gates.

Lining up behind the other visitors at the security

checkpoint, Frankie wondered if he would recognize Lacey after all this time. She'd been little more than a child the last time they'd met, even though she'd been tried as an adult.

As a bored guard waved Frankie down a wide corridor and through a set of gray metal doors, another guard waited to scan him for weapons using a metal-detecting wand.

Finally, he stepped out into a crowded visiting room where inmates in blue jumpers sat at round-top tables with their visitors. He saw Lacey Emerson straight away.

The pretty teenager he'd known was now an attractive woman. Her long hair was still dark and thick, and her skin was unlined and clear of marks or blemishes.

She'd turned thirty a year before, but Frankie decided she looked younger than her age. Prison had been good to her.

"What are you doing here, Frankie?" Lacey asked before he'd gotten a chance to sit down. "When they told me you were coming, I thought it had to be a mistake."

"It could be a huge mistake," he said, sinking into a chair. "But I guess that all depends on what you can tell me about my sister's death. Cause someone told me it wasn't an accident after all. What do you think about that?"

Leaning forward, Lacey lowered her voice as if someone around them might be listening in.

"I think it's taken you a hell of a long time to figure that out," she said, her eyes blazing. "Franny didn't overdose on heroin any more than I shot Booker in the back of the head."

Frankie held her gaze, trying to decide if she was telling

177

the truth, or if she was playing some sort of game.

"So, you're innocent and my sister was murdered?" he said, raising his eyebrows. "Is that your story?"

"It's not a story, it's the truth. I'm *innocent*," she insisted. "Only no one will believe me. They never would."

After so many years of blaming Lacey for her role in Franny's death, it was hard to feel sorry for her.

"Even if you didn't pull the trigger and kill Booker, the two of you still got Franny hooked on smack," he said, crossing his arms over his chest. "You're still responsible for-"

"She wasn't hooked on smack!" Lacey hissed. "Franny wasn't hooked on *anything*. She never took any drugs. She hated the stuff. She was always after me to stop."

Shaking her head, she shrugged.

"What's the use of telling you all this, anyway?" she said. "You're never gonna believe me. I'm wasting my breath."

"I believe you," Frankie said, his tone softening. "At least, I believe that Franny wasn't an addict and that she didn't overdose. In fact, I believe someone killed her. What I came here to find out from you, is who killed her, and why."

Lacey stared at him as if he were crazy.

"You don't have a clue what's going on, do you?" she said. "I was framed for a murder I didn't commit and have spent *fifteen years* in prison. With good behavior, I could be out in another two or three years. I could still have a life."

Tears sprang to her eyes, but she blinked them away.

"But the people who framed me and put me in here,

wouldn't take kindly to me ratting them out. If I do that, they may decide to get rid of me once and for all."

The realization that the woman in front of him knew who was responsible for Franny's death and had chosen not to say anything all this time, hit him like a punch in the gut.

Dropping his head in his hands to hide the rage that surged through him, he forced himself to suck in a deep breath of air, count to ten, and then exhale.

Finally, he lifted his head.

"So, you know who killed my baby sister."

It wasn't a question. It was a statement.

"I know who's responsible for both Franny and Booker's deaths," she agreed. "But if I tell you or that FBI agent who was here last week, I'm dead. If I talk, I'll never walk out those doors. They'll take me out of here in a body bag."

Frankie brought both his fists down hard on the table, causing Lacey to jump back in her chair.

"My sister was taken out of your drug-dealing boyfriend's apartment in a fucking body bag," he hissed as a guard started to move in their direction. "And you've sat in here with your mouth shut in order to save your own ass?"

"Is there a problem here?"

The guard stood beside the table frowning down at them.

"No problem," Frankie said, putting up both hands and pasting on a thin smile. "Sorry...we'll keep it down."

Giving him a warning look, the guard moved away.

"And what do you mean by an FBI agent?" Frankie asked. "Are you saying the feds are investigating your case?"

"I don't know what they're doing," she said, her face now closed off and sullen. "Some agent came here trying to get me to tell him what I knew about Dwight Atkins."

Frankie raised his eyebrows.

"And what did you tell him?"

"I told him that Dwight had been working with some pretty dangerous men. They were supplying Booker with the drugs he was selling, and dealing in other stuff, too. Mainly guns, I think. They had connections in high places. Which is why I'm sitting here. And why Franny's death was never investigated properly."

She looked around as if she was suddenly worried she'd said too much. That someone might have overheard.

"But like I told that FBI guy, I'm not giving out any names, and I won't testify in court or any of that. If they find out I'm talking, they'll make sure to shut me up."

CHAPTER TWENTY-FOUR

Lacey stood and looked down at Frankie, fearing she may have already said too much. It wasn't like she wanted to hold back what she knew about the ruthless men who'd killed her best friend and her boyfriend. But they had power and connections, and all she had was the hope of someday walking out a free woman.

"I'm sorry," she said with a sigh. "I loved Franny. I really did. She tried to help me. Even after I got hooked on smack, she didn't give up on me. But I was too weak. I let her down."

She motioned to the guard.

"The man who killed her...he's killing other women, too," Frankie said, talking fast. "This isn't just about Franny. And it isn't all in the past. It's happening now. It'll keep happening if you don't tell me who-"

"Okay, let's go," the guard said, waving her toward the door. "Visiting time is over."

As she walked toward the exit, Frankie called after her.

"Just think about it, Lacey. Think about the other women."

Glancing back when she got to the door, she caught a

final glimpse of Frankie's troubled brown eyes. Eyes that reminded her so much of Franny. And of all the mistakes she'd made.

As she followed the guard back to her cellblock, she wondered what Frankie had meant when he'd told her to think of the other women.

She rarely watched the news, but even she had seen the stories about the bones in the Wolf River and the women who had gone missing or been killed.

Could he really suspect that the men who'd been running drugs and guns with Dwight were killing those women?

She thought back to the last time she'd seen Booker.

He'd wanted to borrow her car, and she'd been scheduled to work, but had ended up getting high at a friend's house instead. She hadn't returned to her apartment for days, and by then Booker was dead.

But what had he said before he'd left?

Going into her cell, she lay down on her bunk and tried to think. It had been so long ago, and she'd been high most of the time, but hadn't Booker said something about a missing girl? About seeing her in someone's car?

Yes, they put up all those posters about that singer from Nashville. Georgia something or other. And Booker had seen her leaving Rowdy's with someone in a black Bronco.

Who had driven a black Bronco?

A face materialized in Lacey's mind.

Maybe Booker wasn't killed because he'd been siphoning off some of the smack. Maybe it was because he'd seen something. Maybe he knew who'd taken that girl. Maybe Franny knew too, and that's why she...

Jumping up from her bunk, Lacey felt under her mattress for the FBI agent's business card. She'd been so impressed by the fancy title and silver lettering when she'd seen it.

Special Agent Kade Mabry.

She felt a spark of hope for the first time in a long time. Maybe there really was a way she could get out of Larksville before her sentence was over. Before her life was over.

Her fingers prodded the thin material without luck. Lifting the flimsy mattress completely off the bed she saw that the card was gone, along with the small fold of one-dollar bills she had tucked away.

A voice spoke up from her cell doorway.

"Looking for something?"

Dropping the mattress back on the frame, Lacey spun around to see a tall inmate with a blonde crewcut standing just outside her cell.

The woman was muscular, with tattoo sleeves visible on both of her bulky forearms.

"Just cleaning up," Lacey said, trying to remember the woman's name.

Is it Rhoda? No...Rhonda.

The buff woman had arrived at Larksville about six months earlier. Lacey often saw her working out with the other fitness fanatics in the yard.

"I was told you may be interested in some of this."

Rhonda stepped into the cell and held up a small baggie of white powder.

Lacey's eyes widened.

"Who told you that?"

"A mutual friend," Rhonda said with a sly grin. "Someone who owes you a favor. For keeping your mouth shut."

She dangled the baggie in front of Lacey's face.

"Apparently, this one's on the house."

Staring at the powder, Lacey felt an instant pull in her gut. She hadn't seen a bag like that for a long time.

There weren't many opportunities to achieve a proper high in Larksville if you weren't connected and didn't have cash coming in from outside.

"But...why now?" Lacey asked. "What-"

"I wasn't given details," Rhonda said, starting to get impatient. "I was just told to deliver this to you."

When Lacey still didn't reach for the bag, Rhonda's smile faded, and her tone darkened.

"Do you want it or not? I can take it back and tell-"

"Yes," Lacey said, snatching the baggie from the woman's hand. "Yes, I want it."

She stepped back and sat on her bunk, staring down at the powder, knowing she should wait until the intimidating woman in front of her left, and then flush it down the toilet.

"Good girl," Rhonda said, backing toward the door.

She stopped before stepping into the corridor.

"Oh...and remember..."

She made a quick zipping motion in front of her mouth, then slipped out of sight.

Gripping the bag, Lacey stood and walked to the small metal toilet. She hesitated as she looked down at the powder, unable to spill it in as she knew she should.

It had the power to make the miserable little cell disappear. To turn all her problems and pain into the best kind of bliss. At least, for a while.

I'll just snort a little bit. Just enough to take the edge off.

She crossed to the metal ledge on the wall that acted as a desk and tipped some of the powder out.

Pulling an open envelope off the stack of letters she kept from her mother, Lacey tore off a piece of paper and rolled it into a tube. She paused as she bent over the powder, relishing the thrill of anticipation.

It's been so long. Too long...

The thought was lost as she inhaled, snorting in all of the white powder at once.

She knew the effect of heroin was usually less intense and took longer to kick in when snorted rather than injected, so the immediate wave of dizziness took her by surprise.

Swaying on her feet, she tried to make it back to her bunk, but her feet wouldn't cooperate as the room began to fade in and out around her.

The next thing she knew her face was pressed against the concrete floor of her cell. Too weak to move, she tried to call for help, but her throat had closed, blocking her airway.

As the blackness descended, an image of Franny flashed through her panicked mind. Her best friend alone on the floor, gasping for air.

No, not alone. That bastard was with her. He must have forced her. She hated drugs. She begged me to stop. But I wouldn't listen.

She clawed weakly at her throat, desperate for air as Rhonda's sly smile hovered in her mind's eye.

Whoever had sent the powder hadn't wanted to just keep Lacey quiet, they had intended to silence her for good.

CHAPTER TWENTY-FIVE

Ranger let the door to the office slam shut with a loud bang, then turned to Kinsey, who sat at her desk reading the preliminary autopsy report on Dwight and Cheryl Atkins. Sucking in a deep breath, he forced himself to stay calm and keep his voice down.

"Explain to me again why, after you found Josie Atkins, you let her go again before we could question her?"

"The girl was upset," Kinsey said, not taking her eyes off the report. "She was going to come in today for an interview, but then we got the call on Tara Wilder, so I postponed it. She'll come in tomorrow morning."

Heat rushed into Ranger's cheeks, turning them red.

"*If* she's alive tomorrow," he snapped, forgetting to keep his voice down. "And if she did see something, then whoever killed her parents could be looking for her right now."

Kinsey finally looked up. He could see from the defiant tilt of her chin that she wasn't ready to back down.

"Josie told us at the scene she didn't see anything. So why are you so sure she's in danger?"

Her eyes narrowed.

"Is there something you're not telling me?"

Plowing a frustrated hand through his neatly gelled hair, Ranger forced himself to lower his voice.

"The man shot two people in cold blood, one of whom was dying of cancer. He's ruthless. If he even suspects their daughter knows who he is, he'll go after her. I'm sure of it."

Kinsey nodded.

"I agree the man is ruthless. But he has no idea where Josie Atkins is right now. Besides, it looks as if he's moved on."

She glanced toward the stack of crime scene photos that lay on her desk. The one on top contained a close-up image of the bullet wound to the back of Tara Wilder's head.

"It's likely the same shooter is responsible for yet another death. Which means he's escalating. He could go after someone else next. And we have no idea why."

Ranger stared into Kinsey's anxious eyes, wondering how everything had spiraled so quickly out of control.

"The only way we can do everything we need to do is by prioritizing our time and resources. And right now, questioning Josie Atkins is not my top priority."

She held up the file in her hand and then motioned to the stack of crime scene photos on the desk and the boxes stacked in the corner that held the files on the other Wolf River Killer cases.

Biting her lip, she sighed.

"Maybe we should ask Shipley to assign more detectives to the case, or maybe even call in the feds to help us. I mean, we're dealing with a serial killer and-"

"No!" Ranger barked before he could stop himself.

Seeing the flash of surprise on Kinsey's face, he held up his hands and sighed.

"I'm sorry. I'm just stressed," he said, backing toward the door. "I need some caffeine...maybe some air. I'll be back."

He turned and strode out the door, his hands clenched into fists as he stormed down the hall and out through the exit into the parking lot.

Brushing past two officers climbing out of a patrol car, he hurried to his Interceptor, in no mood for small talk.

As he slipped into the driver's seat, he pulled out his phone and angrily tapped out a number he knew by memory.

"Ranger? What's up?"

The voice on the other end of the call sounded stressed.

"I still haven't talked to the girl," Ranger said. "But I think I know where she is. Kinsey sent her off with that P.I. Frankie Dawson even after I told her to bring her in. But I plan to-"

"Lacey Emerson is dead."

The man's words stopped Ranger's rant.

"When?" he asked numbly. "How?"

"She overdosed on fentanyl. The warden says he doesn't know how she got it, but she did have a visitor earlier."

Ranger frowned.

"Who?"

"Frankie Dawson."

Staring down at the phone, he tried to process the

information. It didn't make sense.

"What was he even doing there? Why would he–"

He jumped as a loud knock sounded on the window.

Chief Shipley stood outside staring in at him.

The police chief's face was twisted into an angry scowl as he motioned for him to roll down the window.

"Shipley's here and he's not happy," Ranger said under his breath. "I gotta go."

Ending the call, he reluctantly opened the door and stepped out, preferring to face the older man face to face.

"What the hell are you doing to find the Atkins girl?" Shipley demanded as soon as he was standing in front of him. "And who's working the Tara Wilder case?"

"Josie Atkins is coming in for an interview tomorrow, and Kinsey and I are all over the Wilder case," Ranger said.

He kept his eyes on Shipley's flushed face, ignoring the curious stares they were getting from the officers standing near the building's entrance.

"You know, I'm starting to have doubts about you and that partner of yours," Shipley said. "I thought it would be good to have some fresh detectives in the field, but now I'm not so sure you have what it takes."

Ranger started to protest, but Shipley held up a hand.

When the police chief spoke again, he was using the same *man-to-man* tone his father had always used with Ranger when he'd been trying to make excuses for not showing up to his ballgame, or for arriving at his birthday party after they'd already sung *Happy Birthday* and cut the cake.

"Don't you know there's a killer out there?" he said. "We don't have time to play this by the book."

He lowered his voice and cocked his head.

"Sometimes we've got to use our guts and just take action, even if we don't have all the evidence yet. It'll come. We can make sure of that."

When Ranger just stared at him, Shipley gave a deep sigh.

"I'm disappointed in you, son. When I promoted you to Major Crimes I thought you'd be a chip off the old block."

He hitched up his pants and cleared his throat.

"With a case like this, your father would have zeroed in on a suspect by now. You wouldn't catch Ike Ranger out here talking on his phone like a twelve-year-old girl."

Resisting the urge to swing a punch at the older man, Ranger managed to swallow back his rage.

He would act, alright. But it wasn't the right time yet.

"I'm sorry, Chief," he forced himself to say. "Believe me, you did the right thing by promoting me. Don't worry, from now on, I'm going to surprise you."

CHAPTER TWENTY-SIX

The phone buzzed beside Frankie's open laptop, making him jump and causing Sherlock to shift on the floor beside him and perk up his ears. His heart skipped a beat when he saw Peyton's name on the display.

Lifting the phone to his ear, he felt the same burst of hope he still felt every time she called.

"Peyton, you okay?"

"Yeah, I'm okay, Frankie. It's *you* I'm worried about."

The sound of her voice after everything he'd been through during the last few days brought a lump to his throat.

"I'm fine," he said. "I couldn't make the thing with the lawyer because I'm up in Tennessee. But we can reschedule."

"That's not why I'm worried," she said. "It's not about the meeting. I got a call from your mother. She said you were in some trouble, and I did some digging, and it looks as if she was right."

Frankie rolled his eyes at the thought of his mother once again announcing his personal problems to everyone in her contact list. They definitely needed to have a serious talk.

"Ma shouldn't have called you," he said. "And what do you mean that you *did some digging*? Have you been checking up on me?"

"It didn't take much effort," she said. "You're on the front page of the *Memphis Gazette*. You really should learn to keep your temper with reporters."

He grimaced as he thought of the video clip Dusty Fontaine had posted of his outburst by the river.

"But I'm more worried about you being called a person of interest in a double murder," she admitted. "The Barrel Creek PD has a reputation. And it isn't a good one."

"I know how to look after myself," Frankie assured her. "They already tried to railroad me and failed. Believe me, I know not to trust the cops. I learned that from you."

He regretted the words as soon as they'd left his mouth.

"I didn't mean it that way..."

"Yes, you did," she said. "But that's okay. I deserve that. You were arrested and went to prison, and I didn't stop it from happening even though I knew it was wrong."

She exhaled softly.

"I made a mistake. One I regret every day. Which is why I don't want you to go through something like that again."

Before he could respond, she continued.

"Which is why I spoke to an old friend in the FBI's Memphis Field office," she said. "Special Agent Kade Mabry. He said there have been complaints about the Barrel Creek PD for years. He couldn't say much, but he implied there's an ongoing investigation. He advised you to stay away."

"What do you mean by an *old friend*?" Frankie asked.

"That's not important," Peyton said. "Kade said the feds were handling it. He said you shouldn't get involved."

Frankie's back instantly stiffened.

"Well, if *Kade* knows so much, he should know I'm already involved. And why were you telling him about me anyway?"

She sighed heavily.

"I *didn't* tell him about you. At least, not who you are," she said. "I just told him I had a friend, and-"

"A friend? Is that all we are now? Just friends?"

Frankie closed his eyes and gripped the phone to his ear, knowing he sounded pathetic but unable to help himself.

"I'm trying to help you," she said in a small voice. "I saw the *Memphis Gazette* website, and I was worried about you."

"I know...and I appreciate it," he said, suddenly feeling every one of the eight hundred miles between them. "But I got this. I'm not gonna screw up, okay? In fact, I'm getting close to finding out what's going on around here."

He looked at his laptop and silently cursed Dusty Fontaine.

"Maybe next time you read the *Gazette*, you'll see a headline saying *Frankie Dawson Catches the Wolf River Killer*."

Forcing out a thin laugh, he grabbed his keys off the desk and jingled them by the receiver.

He had to get off the phone before he broke down and started begging her not to sign the papers. A man needed to keep some dignity after all.

"I actually gotta run," he said as he scratched at his

stubble, which was now more like a beard. "I got me a serial killer to catch. But it was good to hear your voice."

Ending the call with a lump in his throat, he looked at the keys in his hand, and then at the website on his screen.

Making a quick decision, he walked out to his Mustang.

* * *

Frankie slowed to a stop at the light then took a right onto Arcadia Street. He was surprised to see a red *For Lease* banner in the window of the *Memphis Gazette* building.

Parking along the street, he got out and went up to the front door and found it locked.

"They closed down the headquarters a few months ago," a voice said behind him. "They outsourced the printing of the physical newspapers, and all the reporters and editors work remotely now."

Frankie turned to see a woman standing in the open door of the Arcadia Coffee Shop next to the defunct building.

"We're about to close down, too," she said with a shrug. "Now that all the reporters and such are gone next door, we don't get enough traffic to make it worth our while."

"Real sorry to hear it," Frankie said, looking past the woman into the sweet-smelling café beyond. "You still selling coffee for now? Maybe a bagel or something, too?"

She smiled and waved him inside.

"I've got a wide selection to choose from," she said, waving at the display counter which was full of croissants, bagels, doughnuts, and cinnamon buns.

Picking out a flaky chocolate croissant, he ordered a black coffee and turned to the row of empty tables by the window.

There was only one customer in the café. A man was seated at a back table, his head bent to his open laptop.

He looked up as Frankie set his coffee cup on the table, then flashed a wide smile.

Frankie did a doubletake as he recognized Dusty Fontaine.

"Mr. Dawson, how nice to see you again."

After a moment's hesitation, Frankie carried his coffee and croissant to the table beside the reporter.

"Actually, you're the one I came to see," he admitted, sinking into a little wooden chair. "I didn't know they'd shut down the *Gazette's* offices."

"It sucks, but what can you do?" Dusty said. "Most of the newspapers in the country are having to do the same."

Sipping at his coffee, Frankie looked around the café.

"So, now you come here instead of going to an office?"

Dusty nodded.

"It's hard to learn a new routine," he said. "Especially for an old dog like me. I've been the entertainment reporter for the Gazette for almost twenty years."

"Entertainment reporter?" Frankie said, looking at the man sideways. "Aren't you on the crime beat?"

The reporter shrugged.

"Those Wolf River Killer stories are special," he said. "I guess you could say they're a pet project of mine."

He sat back in his chair and crossed his legs, giving Frankie a view of his pointy-toed boots. There were no traces left of the mud that had been caked onto the man's two-inch heels the last time Frankie had seen him.

"You see, I've covered the Nashville and Memphis music scene for two decades. I'd been working the scene for maybe five or six years when I started noticing women were going missing."

Taking a bite of his croissant, Frankie leaned forward and propped his elbows on the table.

"What women?" he asked, still chewing his bite.

"Aspiring singers, fans, groupies. Could be anyone who was traveling alone between the two cities."

Dusty gestured toward his computer.

"I have a list. I actually brought it to the Barrel Creek PD, the Memphis PD, and even the FBI after I decided it wasn't all in my imagination."

"What'd they say?" Frankie asked.

An angry smile twisted the reporter's narrow face.

"They laughed and advised me to stick to entertainment reporting. But I was keeping track. I didn't give up," he said. "And when they found all those bones in the river? That's when I started my own investigation."

"And what'd you find out?"

A suspicious gleam entered Dusty's eyes.

"Aren't you Rowdy Dawson's nephew?" he asked.

Frankie nodded, confused.

"Yeah, I am, what about it?"

"Well, according to my research, the one thing all these women have in common is that they stopped by Rowdy's Bar and Grill just before they went missing."

Producing a thick file from a backpack on the chair beside him, Dusty pushed it across the table toward Frankie.

"This is pretty much everything I've collected. All my notes and research. It all points to Rowdy's."

As Frankie began to flip through the contents of the folder, he became aware of the radio playing behind the counter.

A breaking news report had interrupted the music, filling the coffee shop with the reporter's somber voice.

"Lacey Emerson, a local woman previously convicted of killing small-time drug dealer Booker Boudreaux, died this morning while in custody at Larksville Correctional Facility. Administrators at the facility say she committed suicide in her cell."

The report went on to say that foul play was not suspected.

"Bullshit," Frankie muttered.

He lifted a shaking hand to push back a shaggy section of hair that had fallen over his eyes.

Dusty looked confused.

"What's bullshit, Mr. Dawson?"

"Frankie," he said, staring down at the reporter's bulging folder. "My name is Frankie. And it's bullshit that Lacey Emerson committed suicide."

After a surprised pause, Dusty lifted his sparse eyebrows.

"You knew her?"

"Yep, I knew her," Frankie nodded. "I saw her this morning in Larksville. She didn't seem suicidal to me, although she did claim she was innocent. Said she'd been set up by the Barrel Creek PD."

Dropping his head in his hands, he suddenly wondered where the nearest bar was, eager to trade his cup of black coffee for a tall glass of whiskey.

He heard Dusty's fingers flying across his keyboard.

"It figures," the reporter scoffed.

"What does?" Frankie asked, looking up with a frown.

"I just checked the *Gazette's* archives," Dusty said.

He turned his screen to face Frankie.

"Lacey Emerson's arresting officers were Otto Shipley and Ike Ranger, both detectives in Vice at the time."

"Isn't Shipley the chief now?" Frankie asked. "And Ranger? He's pretty young to have been working a homicide case back then."

Dusty shook his head.

"You're thinking of Sheldon Ranger, who works Major Crimes. He's Ike Ranger's son."

"So, you think Shipley and Ike Ranger were dirty?"

The reporter stared at the screen, scanning the article he'd pulled up with a deepening frown.

"Ike Ranger's dead now," he said. "But if you look through my notes, you'll see I interviewed plenty of people who claimed he was on the take. Only problem was, these people were dealers, addicts, and street people. Not exactly the most convincing witnesses."

He took a small sip of what appeared to be green tea.

"And the guy had been awarded plenty of medals and commendations by the chief, the city council, even the mayor. When he was killed in the line of duty, they had a big funeral. Made a huge fuss about losing a valuable member of the Barrel Creek PD. Acted like he was some kind of hero."

As Dusty spoke, Frankie pictured Lacey's face as she had glanced back at him in Larksville. She'd looked like a woman trying to save her own hide, not a woman planning suicide.

There's no damn way she killed herself. Someone must have wanted to shut her up. They must have known she could start talking at any minute.

It seemed as if someone was taking out anyone he'd spoken to. Dwight and Cheryl. Tara Wilder. And now Lacey.

"I've got to go," he said, standing abruptly and moving toward the door. "But I'll be in touch soon. I have a good idea I know what's going on, and I might need some of your research to prove it."

Heading out the door and back to his Mustang, he sped back toward Monarch Ave, suddenly wanting to get home.

People around him were dropping like flies, and he needed to check on Josie.

CHAPTER TWENTY-SEVEN

Rosalie stepped into the lab, surprised to see that Uma Chandra was still there. The forensic anthropologist leaned over a microscope studying what appeared to be a bone fragment. She lifted her eyes to Rosalie, who held up the printout in her hand.

"I got the DNA results back from the blood and tissue found in Tara Wilder's mouth," she said, her voice practically vibrating with frustration. "And there's a match in CODIS."

Uma's eyes widened.

"So, you got lucky. You've got your killer."

"Not quite," Rosalie sighed. "It matched a DNA profile collected from the scene of an unsolved murder in Nashville a few years ago."

She let her hand fall to her side.

"So, what's next?" Uma asked.

"I already called the detective who worked the case," she admitted. "I was too hyped to wait. The victim was twenty-year-old Krystal Carter. She was found in an alley behind a bar with defensive wounds and blood under her fingernails. She'd also been shot in the back of the head."

The two women stared at each other for a long beat as Uma silently processed the information.

It seemed likely that Tara Wilder had been the victim of a serial killer. Perhaps the same killer who'd been dumping bones in the Wolf River.

"So, your guy is willing to travel," Uma mused. "I wonder how far he's been...how many victims he's killed?"

The question sent a ripple of unease down Rosalie's spine.

"That's up to the police to figure out," she said. "I guess the Barrel Creek PD may decide to call in the state bureau or maybe the FBI, seeing that this is now a multijurisdictional investigation."

Studying the printout, Rosalie turned and left Uma to her work, deciding she'd stop and talk to Detective Kinsey on her way home. But when she walked into the Barrel Creek police station an hour later and approached the desk sergeant, the detective wasn't there.

"I can leave her a message, Dr. Quintero," the officer said. "Or I can give you her card, which has her cell number on it."

"Thanks, that would be great."

But before she could reach out and take the offered card, a deep voice spoke up behind her

"Dr. Quintero, is everything okay?"

Turning at the sound of her name, she saw Chief Shipley standing behind her, his tall frame blocking out the light coming in from the windows and tried to summon a smile.

She wasn't sure why but something about the police chief

had always made her slightly uncomfortable. Perhaps it was the way he always stood a little too close, or maybe the fact that he usually found a reason to touch her arm or back.

"I was hoping to speak to Detective Kinsey," she said, stepping to the side so as not to block the desk. "But it seems she's gone for the day. Or perhaps she's out investigating."

"Is there an update on one of the homicides she and Detective Ranger are working on?" Shipley asked.

Putting a firm hand under her elbow, he led her toward the window, sticking close beside her.

"Yes, actually," she said, pulling her elbow out of his grip and taking a step back. "There was a DNA match in CODIS for a sample taken from Tara Wilder's body."

Shipley's eyes widened.

"That is big news," he said, glancing around the lobby. "Probably not something we should be discussing out here."

He gestured toward the back.

"Let's go to my office where we can speak alone."

Knowing there was no reasonable way she could refuse to go with him, Rosalie reluctantly followed him into the back and down the hall.

"So, there was a match in CODIS," Shipley said, closing the door behind her. "Do we have a name then?"

Standing in front of her, he looked down into Rosalie's face, his eyes never leaving hers.

"Not quite," she said. "The sample we recovered from Tara's body matched a DNA profile collected from the scene of an unsolved murder in Nashville."

She cleared her throat and inched backward.

"I hope Detective Kinsey won't mind, but I took the liberty of calling the Nashville detective who was listed on the case file," she said. "The victim in that case matches our profile. A young woman was shot in the head. So, it looks like our killer isn't sticking to the Wolf River or to Barrel Creek."

To her relief, Shipley took a step back as she continued.

"I think it may be time to call in the state or federal bureau," she suggested. "I mean, now that several jurisdictions will be involved..."

Looking up, she recoiled at the rage evident on his face.

"You took it upon yourself to call the detective directly?"

His words were thick with outrage.

"And now you're telling me to bring in outside agencies to help run my cases? Just who do you think you are?"

Adrenaline surged through her at the hostility in his voice.

"I'm the medical examiner assigned to these cases," she said, backing toward the door. "And I have every right to fully investigate any unnatural death, with or without your department's cooperation."

She reached for the doorknob, but he stuck out a hand to prevent her from leaving.

"Be careful, Dr. Quintero," he said, leaning forward so that his mouth was mere inches from her ear. "Or you might find that you're getting in over your head."

Spinning around, she twisted the knob and yanked hard

on the door, only to find that Shipley had removed his hand.

She stumbled back as the door swung open, then darted forward into the hall, not stopping until she was standing beside her car.

Once safely locked inside, she pulled her phone out of her purse. If the thought of bringing in the FBI had sent Shipley over the edge, then that was just what she intended to do.

*   *   *

Special Agent Kade Mabry was waiting outside the FBI field office when Rosalie arrived.

He was tall and broad, with thick dark hair and intensely blue eyes. Escorting her into the five-story, redbrick building, he walked her through security and led her into a small conference room overlooking a thick forest of trees.

Dressed casually for an FBI agent in a black polo shirt and khaki pants, he had a matter-of-fact, no-nonsense air that immediately set Rosalie at ease.

"You said on the phone that you're working on several homicides in Barrel Creek with a DNA link to a case in Nashville," he said, once they were seated across from reach other at the sleek wooden conference table. "And that you're concerned about the handling of the case by the local police department."

"Not the whole department."

She suddenly felt awkward, as if she was a student tattle-telling on someone in the principal's office.

"But something was off with Chief Shipley's reaction to

the news that we got a DNA match in CODIS. And he became enraged when I suggested calling in the FBI."

Kade nodded and jotted something on his notepad.

"Okay, so he didn't want any outsiders getting involved," he said. "Is that about right?"

Rosalie nodded, wondering if he thought she was overreacting. It probably was pretty common for local police departments to try to keep the feds out.

"So, why did you feel the need to contact us directly?" he asked. "What do you think is going on?"

"I think too many women are turning up dead in Barrel Creek, for one thing," she said, knowing she must sound defensive. "You had to have heard it on the news. All the bones that have been discovered. So far we've identified the skulls of three different female victims, along with a hoodie belonging to a missing woman named Vicky Vaughn."

She sucked in a deep breath, trying to gauge his reaction, but his face was unreadable.

"Then there was the double murder of Dwight and Cheryl Atkins," she said. "They were both shot in the head. The bullets are in the FBI lab now getting tested."

"And Tara Wilder?" he said. "Is that also your case?"

Rosalie nodded.

"Yes, she was the latest victim. The one that got Chief Shipley all worked up."

Remembering Shipley's voice in her ear, she grimaced.

"We recovered DNA from Tara Wilder that was linked to a homicide victim in Nashville named Krystal Carter," she said. "And Shipley didn't seem to like that at all. Maybe you think I'm just being paranoid or overreacting, but-"

"You're not paranoid, and you've done exactly the right thing," Kade said. "In fact, I'm very glad you're here."

He leaned back in his chair and sighed.

"You see, we've been working on an investigation into the Barrel Creek PD for quite some time, and our scope has recently expanded to include their handling of several homicide cases going back as far as fifteen years ago."

Rosalie blinked in surprise.

"You're already investigating Shipley?"

"Him and others in the department," he confirmed. "And your information will prove very helpful I'm sure. We'll want to see the DNA profile and autopsy reports. But going forward, I need you to keep all this quiet. Tell no one."

Standing up, he crossed to the window and stared out at the army of trees below. When he turned back, she saw that his eyes had darkened into a deep, stormy blue.

"I have a feeling that the investigation is going to start moving very fast now," he said. "We'll all need to be careful until we know for sure who's been pulling the trigger."

CHAPTER TWENTY-EIGHT

The Wolf drove slowly past the two-story house on Monarch Avenue, keeping an eye out for Josie Atkins. The pretty blonde teen had been holed up inside the house for the last few days, making it impossible to get his hands on her. But he wasn't about to give up. Not until he made sure she couldn't tell anyone what she might have seen or heard the night of her parents' death.

As he circled the block, his phone buzzed on the dashboard, flashing the words *Unknown Number*.

Tapping on his Bluetooth earpiece to answer the call, he didn't bother with a greeting.

"What's happened?" he asked.

"That bitch at the medical examiner's office wants to bring in the feds. She's already involved some detective in Nashville. And she claims she has a DNA match."

The Wolf gripped the steering wheel and looked down at the sleeve covering the throbbing wound on his wrist, which had swollen to twice its normal size and turned an angry red.

"A DNA match to *what* exactly?"

"She says that whoever killed Tara Wilder also killed

some woman in Nashville. She says there's DNA evidence."

"And what does that have to do with me?" the Wolf asked, his voice low and dangerous. "You don't think I had something to do with Tara Wilder's death, do you?"

The long silence on the other end of the call told him everything he needed to know.

The pretense that he was just one of the crew, just one of several otherwise respectable men willing to smuggle drugs and guns to make some extra cash, was over.

Long-held suspicions could no longer be explained away when held up to the evidence of bones, blood, and DNA.

"If the M.E. brings in outsiders, I won't be able to protect you. There will be nothing for me to do.

"Then you need to stop the bitch from bringing them in," the Wolf snarled. "You need to destroy the DNA."

Pulling onto Hastings Highway, he headed west toward Barrel Creek, stopping at a red light as the caller's scornful laugh rang in his ear.

"It's too late for that. I tried to warn you before, but you never listened. You've screwed up too many times."

"And I've already told you if I'm going down, so are you."

The Wolf's voice was as hard and cold as ice.

"And don't even think of ratting me out or you'll end up like Dwight. He tried to snitch me out and look what happened to him."

"Are you threatening me?"

The light turned green.

"It's a threat if you want it to be," the Wolf said,

pressing his foot down hard on the accelerator. "All I know is we had a deal and I did my part. Now you do yours."

"If the feds come in, it's out of my hands."

The fear and resignation in the caller's voice told the Wolf he was wasting his time.

"Fine, then I'll take care of it myself before it gets that far," the Wolf said. "Leave it to me."

* * *

The big white medical examiner's van was parked outside Rosalie Quintero's office when the Wolf turned onto Sandstone Boulevard and drove past the otherwise empty parking lot.

It looked as if the interfering woman had gone home for the day, which should make it easier to find what he was looking for. He would just need to figure out how to gain access to the locked building.

Parking the old Bronco on a deserted backstreet a block north, the Wolf made sure he wasn't being observed, then opened the glove compartment and retrieved the locksmith's toolkit he'd ordered online.

He stuck the small kit in his jacket pocket, then dropped in his old Swiss Army knife after it for good measure.

A quick doublecheck of his belt and ankle holsters reassured him that both his Glock and Ruger were in place.

Feeling slightly over-equipped for the task at hand, the Wolf climbed out of the SUV and walked back to the office.

He ignored the throbbing that had started up again in his

wrist as the oxycodone he'd taken earlier started to wear off.

As he neared the back of the building, he took out a lightweight ski mask and pulled it down over his head, pretty sure the medical examiner's office would have security cameras installed outside.

And what about an alarm? Have you thought of that?

Ignoring the voice in his head, the Wolf walked swiftly to the back door, then hesitated. A silver sedan was parked beside the dumpster, hidden from the road.

I guess the place might not be deserted after all.

Tension tightened his shoulders as he looked around to make sure he wasn't being observed, then shrugged.

There was no going back now, not if he wanted to find the bones and DNA evidence they were trying to use against him.

If he could steal or destroy the collection, they would have nothing to show a jury. Nothing to tie him to the killings.

Sucking in a deep breath, he reached a gloved hand toward the door, wondering which tool might work best on the lock as he tried the handle.

His heart skipped a beat as the handle gave way and the door swung open.

The Wolf looked back at the silver sedan, quickly recalculating his plan. Whoever had driven it must still be inside the building.

Perhaps they'd run in to get something and left the door unlocked, assuming that they'd be back before anyone could happen by. Or perhaps they'd simply been careless.

Either way, whoever was in there had made a common mistake by letting down their guard, forgoing commonsense safety measures, and assuming they'd be safe.

Assuming bad things could only happen to other people.

The Wolf had seen people make the same mistake many times before. It was usually the last mistake they ever made.

Stepping into a cool, windowless corridor, he crept forward, pushing his way past a swinging door into a large storeroom.

He made his way forward, exiting into another hall that had a row of offices along one side. The second office on the right had a nameplate affixed to the closed door.

Rosalie Quintero – Medical Examiner.

The small glow of anticipation in his belly ignited into a flame as the Wolf pictured the pretty, dark-haired woman who was so intent on causing him trouble.

He listened at the door but heard nothing.

Pulling his gun from his holster, he reached down and tried the handle. This time, the door had been locked.

He cursed under his breath as he reached for the little kit in his pocket, bypassing the ineffectual knob lock after a short bout of tinkering with the cheap tools.

As soon as the lock clicked open, he pushed into the room, already knowing the medical examiner wasn't sitting inside patiently waiting for him to break in.

But then, he hadn't come for the woman.

Although that would have been a bonus.

No, he'd come for the bones and the DNA.

And now that he'd gotten inside, and no one had appeared to confront him, his only problem was finding them.

Flipping on the light, he decided to start his search by going through Rosalie Quintero's desk, looking for keys or passcodes he might be able to use elsewhere in the building.

But before he could even open the top drawer, his eyes fell on a document lying on the desk in full view.

He scanned it, seeing that it was a report on the ballistics testing of two bullets. A handwritten Post-it note had been stuck to the top of the report.

Rosalie,
Results just came in. I was right.
Two different guns used. The
Glock showed up in NIBIN with
link to a cold case homicide.
We need to talk!
Marty

The Wolf scowled and crumpled the note and the report in one big hand. He knew that the NIBIN was the National Integrated Ballistic Information Network run by the ATF.

And the report meant that they now had forensic evidence linking his gun to Dwight and Cheryl's murders, as well as a previous crime that hadn't yet been solved.

He had just rammed the paper into the front pocket of

his pants when he heard a faint sound down the hall.

Someone had coughed.

Sticking his head out of the office door, he listened carefully, then stepped into the hall and headed to the end.

He turned left in the direction of the sound, then stopped in front of a glass-paneled door that revealed a small lab.

A slim woman in a white lab coat had her back to him. Her dark hair had been pulled back into a low bun, and she was looking into a microscope.

The Wolf allowed his mouth to spread into a nasty smile. Rosalie Quintero hadn't left the building after all.

Keeping his Glock at the ready in one hand, he used the other hand to slowly push the door open.

The woman at the microscope didn't hear him coming up behind her until he was halfway across the room.

As he approached, she lifted her head and turned around, staring at him in wide-eyed shock that was mirrored by his own surprise.

The woman wasn't Rosalie Quintero.

The Wolf's momentary hesitation gave the woman time to react. She moved quickly, delivering a sharp, swift kick to his hand that sent the Glock flying across the room.

The gun smashed into a glass beaker on the counter, sending shards of glass scattering across the floor as the woman made a dash for the door.

His hand now empty of a weapon, the Wolf charged forward, managing to grab the back of her lab coat just before she made it out the door.

"Where are the bones?" he demanded, jerking her

backward, holding her against him. "I want every last one."

The woman let out a bloodcurdling scream and stomped on his foot, then grabbed his wounded arm, pulling with all her might.

Releasing his grip, he howled in pain, clutching at his arm as she made another break toward the door.

She'd made it halfway down the hall when he caught up to her, his Swiss Army knife now clutched in his hand.

"Where are the bones?" he growled in her ear as he held the knife to her throat. "Tell me before I–"

"They're all gone," she gasped out. "We sent them to the FBI lab this afternoon for testing."

He twisted her around and stared into her wide, terrified eyes, trying to see if she was lying.

"Are you the one who called in the feds?" he demanded. "Is it you who's causing all this trouble?"

There was a flash of something in her hand and then a stab of pain in his side.

Staring down, he saw a small scalpel protruding from his ribs, a bright patch of blood already soaking into his shirt.

"Look what you've done!" he said between clenched teeth as he wrenched the scalpel out and dropped it on the floor.

Still holding the Swiss Army knife, he thrust it forward.

A warm gush of blood ran over his hand as the blade sank into the soft flesh of the woman's stomach and she collapsed to the floor.

Clutching at his blood-sodden shirt, the Wolf backed away, stopping only to pick up his Glock before he ran out of the lab, down the hall, and through the exit.

CHAPTER TWENTY-NINE

The morning air was cool and crisp as Frankie stepped onto the porch and surveyed Monarch Avenue. Leading Sherlock down the steps, he was careful to stay on the sidewalk as a black Ford Bronco sped past and disappeared around the corner.

Glancing at his watch, he quickened his step. He and Josie would need to leave soon if they were going to make it to the medical examiner's office on time.

The girl had urged him to schedule the viewing for the first available timeslot that morning.

She was anxious to see her parents and have a chance to say a proper good-bye, although Frankie was beginning to wonder if it was such a good idea.

He suspected that seeing the damage that had been done to the people she loved most would only make things worse.

Sometimes ignorance is bliss.

By the time he and Sherlock had circled the block and returned to the house, Josie was waiting on the porch.

She'd found a drawerful of clothes Franny had left behind, and she was wearing a pair of faded jeans and a Memphis Grizzlies sweatshirt.

Frankie stopped still when he saw the shirt, transported back in time to the day he and Franny had gotten a rare chance to go to one of the Grizzlies' home games after Dwight had given him comp tickets his father hadn't wanted.

The sweatshirt, along with a slice of cheese pizza and a soda, had cost him half a day's wages, but the smile on Franny's face as she'd left the arena had been priceless.

"Nice shirt," he said as he opened the car door.

Josie looked down at it self-consciously, then smiled.

"My dad took me to a few Grizzlies' games," she said, biting her lip. "But he said these shirts were overpriced."

"Well, your dad was a smart guy when it came to money," Frankie said with a laugh. "Lucky for you, I'm not so smart."

Before he could close the door, she stopped him.

"Sherlock's coming with us, right?"

She looked down at the black Labrador who waited patiently behind Frankie.

"I was thinking we'd leave him here."

His resolve weakened at the crestfallen look on her face.

"But if it would make you feel better..."

"It will," she said, her frown instantly clearing as Frankie opened the back door and waited for the dog to jump in.

But as they drew nearer to the medical examiner's office, Josie's face began to cloud over again.

"You sure you want to do this?" Frankie asked as they turned onto Sandstone Boulevard. "No one would blame you if you changed your mind."

"I'm sure," Josie said, swallowing hard.

Pulling into the parking lot, Frankie saw that the only vehicle parked outside was the big white medical examiner's van, which had probably been left there overnight.

"Looks like we might be the first ones here," he said, sensing Josie's anxiety. "Let's go check the doors to see if they're open yet. It'll give us a chance to stretch our legs."

Finding the front doors locked, Frankie started to head back to the car, but Sherlock strained against the leash.

"I think he wants to explore," Josie said, taking the leash from his hand. "Don't worry, we'll stay on the grass."

Frankie hesitated, then nodded.

"Okay, but stay close by," he cautioned. "I don't want to lose you again."

She waved a hand and followed after Sherlock as he sniffed the ground, heading around the side of the building.

Starting to get nervous as the duo wandered out of sight, Frankie was just about to go after them when Josie came running back with Sherlock on her heels.

"I think you'd better see this!" she called, waving for him to follow her as she turned and ran back the way she'd come.

With a groan, Frankie jogged after her, wincing as the blister on his toe started to sting.

When he came around the corner, Josie was standing beside the back door, which stood open, revealing a dimly lit corridor inside.

"Look," Josie said, pointing a small finger at a large reddish smudge on the door. "Isn't that blood?"

Moving closer, Frankie stared down at the open door and what appeared to be a bloody palm print.

He jumped as Sherlock barked from somewhere inside the building, then turned to Josie, who wore a guilty expression.

"Sherlock wanted to follow the trail," she said with an apologetic grimace. "I tried to stop him, but he kept pulling on the leash."

"Stay here," Frankie said, wishing he'd thought to bring his Glock. "I'm going to go and grab Sherlock, and then we're going to go back to the car and call 911."

Stepping through the door, careful not to touch the blood, Frankie hurried down a windowless corridor that led past a storeroom and a row of closed offices.

He followed Sherlock's barks to the open door of a small lab, which appeared to be empty.

"Come on, Sherlock!" he called, noticing several shards of glass on the floor. "What have you-"

A hand settled on his arm.

Spinning around, he saw Josie standing behind him.

"I told you to stay out there," he said, shaking his head. "You're as bad as Sherlock when it comes to listening."

The Labrador barked again.

Frankie stepped forward, determined to grab his leash, then froze when he saw a woman in a white lab coat lying on the floor in a dried puddle of blood.

"Dr. Quintero!" Frankie called.

His foot crunched over a thick shard of glass as he moved forward to crouch next to the unconscious figure.

Bending over her, he saw that the woman wasn't Rosalie Quintero. His eyes scanned the badge pinned to her lab coat.

Dr. Uma Chandra.

Now that he could see her face, he recognized the woman from Tara Wilder's crime scene. She'd been with the M.E. when she'd examined the body on the dock.

"Is she dead?"

Josie's voice wavered as she stared down at the woman.

Reaching out two fingers, Frankie checked the pulse in Uma's throat. His heart jumped at the light *thump, thump, thump* under his fingertips.

He bent closer and felt a soft puff of breath escape her lips.

"She's alive," he said, fumbling to take out the phone in his pocket and jabbing *9-1-1* with shaky fingers.

"9-1-1, what's your emergency?"

Frankie almost dropped the phone when Uma groaned and shifted on the floor beside him.

"I need an ambulance at the Barrel Creek M.E.'s Office," he said. "A woman's bleeding and unconscious. I don't know what happened to her, but we need someone here fast."

Uma groaned again as Frankie ended the call, and her eyes fluttered open.

"He...stabbed me," she gasped, clutching at her stomach. "He wanted the bones. But I wouldn't...give them to him."

"Who stabbed you?" Frankie asked.

He stared down into the woman's anguished eyes and took her cold hand in his.

"Who did this?"

"I...couldn't see his face," she said. "He...wore a mask."

Grimacing again, she grasped Frankie's hand.

"He must have mistaken me for...Rosalie. He told me I caused trouble...by calling in the feds."

"I think I hear the ambulance," Josie said, turning and running toward the front door.

Moments later she was leading two paramedics into the lab. One bent to examine Uma's wound as the other crouched beside her and began checking her vitals.

Frankie waved Josie and Sherlock out to the lobby, then paced back and forth until one of the paramedics came out to give them an update.

"She's suffered a serious injury, and has lost quite a bit of blood, but her condition is surprisingly stable. Now, we need to get her to the hospital and let the doctors fix her up."

As they were wheeling Uma out to the ambulance, a startled face appeared in the doorway.

"What's happened?" Rosalie asked.

Her face was a mask of shocked concern.

"What's happened is the Wolf River Killer was here," Frankie said. "According to Uma, he wanted his bones back."

CHAPTER THIRTY

Josie wrapped her thin arms tightly around Sherlock's neck as he sat on the floor beside her. Both she and the dog watched Frankie as he paced anxiously back and forth inside Rosalie's office, waiting for the police to arrive.

"So, Uma said she hadn't seen the man's face?" Rosalie asked again as if she hoped the answer would be different this time around. "She didn't recognize his voice?"

Stopping in midstride, Frankie sighed and shook his head.

"She didn't know him," he said. "He must have thought she was you. I know I did when I saw her on the floor."

Rosalie wrapped her arms around herself and shivered.

"I feel so terrible," she said. "I should have been here with poor Uma. Maybe then..."

"Maybe then you would have been killed," Frankie said bluntly. "The guy was out for blood, and it was your blood he wanted. That, and those bones."

The M.E. looked at him with red-rimmed eyes.

"You think the man who attacked Uma is the Wolf River Killer? You think he was coming to take the bones back?"

"Who else would want them?"

Frankie began to pace again.

"He was mad at you," Josie said, keeping her arms around Sherlock. "Because you called in the feds. That's what he told Uma. That's why he came here looking for the bones."

Turning to stare at Josie, the M.E. shook her head.

"He couldn't have known that I..."

Her voice faltered, and she dropped her eyes.

"That you what?" Frankie demanded. "What did you do?"

"I went to see Detective Kinsey," she said weakly. "But she wasn't there, and Chief Shipley came out. He asked about the case. I told him...I told him he should call in the feds."

A look of panic entered her eyes.

"How would the man who did this...how would he have known?" she murmured. "I didn't tell anyone but the agent."

Frankie frowned.

"What agent?"

Rosalie hesitated, her face twisting with indecision as if she was fighting an internal battle with her own conscience.

"He said I'm not supposed to tell anyone," she finally admitted with a resigned shrug of her narrow shoulders.

Lifting a hand, she pushed back a wisp of dark hair that had escaped her bun.

"But now I don't know who to trust."

"Slow down a minute," Frankie said, stopping his pacing directly in front of Rosalie. "What did you tell this agent?"

The M.E. sank into the chair behind her desk.

"I called the FBI field office in Memphis and spoke to an agent named Kade Mabry," she said. "I told him that Chief Shipley had acted strangely when he'd heard about the DNA results we'd found linking some of the cases."

Frankie lifted his eyebrows.

"You think Shipley's got something to hide?"

The M.E. shrugged.

"I don't know what it is, but that man has always given me the creeps. And when he heard I'd called the Nashville PD to check on a link to our case, and that I wanted to bring in the FBI, he lost it. He even had the nerve to threaten me."

"And this Agent Kade Mabry told you what exactly?"

Rosalie sighed.

"He told me that the FBI has been investigating Shipley and his department for a while. That they'd received multiple complaints," she admitted. "But he said I should be careful not to let anyone know."

As Rosalie spoke, Josie thought back to the night her parents had been killed. Closing her eyes, she replayed her father's words.

"You know it's too dangerous to involve the police. I tried to tell the feds, but I don't think they believed me."

Realizing what it might mean, she jumped to her feet.

"My dad talked to the FBI, too," she said.

Both Frankie and Rosalie turned to stare at her.

"Before he died, he told my mom he'd been too scared to go to the police and tell them he knew who was killing girls and dumping their bones in the river. He didn't trust them."

She tucked a strand of dark blonde hair behind her ear and shifted from foot to foot, too worked up to stand still.

"Dad said he'd tried to tell the feds, but he didn't think they'd believed him. But maybe they did. Maybe he started off an investigation and now-"

Her words were interrupted by a knock on the door.

Seconds later, Marty Prince stuck his head into the room.

"I'm ready in the viewing room," he said. "Oh, and Detective Kinsey called to say she's on her way to investigate the break-in and take a statement."

"Thanks, Marty. Let me know when she gets here."

As the forensic technician nodded and closed the door, the M.E. turned to Frankie and Josie with a look of panic.

"What should we tell her?" she asked.

"We'll just tell her what happened to Uma," Frankie said. "Nothing about the feds. If she finds out the Barrel Creek PD is under investigation, it could ruin the whole operation."

Rosalie nodded weakly, then turned toward Josie.

"I haven't forgotten about you seeing your parents," she said. "Marty has everything set up in the viewing room. I'll ask him to take you in there now."

The words sent a ripple of anxiety through Josie, but she nodded solemnly, steeling herself for her final goodbyes.

Minutes later she was following Marty toward the viewing room, her heart thumping loudly under the blue Memphis Grizzlies sweatshirt.

Looking back, she saw Frankie and Sherlock standing in the hall staring after her with dark, worried eyes.

"You can always have company, you know," Marty said as he followed her gaze. "They can both come in with you if you want. I won't tell anyone."

She saw Frankie raise his eyebrows in a silent question.

Meeting his steadfast gaze, Josie nodded.

She didn't want to go into the room all alone, and right now Frankie and Sherlock were all she had.

As the trio walked into the small room, Marty positioned himself next to two metal tables arranged side by side.

"Normally we would have you stand behind a glass partition since we haven't officially released the bodies yet," he said. "But Rosalie made an exception in this case."

Not sure if she was supposed to say thank you or not, Josie just nodded, keeping her eyes resting on the two figures hidden under the white sheets.

"Oh, and there's a box of tissues and a pitcher of water on the table," Marty added with a sympathetic smile. "And I'll stay in the room in case you need anything. Just tell me when you're ready."

Reaching for Frankie's hand, Josie exhaled.

"Okay," she said. "I think I'm ready now."

CHAPTER THIRTY-ONE

Kinsey brought the Interceptor to a stop in front of the station and waited for Ranger to settle into the passenger's seat before pulling back onto Hastings Highway. A break-in and assault had been reported by the medical examiner's office as she'd been driving into work.

"I bet you can't guess who called 911," Kinsey said with a sideways glance at Ranger.

"Frankie Dawson," he instantly replied. "The dispatcher already told me. The guy must go looking for trouble."

Thinking back to the last few days, Kinsey wasn't so sure. It was starting to seem the other way around. Trouble seemed to find the lanky private investigator at every turn.

"Well, he is a P.I., right?" she said, not liking the tense atmosphere she was sensing between them. "Isn't that what he's supposed to do?"

Ranger just grunted and stared out the window, obviously distracted and in a foul mood.

They rode in silence until the Interceptor pulled up in front of the M.E.'s office.

Walking into the lobby, Kinsey was surprised to see Rosalie Quintero already waiting for them.

"You certainly took your time getting here," the medical examiner said stiffly. "I assume you were told that Dr. Chandra was attacked in the lab last night and has been taken to the hospital?"

Kinsey had never seen Rosalie so agitated.

"Dr. Chandra?"

The name sounded familiar.

"Uma Chandra, the forensics anthropologist who's been assisting with the analysis of the Wolf River bones," Rosalie explained. "She came with me to the Tara Wilder scene."

An image of the petite woman with friendly brown eyes flashed into Kinsey's mind.

"No, I mean, I knew there was a break-in, and that someone had been assaulted," she stammered, glancing at Ranger. "But I didn't realize it was Dr. Chandra."

Ranger wasn't listening, he was looking down the hall as Marty Prince emerged from a door marked *Authorized Personnel Only*, followed by Frankie Dawson and Josie Atkins.

"What's going on?" he asked. "Why's Josie Atkins here?"

Rosalie pursed her lips.

"She came to view her parents' bodies," she said. "She is their next of kin. But I'm not sure what that has to do with our break-in and the attack on Uma Chandra."

Turning back to see the look of reproach on the M.E.'s face, Ranger nodded.

"Uh, yes, you say the assault took place last night? Why was it only called in this morning, then?" he asked. "Can you show us where it happened?"

They followed Rosalie into the lab.

"We haven't cleaned anything up yet," she said, pointing around to the broken glass and the blood on the floor.

Kinsey gaped at the scene, her eyes falling on a bloody scalpel lying on the floor. There'd obviously been quite a struggle between Dr. Chandra and her attacker.

"We need to get a CSI team out here right away," she said, reaching for her phone. "You were right not to touch anything. We'll need to collect the evidence first."

Once she'd made the call, Kinsey turned back to Rosalie.

"Maybe we should go to your office," she suggested. "You can give us more details and we can take a statement."

The M.E. led them down the hall, then stopped short as she opened her office door, looking down at the lock with a perplexed frown.

"You know, my office was locked last night but when I came in this morning..."

She shook her head in confusion.

"I think it was open. The man who came in must have broken into my office, too," she said, sounding shaken.

"Did he take anything?" Kinsey asked.

She saw Rosalie's eyes shift to her desk, which was empty.

"I'm not sure," the M.E. said quickly, suddenly flustered. "I had some paperwork lying around. Ballistics results, and maybe a DNA profile."

Before she could continue, Ranger spoke up.

"You said *the man who came in.* You know it was a man?"

Rosalie nodded.

"I haven't spoken to Uma myself, but from what she told Frankie Dawson, a man attacked her as she was working in the lab. He said he was looking for the bones, and...and then he stabbed her."

"The bones?" Kinsey asked. "Did he mean the bones recovered from the Wolf River? Did he take them?"

The idea was disturbing. She'd never heard of a criminal trying to steal back human remains.

"Yes, I think he meant the bones from the river, which we've been examining. And no, he didn't take them. I checked the cooler and they were all still there. Somehow Uma must have dissuaded him."

"Of course, we'll need to interview both Mr. Dawson and Dr. Chandra," Kinsey said, making a note on her pad. "And while the CSI team is working in the lab, Detective Ranger and I can look around the rest of the building and try to find out how this man got inside."

As she stood to leave the office, Ranger held up a hand.

"Just a minute," he said, leaning forward to address Rosalie. "You said there were ballistics results and a DNA profile on your desk that might be missing. Can you tell us more about that? Is there some reason the attacker would want to take them?"

The M.E. put a nervous hand to her throat as she explained the DNA profile had been taken from blood and tissue found in Tara Wilder's mouth.

"We ran the profile through CODIS, and it matched DNA recovered from the body of a twenty-year-old homicide victim named Krystal Carter," Rosalie said. "She was found in an alley behind a Nashville bar. She'd been shot in the back of the head."

"When did you learn all of this?" Ranger asked. "And why didn't you let us know what you'd found?"

Rosalie shifted uncomfortably.

"I did try to speak to Detective Kinsey, but she wasn't available, so I told Chief Shipley. He wasn't happy that I'd called the Nashville PD about the matching profile in CODIS. I guess he thinks I've overstepped my responsibilities."

Before the medical examiner could say more, Kinsey's phone buzzed in her pocket.

She looked down at the display and winced.

"Sorry, I should probably take this," she said as she made her way out of the office.

Once she'd closed the door behind her, Kinsey answered the call and held the phone to her ear.

"Chief Shipley, how can I help you?"

"Is it true?" he demanded. "Do we have another body?"

Kinsey hesitated, wondering who he'd been talking to. Could Dr. Chandra have died on the way to the hospital? Did he know something she didn't know?

"I don't think so," she finally said. "Although another woman's been attacked. But luckily, this one's still alive."

"Still alive?"

Shipley sounded surprised.

"Yes, a forensic anthropologist working at the M.E.'s office was attacked in the lab. The assailant left her for dead. She wasn't discovered until this morning, but she survived."

"That's wonderful," Shipley said. "Has she been able to ID the man who attacked her? What do we know so far?"

"We're still investigating the scene, and we still need to interview the victim and the man who found her."

She wasn't planning to mention Frankie Dawson's name, but the dispatcher must have already spread the news.

"Is it true? Was Frankie Dawson the one who found her and called it in?"

"Yes," she said, relieved he didn't seem to know that Josie Atkins had been with Frankie when he'd found Uma. "And we'll be talking to him soon, but–"

The chief didn't let her finish.

"Bring him in," he ordered. "Get him down here for questioning as soon as possible. If he won't come willingly, then arrest him."

"On what charge?" Kinsey asked, startled by the demand.

Shipley scoffed.

"Didn't you tell me Frankie Dawson had been trespassing at a crime scene the other day?"

He was starting to sound angry.

"Well, yes..."

"Then use your brain," he thundered. "This is the second time that man has discovered a crime scene and we need to stop him from interfering."

Kinsey shook her head in disbelief.

"Finding an assault victim and calling 911 for help is hardly *interfering*," she protested, unable to hold back her outrage any longer. "He probably saved Uma Chandra's life."

"Spare me the hero story. Just bring him down here, Kinsey. No more excuses and no more screw-ups."

Realizing Shipley had ended the call, Kinsey dropped the phone back in her pocket, turning to see Ranger behind her.

"Did you hear any of that?" she asked.

"Enough to know the chief wants you to bring in Frankie Dawson," he said. "Did you tell him about the girl?"

She shook her head.

"No, and I'm not going to. You stay here and wait for the crime scene crew. I'll take Frankie to the station. But I plan to drop Josie off at his grandmother's house on the way."

"I thought he said she lives over in Chesterville," he said. "That's hardly on the way."

"It's close enough," Kinsey snapped. "The girl's been through hell. She doesn't need to put up with Shipley's bullshit, too."

Ranger blinked in surprise, then inclined his head.

"I agree," he said. "But don't let him hear you say that."

He had disappeared down the hall in the direction of the lab when Josie and Frankie came out to the lobby.

"I'm sorry, Frankie," she said, remembering his anger the last time she'd called him Mr. Dawson. "But I'm going to need to take you down to the station to get a full statement from you."

Avoiding the accusing stare Josie was shooting in her direction, Kinsey continued.

"We just need to understand what happened this morning when you discovered Uma Chandra. I can drop

Josie and Sherlock off at your grandmother's house on the way."

To her surprise, Frankie didn't argue.

"Fine, as long as Josie can go straight home. She's been through a hell of a lot this morning."

The drive to Chesterville was tense and quiet, and when they arrived at the house on Monarch Avenue, Josie and Sherlock got out and walked to the door without a goodbye.

"So, did Shipley put you up to this?" Frankie asked once they were alone in the SUV.

"It's standard protocol," Kinsey said, avoiding his eyes. "A woman has been assaulted, after all."

Frankie snorted.

"Yeah, and you should be out there looking for the guy who tried to off her, not chauffeuring me around town."

Knowing he was probably right, she fell silent until they'd made it to the station. When they arrived, she led him into the same interview room as the last time.

"This place is beginning to feel like home," Frankie said as he sank onto a metal chair, kicked his loafers up onto the table, and pulled out a stick of gum.

Kinsey suppressed a smile as she left the room.

She walked down to Shipley's office and rapped on the open door, trying to keep the resentment out of her eyes as the chief looked up.

"I've got Mr. Dawson in the interview room," she said. "I'll take a full statement and–"

"No, I'll handle Mr. Dawson from here," Shipley said, getting to his feet. "You can go."

Staring at him in surprise, Kinsey made no move to leave. "But–"

"I said I will handle it from here," the chief barked. "I will question Frankie Dawson personally. He won't get anything over on me, I assure you."

He waved a hand to dismiss her.

"Continue working on your other cases," he said. "I'll assign another team to the break-in at the M.E.'s office."

"It's not just a simple break-in," she tried to protest. "This could be connected to the bones in the–"

"I said *I'll handle it*, detective, now go."

* * *

Kinsey was still fuming when she stormed out of the Barrel Creek Police Station and jumped into the Interceptor.

She sped out of the parking lot, not sure where she was headed until she turned onto Ironstone Way.

The Atkins house was still blocked off with yellow crime scene tape and appeared to be empty.

Kinsey knew that, in addition to the CSI team and the medical examiner's office, either she or Ranger would need to give their approval to release the house back to its owner.

Might as well have one last look around. Who knows what I might find in the light of day?

Parking the Interceptor in the back, Kinsey went in through the kitchen door, surprised to find it unlocked.

Careless investigators are going to allow the place to get robbed.

As she stepped inside and began looking around, she saw that her fears had not been unfounded. The place appeared to have been ransacked.

No way our team did this. It had to be someone else. Someone looking for something? But what?

The questioned lingered in her mind as she took out her phone and began recording the mess that had been made, trying to find a pattern as to what the intruders had been trying to find.

Seeing that all the drawers had been tipped out and that papers and receipts had been rifled through, she wondered if they'd been looking for some kind of documents or records.

After she had assessed all the rooms on both the first and second floors, she stood in the hallway between Josie's bedroom and her parents' bedroom, hands on hips.

What the hell were they after?

She had taken several steps toward the landing when she stopped and looked up at the ceiling.

The hatch to the attic was well concealed, but she could see the faint outline in the wood above. Unable to see a string hanging down, she looked at the light switch on the wall and tried each one.

The last switch she tried started up a soft electric whirring from above. As the hatch above began to open, a step ladder automatically lowered down.

Kinsey waited until the ladder was securely in place, then climbed up, sticking her head into a cozy space that appeared to have served as part storage room and part craft studio.

Imagining Cheryl Atkins sitting at the sewing machine by the tiny window or working on the scrapbooks stacked on the table, Kinsey climbed up the rest of the way and stepped into the attic, her head nearly reaching the sloped ceiling.

The small room hadn't been disturbed, and Kinsey figured the intruders hadn't discovered the electronic attic stairs.

Running an eye over all the boxes piled in the corner, and the file cabinet and steamer trunk lining the back wall, Kinsey figured they'd missed the payload.

She decided to start with the old-fashioned trunk and work her way clockwise around the room. Opening the heavy lid, she reached in and pulled out a stack of old letters.

Underneath the letters, she saw a bundle of writing journals, tied with a pink ribbon.

Picking up the bundle, she untied the ribbon and flipped through the top journal, her eyes skimming over the words with growing excitement.

It appeared as if Cheryl Atkins had kept a journal for much of her life, and from what Kinsey was reading, she hadn't felt the need to hold anything back.

Pulse quickening as she turned to the next page, the detective realized that Dwight and Cheryl hadn't taken their secrets with them to their graves after all.

CHAPTER THIRTY-TWO

Frankie sat in the little metal folding chair, his elbows propped on the wooden table and his hands folded into a prayer position under his chin. Tapping his foot nervously on the sticky concrete floor of the interview room, he stared at the door, willing Detective Kinsey to come in.

He was eager to get home to Josie and make sure she was alright. After what she'd seen, he didn't want her to be left on her own, although the thought that she was with Sherlock made him feel slightly less anxious.

Hearing footsteps outside the door, Frankie tensed and prepared to make his case.

He wasn't prepared to see Chief Shipley's hostile face, and the shock must have shown in his expression.

"Sorry to disappoint you, Mr. Dawson. You were probably expecting Detective Kinsey. But you've messed her and Ranger around long enough. I thought it was time for you and me to have a talk. You know, *man to man*."

Frankie felt his stomach drop.

Although he'd never officially met the man in front of him, he knew the type. He'd met many just like him.

Bullies, hypocrites, and frauds.

Those who'd sworn to uphold the law, but who considered themselves to be above the law.

In some ways, they were worse than the outright criminals Frankie had met throughout his life, both in and out of prison. At least the career crooks didn't pretend to be something they weren't.

"Kinsey's green, but she's smart," Frankie said, folding his arms over his chest. "And she's trying to find a man who has killed a busload of people in this town, which is more than I can say for you."

Shipley frowned.

"What do you mean by that?"

"Finding the Wolf River Killer isn't your top priority, is it, Chief? The whole town is desperate to find this guy, but you're holed up in your little office trying to stop Kinsey and Ranger from doing their jobs. Hoping to pin the murders on some chump, like me. Why is that?"

An angry red flush crept up Shipley's face.

"Don't you come in here talking to me like that," Shipley said, his voice low and hard. "I know about you."

He jabbed a thick finger in Frankie's face.

"You're an ex-con who got some hack to overturn your sentence. An alcoholic who became a P.I. because he couldn't hold down a real job. A man who left his hometown with his tail between his legs fifteen years ago after his drugged-up sister overdosed."

Shipley let out a nasty laugh.

"And now you're going to come in here and tell me I'm

not doing my job? Accusing me of what exactly?"

He cocked his head and raised his thick eyebrows in mock curiosity. But there was a warning gleam in his eyes.

"I think you've got this a little backward, pal. You're the one who brought me in here to make some kind of trumped-up accusation," Frankie said. "So, get on with it."

The comment caused a vein to start pulsing in Shipley's forehead. The chief squeezed both his hands into fists and banged them down hard on the table in front of Frankie.

"I want you out of my town!"

Frankie jumped back in surprise as the words exploded from Shipley's mouth.

He leaned back as Shipley bent over the table to put his face only inches from Frankie's.

"You need to leave," he gritted out. "You have no idea what kind of trouble you'll find yourself in if you stay."

Frankie saw something in the older man's eyes that he hadn't expected to see. The chief was afraid.

"So, if I don't leave, you'll do what?" Frankie asked. "Frame me for Dwight and Cheryl's murders? Maybe throw in a charge for Tara Wilder's murder, too?"

Shipley stood and ran a hand through his hair, smoothing back a grayish curl that had fallen over his forehead.

"That sounds like a good start," the police chief said, regaining his composure. "I'm sure by the time I'm done, you'll have enough charges to earn you even more time than poor Lacey Emerson got."

A look of satisfaction fell over Shipley's face as he saw

Frankie's eyes narrow.

"So, you admit you railroaded Lacey Emerson?"

"I admit nothing to the likes of you," Shipley said. "But I was sorry to hear that Lacey wouldn't get to complete the remainder of her sentence. I hate to see justice go unserved."

Now it was Frankie's turn to slam his fist on the table.

"You really are a cold bastard, aren't you?"

"You were out at Larksville the day she died, weren't you, Frankie?" Shipley asked. "You know, they think somehow the drugs she ingested were mixed with fentanyl. You wouldn't know anything about that, would you?"

A cold finger of fear ran down Frankie's back.

"It just so happens that one of the guards said you two were arguing in the visiting room, and an inmate swears that she saw you handing Lacey something in a plastic baggie."

"That's bullshit and you know it," Frankie said, struggling to stop himself from lunging at Shipley's head. "If I didn't have Josie to think about, I'd..."

The words spilled out before he could stop them.

"Oh yes, Josie Atkins," Shipley said. "She is a problem."

He stared down into Frankie's face, then pulled his phone out of his jacket pocket.

After tapping in a number, he held the phone to his ear.

"Detective Ranger? I have Frankie Dawson here, and I need you to do me a favor. I need you to go pick up the Atkins' brat and bring her to the station for questioning."

The chief paused to listen to Ranger's reply.

"I know you're at a crime scene, but this is important," Shipley said. "I have reason to believe the girl's the one who pulled the trigger."

Frankie jumped up from his chair and stood in front of the chief with both hands clenched into fists.

"Mr. Dawson says that you'll know where the girl is. Now, go get her and bring her here."

Shipley listened again, then slammed down the phone.

Before Frankie could react, he charged to the door and flung it open to reveal Will Jackson standing in the hall.

"Officer Jackson, I've got an errand to run," he said. "See that Mr. Dawson doesn't leave this room until I return."

Without another word, Shipley strode off down the hall, leaving Frankie face-to-face with the uniformed officer.

"Listen, I gotta get out of here," Frankie said, looking past Jackson into the hall, gauging his chance of escape.

"Forget about it," Jackson said, stepping out of the room.

As he heard the lock turn, Frankie took out his phone and dialed his mother's number, but it went to voicemail.

"Ma, as soon as you hear this take Josie out of the house," he said, beginning to panic. "Take her to the mall or the movies or something. Just keep her out of the house until you hear from me again."

Knowing his mother rarely checked her voicemails, he tried calling the landline to Granny Davis' house, but it just rang and rang without answer.

He was considering calling Kinsey and appealing to her better nature when he heard loud voices in the hall.

The interview room door swung open, and Ranger

charged into the room, looking around as if he expected to see someone with Frankie.

"Shipley asked me to watch him until he got back," Jackson said, nodding toward Frankie.

"That's okay, Jackson. I'll take watch now," Ranger said, sounding slightly out of breath. "I've got to wait for Shipley to get back anyway. I've got something to tell him."

Jackson hesitated, then nodded and disappeared down the hall. As soon as he was gone, Ranger turned to Frankie.

"Okay, let's go," he said, stepping out into the hall.

"Where are we going? I need to find Josie."

Ranger shook his head.

"Shipley won't hurt her, and he doesn't know where she is right now anyway. Not unless you told him."

As he opened his mouth to ask where they were going, Ranger lifted a hand to silence him.

"If you really do care about Josie, you'll stop asking questions and come with me before it's too late."

CHAPTER THIRTY-THREE

anger quickly scanned the parking lot, then led Frankie toward a black Ford Interceptor that matched the vehicle Kinsey had been driving. Waiting for the P.I. to jump into the passenger's seat, he glanced nervously at the street, expecting Shipley to appear at any moment, anxious to get away before the chief started looking for him.

He pulled onto Hastings Highway, then merged onto the interstate heading east. Checking his rearview mirror, he half-expected to see Shipley zooming up behind him.

"Who's chasing us, man?" Frankie asked, turning to see what Ranger kept looking at in the review mirror. "And what does this have to do with Josie?"

Ranger flicked his eyes back to the interstate, which ran beside the winding Wolf River for much of the journey.

"She's in danger," Ranger said. "But not from Shipley. At least, I don't think so. It's possible the chief might try to throw her in a cell, but I doubt he'd hurt her. Not physically."

"If it isn't Shipley you're worried about, then who?"

Knowing it was no longer possible to keep Frankie in the

dark, Ranger glanced over at the P.I., unsure where to begin.

"We believe the man who killed Josie's parents is an associate of Shipley's. Someone who is determined to keep her from telling anyone what she may have seen or heard."

Frankie's eyes narrowed, and he stiffened beside Ranger.

"Are you playing some kind of game to get Josie to talk to you?" Frankie asked. "Cause, you can forget it. She doesn't trust the Barrel Creek PD, and I don't either."

"I don't blame her," Ranger said with a sigh. "But we need to know what she's been told. What she may have seen or heard that night. It could be a matter of life or death for the Wolf's next victim."

A frown creased Frankie's forehead.

"The Wolf?"

"That's what Dwight called him," Ranger said. "Before he died, he was prepared to give evidence against a man he believed was the Wolf River Killer. But he knew the man was protected by the Barrel Creek PD. Or at least some of the officers there. Shipley was just one of them."

Ranger took a deep breath.

"My father...Ike Ranger...he was another."

"Your father was crooked?" Frankie asked.

But the P.I. didn't look surprised.

"I guess you've spoken to Dusty Fontaine, then," Ranger said. "He'll tell anyone who will listen that my father was on the take. The problem is very few people will listen."

He thought of the first time Dusty had approached him. Ranger had been so angry, even though deep down, he'd suspected the reporter had been telling the truth.

"I'm guessing the *Gazette* won't publish his suspicions because they're afraid they'll get sued."

Frankie didn't reply as Ranger circled a redbrick building, then parked the SUV in a nearby lot.

Pulling out his phone, he tapped in a text message and pressed *Send*, then turned to face Frankie.

"After my father died, I found evidence that he and Shipley, and some of the others, mostly old-timers, had been involved in a smuggling ring," Ranger said. "Most of them had already retired. A few died in suspicious circumstances, like my father."

He glanced in the rearview mirror just as a man stepped out of the building and approached the car. He appeared beside Frankie's window and flashed his FBI credentials.

"Diesel? What are you doing here?" Frankie asked, his eyes widening as he rolled down the window.

"It's Special Agent Kade Mabry," the man said. "Diesel is the name I've been using undercover as part of an investigation into the Barrel Creek police department. Come on in and we'll tell you what we can."

Frankie turned to stare at Ranger.

"You've been working with the feds?"

Ranger nodded as Kade led them into the FBI field office.

"Detective Ranger has been helping us from the start," the agent confirmed as he walked them through security and ushered them into a small conference room.

"Dwight Atkins made contact almost a year ago," he explained after they were seated around a sleek conference table. "Right after he was told his cancer was terminal."

Leaning back in his chair, the agent looked somber.

"He suspected he knew who was responsible for dumping the bones found in the Wolf River," he said. "He called the man the Wolf, but he refused to reveal his true identity until we could guarantee he and his family wouldn't face retribution."

Frankie shook his head.

"What do you mean by retribution?"

"Dwight said the Barrel Creek PD had been infiltrated by men involved in several illegal activities," Kade said. "Mainly dealing and shipping drugs and guns out of his barrel factory. He claimed he'd tried to pull out over the years but had faced threats from Shipley. He believed if he turned the Wolf in, Shipley would protect the man, leaving him free to retaliate."

Getting to his feet, he started pacing the floor.

"So, when we made contact with Detective Ranger, and he agreed to work with us from the inside, it seemed we were close to taking down Shipley and convincing Dwight to tell us who the Wolf really is. But then..."

"Then Dwight ended up dead, along with his wife, and you guys still don't know who the killer is," Frankie said. "And you're afraid to take down Shipley in case it tips the guy off and he makes a run for it. Am I understanding the situation?"

Kade nodded.

"We think the Wolf suspects Josie saw or heard him that night and has been putting pressure on Shipley to question her and find out," Ranger added. "Which is why I wanted to be the one to question her, so that I could tell Shipley she hadn't seen anything. I figured that might convince him to contact the Wolf and put his mind at ease."

"You really think that would have satisfied this Wolf guy?" Frankie asked. "I mean, the kind of guy who gets off on putting bullets in the backs of people's heads isn't going to take any chances. I wouldn't doubt the guy plans on taking care of Josie personally."

The idea had already crossed Ranger's mind.

"Yeah, it's possible," he admitted. "Which is one of the reasons we've decided we can't wait any longer. We're going to move on Shipley soon. We think we have enough evidence built up against him and his associates now to make it stick."

Kade paced back to the table, full of nervous energy.

"Based on our investigation, I'm pretty sure someone in Shipley's inner circle has to be the Wolf," he said. "If we bring them all in, one of them is sure to crack and make a deal. We agree on a reduced sentence if they put the finger on the Wolf."

Ranger saw the doubt in Frankie's eyes.

"What's the connection to Rowdy's?" Frankie asked. "You seem to spend a lot of time there."

Dropping into his chair, Kade hesitated.

"Look, I know your uncle owns the place," he finally said. "But you might not be aware that an unusually high number of missing women have been last seen at your uncle's bar."

"You mean women like Tara Wilder?" Frankie asked.

The FBI agent's face hardened.

"That one hurt," he said, his voice thick with regret. "The Wolf got to Tara under my watch. That's when I decided it had to end. That we can't wait any longer."

Frankie fell silent as if thinking.

"Have you ever considered that Shipley himself could be the Wolf?" he asked. "That he's killing these women?"

Kade Mabry sat back in his chair, considering the question.

"Otto Shipley has been on my list of suspects from the beginning," he admitted. "But he's sixty years old and appears to be a happily married family man, which doesn't fit the usual profile."

"Shipley is a bit long in the tooth," Frankie agreed. "But there've been serial killers who weren't caught until they were in their fifties or sixties, so isn't it possible?"

"Shipley's as strong and fit as most men half his age," Ranger added. "And he had the means and opportunity to commit the murders. At least the ones we know about."

Picturing the chief, Ranger felt a surge of anger.

"He had access to plenty of guns," he said. "Hell, the old man's been running illegal guns for the last two decades. And he could have easily tampered with the evidence to throw us off his trail and make us think..."

Kade held up a hand.

"Let's not get too emotional," he cautioned. "We need to follow the evidence...not our anger. But there would be one way to prove it once and for all."

Ranger and Frankie both stared at him, waiting.

"I've spoken to the Barrel Creek M.E. and was able to obtain a DNA profile of the blood and tissue found in Tara Wilder's mouth," he explained. "So, if we get her a sample of Shipley's DNA, she could tell us if he's the Wolf, or eliminate him from the suspect list for good."

All three men fell silent, then Frankie turned to Ranger.

"You work with Shipley at the station, can't you get him to drink a soda or something?" he asked.

"We'd need a warrant," Kade reminded them. "Unless we get a sample that Shipley has discarded in a public place."

Ranger shook his head.

"It wouldn't matter anyway. I'm not going back there as long as Shipley's still in charge," he said. "If I see that man again I may do something I'll regret."

"What about Kinsey?" Frankie asked. "Would she help?"

Shaking his head at the suggestion, Ranger grimaced.

"Kinsey doesn't know anything about this," he admitted. "She's clueless about the criminal activity going on within the department and I wanted to keep it that way. I figured the less she knew about it the safer she'd be."

Kade raised an eyebrow.

"Things are going to start going down pretty quickly from here on out," he said. "I think you're going to need to let her know what's going on."

Frankie nodded.

"She's a decent detective," he added. "She could be an asset to the investigation if given half a chance."

Knowing he couldn't put it off any longer, Ranger pulled out his phone and looked down at Kinsey's number in his contact list.

"Okay, I'll ask her to meet me back at the M.E.'s office to wrap up the scene," he said. "I'll find a way to tell her there."

He tapped on Kinsey's number and held the phone to his ear, suddenly nervous about revealing the duplicitous role he'd been playing with her all along.

"I was just going to call you," Kinsey said as soon as she'd answered the phone. "I'm out at the Atkins house. You'll never believe all the information I found up in the attic."

Ranger heard real excitement in her voice as she continued without pause, giving him no chance to respond.

"According to Cheryl Atkins' journals, Dwight was involved in some highly illegal activity. And that's not all..."

As if fearing she'd be overheard, Kinsey lowered her voice.

"Cheryl's journals implicate Chief Shipley. I always knew there was something fishy about that man."

The statement sent Ranger's pulse racing.

"That may be, but we need to keep the information to ourselves for now," he said. "Are you alone out there?"

"I was the last time I checked," Kinsey said, sounding unafraid. "But I'll be leaving here soon. I'm going to collect some of this evidence and bring it to-"

Ranger quickly jumped in to interrupt her.

"Don't take it to the station," he said. "You can meet me

back at the M.E.'s office. Rosalie Quintero can be trusted. I'll explain everything when I see you there."

There was a short pause.

"Okay," Kinsey said, her voice subdued. "See you there."

Once Ranger had ended the call, he turned to Kade and Frankie with a stunned expression.

"She's found evidence that Shipley's crooked," he said. "Cheryl Atkins kept a journal."

"That's good," Kade said. "Now, we need to find out where Shipley is and find a way to get his DNA."

* * *

Thirty minutes later Ranger drove out of the FBI field office's parking lot with Kade riding shotgun and Frankie sitting in the backseat.

"Agent Cortez has been running electronic surveillance on Shipley for me during the last few weeks," Kade said.

He was using his thumbs to type a message on his phone.

"We know Shipley and his associates use burner phones to communicate, so we haven't been able to trace most of his calls. But Cortez has been tracking his location through a government-issued phone he keeps with him."

Tapping in another message, Kade appeared to be waiting for a response, then frowned.

"That's strange," he said, looking over at Ranger. "Cortez says Shipley's parked on a street just outside Chesterville. His location hasn't changed in the last half-hour."

"Chesterville?" Frankie asked, sticking his head between the front seats. "That's close to my Granny's house."

After another series of taps, Kade looked back at Frankie.

"Shipley's on Viceroy Drive right now," he said. "You want to go check it out?"

Frankie nodded and Kade began calling out directions for Ranger to follow. Soon they were driving along a winding sideroad near the Chesterville city limit.

"Is that Shipley's car?" Kade asked, pointing to a white Interceptor that had pulled off on the side of the road.

As they got closer, they saw the back tire had blown out.

"Pull up behind him," Kade instructed. "I'll go up there and ask if he needs help. If he starts walking back here, you two can duck down."

Stepping out of the vehicle, Kade jogged to the driver's side window and bent to look in.

He froze in place, then turned and motioned for Ranger and Frankie to join him at the car window. The pained grimace on the FBI agent's face made it clear what they could expect to find.

As Ranger approached and looked past Kade into the driver's seat, he saw Shipley slumped over the steering wheel with a gunshot wound to the back of his head.

"It looks and smells fresh," Kade said, sniffing the air, then reaching for his phone. "I've got to call this in. All hell's going to break loose when this gets out. But whoever shot him can't be far away."

"Chesterville isn't far away," Frankie said as Kade turned to talk urgently into his phone. "My Granny's house and

Josie aren't far away."

Ranger stared in at Shipley, still trying to register the fact that the man was dead. When he looked back, he saw that Frankie was climbing into the driver's seat of the Interceptor.

"Frankie?" he yelled, starting after him.

"I'm going home," Frankie called out of the open window as he pulled onto Viceroy Drive. "I've got to check on Josie."

Ranger felt Kade come up beside him as he yelled.

"Wait, Frankie!"

"He'll be back," the agent said. "I'm sure Josie's okay."

CHAPTER THIRTY-FOUR

Josie lay back on the twin bed that had once belonged to Franny Dawson and closed her eyes, willing herself to fall asleep, desperate to escape the nightmarish images that swam inside her head. Why had she ever imagined she'd find comfort in seeing her parents laid out on cold metal tables, their bodies stiff under white sheets and fluorescent lights?

She'd hoped to replace her last memories of them with something other than screams and blood. Had wanted to tell them she was sorry for not knowing how to save them.

But she knew she'd made a terrible mistake as soon as the sheets had been pulled down. Her parents weren't there. They had moved on, and nothing of their energy or essence remained.

Still smelling the sickly-sweet stench of decay in her hair and on her clothes, she tried to read some of the worn copy of *To Kill a Mockingbird* she'd taken from Franny's shelf.

She could still remember watching the movie with her mother one day when she'd stayed home sick from school, and so far she'd already made it halfway through the book.

Eyes growing heavy, she drifted off to the faint sound of

music coming from the radio in the kitchen, where she'd left Granny Davis and Sherlock sitting in companionable silence.

A sudden knock at the front door woke her.

She remained lying down with her eyes closed for a long beat, then sat up as another knock sounded, this time louder.

A man's voice called out.

"Hello, anybody home in there?"

As soon as she heard it, Josie recognized the voice of the man who'd killed her parents.

She froze in horror, then lunged toward the stairs.

"No, Granny! Don't open the door!"

But the old woman had already turned the lock, and the man on the porch pushed the door open and stepped inside.

"Mrs. Davis, it's good to see you."

Josie stood halfway down the stairs, her eyes trained on the gun in the man's hand.

Granny seemed not to notice.

"I was wondering if you'd be back," she said with a vague smile. "I guess you'd better come in and have some tea."

The man lifted his eyes to meet Josie's as he closed the door behind him.

"You..."

She choked out the word before her throat closed, but the fear in her eyes made it clear that she knew who he was and what he'd done.

He was the Wolf River Killer. The monster who had killed

her parents. And he'd come here planning to kill her, next.

"No need to upset the old woman," the man said, blocking Granny's path toward the kitchen. "I'll make it quick and painless for everyone if you come with me quietly."

Sherlock appeared in the kitchen doorway.

At the sight and smell of the man, the Labrador growled low in his throat, then began to bark wildly.

"Get that dog to shut up," the man snarled.

Josie saw him lift his gun in the Labrador's direction.

"No!" she cried out, her eyes hot with angry tears.

Forcing her trembling legs to move, she descended the last few stairs and crossed to Sherlock, grabbing hold of his collar, stroking his soft fur as much to calm him as herself.

"If you use that the neighbors will hear," she warned him in a breathless voice. "They'll come running."

A deep frown appeared on the man's forehead as he slowly lowered the gun.

"I'll come with you," Josie said, knowing she had to get him out of the house, had to stall for time. "Just don't hurt Granny Davis...or the dog."

Sherlock barked again as Josie tried to quiet him, wishing she had her cell phone. If only the police hadn't taken it she may have been able to send a message to Frankie.

He would have come to save me.

Picturing the landline in the kitchen, she tried to calculate how long it would take her to dash in and block the door so she could make a call.

Or maybe I could run out the back door, and...

But no, she couldn't leave Granny Davis and Sherlock with the man. He was a murderer.

He had killed her parents, and he would kill Frankie's grandmother and his dog, too, if she left them at his mercy.

"Lock that mutt in the basement," the man ordered, nodding toward Sherlock. "But the old woman...she'll call for help as soon as we're gone. I'll have to make sure she-"

"She has Alzheimer's," Josie blurted. "She doesn't know who you are or why you're here...do you, Granny Davis? Do you know why he's here?"

The old woman glared at her.

"Of course, I do," Granny said. "He's here...well, he's here to have some tea. I invited him to come back anytime."

She turned to the man with a scowl.

"Although you aren't being very nice I have to say."

Worried that the man would lash out, Josie stepped in front of Granny, willing her legs to stop trembling.

"I'll take them both to the basement," she said quickly. "They won't cause any trouble there."

Before the man could stop her, she took hold of Granny's thin arm and steered her to the door off the hall, which led down into the damp basement.

"I don't like the dark," Granny said as Josie helped her down the narrow stairs.

Switching on the light, Josie turned back for Sherlock, who continued to bark and growl.

"Come on, boy," Josie said. "It's okay."

She took hold of his collar, tugging him toward the open door, tempted to follow the Labrador into the basement and slam the door shut behind her.

But she knew the man would only break through the flimsy wood, scaring Granny and Sherlock in the process.

No, I'll just have to think of something else.

As the basement door closed behind Sherlock, the man grabbed Josie and pulled her toward him, letting the gun fall to the floor.

He wrapped one thick arm around her throat.

"You were right," he grunted. "I can't risk a gunshot in this neighborhood. But I can't let you scream, either."

Reaching into his pocket, he pulled out a syringe.

"This will make it better," he said, jamming the needle into the soft meat above her bicep. "Nighty-night."

Instantly, the room started tilting and spinning, and the light around her faded away into nothingness.

CHAPTER THIRTY-FIVE

Frankie pushed his loafer down hard on the gas pedal, ignoring the speed limit and rolling through stop signs as he sped toward Monarch Avenue. He'd already tried to call the landline at the house a dozen times without success, but Granny Davis rarely answered the old-fashioned phone she still had mounted on the kitchen wall.

His breath was coming fast and hard as he pulled into the driveway and jumped out of the Interceptor.

Whoever had killed Chief Shipley was still out there, perhaps even close by, and he would be looking for Josie next.

Racing up the steps, Frankie grabbed the doorknob and twisted, not sure what he'd do if it didn't turn.

But like most people in the old neighborhood, Granny tended to leave the backdoor unlocked.

As he started to step forward into the house, his eyes registered the muddy footprint on the pale green rug just inside the door.

His heart stopped as recognized a faint star-shaped pattern that had been left behind by the sole of a heavy boot.

"Josie!" he yelled as he hurried forward into the kitchen, slamming the door behind him. "Granny!"

The house was silent as he charged into the hall and surveyed the downstairs rooms with growing panic, before jogging upstairs to look in each bedroom and the attic loft.

Taking the stairs down to the first floor two at a time, he stood in the hall and tried to think.

Where could they be? Did they all go out without telling me?

His mother's little sedan wasn't in the driveway or parked by the curb. He felt a surge of hope. Maybe she'd taken them out somewhere.

Then he heard Sherlock bark.

The sound was faint. It was coming from the basement.

Running to the basement door, he flung the door open.

The light was on, and as he stepped inside, he immediately saw Granny and Sherlock sitting side by side on an old futon that was destined for Goodwill.

"Granny?"

Racing down the stairs, he crouched in front of the futon as Sherlock barked and licked his face.

"Why are you down here?" he asked. "Where's Josie?"

"I don't like it down here," Granny said, attempting to struggle to her feet. "I need a cup of tea."

Frankie took her arm and pulled her to her feet, then led her to the stairs. His stomach clenched with worry as they slowly ascended.

When they got to the kitchen, she crossed to the stove and picked up the kettle as if she'd forgotten Frankie was there.

"Granny. Where is Josie?" he asked, standing behind her and putting a hand on her arm.

She looked over and frowned.

"She must be with the man who came for tea," she said.

Frankie's heart plummeted.

"What man, Granny? Who was it?"

"It was the same man who came for tea the other day," she said as she began to fill the kettle.

Frankie suppressed a groan and turned his face away, trying to hide his frustration. It wasn't his grandmother's fault that he had left her and Josie alone.

I should have protected them. It's my fault Josie's gone.

Raking a hand through his hair, he thought he heard Granny murmur something under her breath.

"What are you saying, Granny?" he asked.

"I said that man needs to work on his manners. Especially if he's going to see Arlene again."

She tutted and pointed to the refrigerator.

"Your mother asked for his number," she said. "I thought it was a little forward of her, but she's always been eager."

Frankie saw that a piece of paper from the notepad by the phone had been stuck to the refrigerator with a magnet. A number had been carefully written in his mother's handwriting.

"Arlene could do better than that man," Granny said. "I told her she could do better. She could have done better than your father, too, if I'm honest."

Sudden footsteps sounded on the front porch and Frankie

put a finger to his lips as the doorknob turned.

"Why are you all standing there?" Arlene asked.

She shifted a bag of groceries to her other hand and stepped into the kitchen, stopping to frown down at the mud on the rug.

"What's going on? Has something happened?"

"Josie's gone," Frankie said. "A man came and took her. He locked Granny and Sherlock in the basement."

Granny shook her head.

"Franny put us down there," she corrected him. "I told her I didn't like the dark, so she turned on the light."

"Josie," Frankie said. "Josie turned on the light."

But Granny wasn't listening as she again turned to the kettle and continued making tea.

"What man?" Arlene asked, her eyes wide and instantly fearful. "Do you think it could be-"

"Granny said the man had been at the house before," Frankie said, cutting her off. "Did you have someone over? Someone who could have taken Josie?"

Arlene shook her head, but her eyes flicked back to the rug.

"I did ask Bill Brewster in when he dropped me off the other night on his way home from Rowdy's. Granny offered him some tea, but he declined."

She set down the bag of groceries and pointed to the rug.

"He had mud on his boots then, too, and I gave him a hard time about it," she said weakly. "Granny told him to come back any time, but I...don't think she liked him."

Dread washed over Frankie as the pieces began to fall

into place. Bill Brewster had worked with Dwight at the Barrel Works for decades, and he hung out at Rowdy's all the time.

Did he spend time with Ma to find out what I knew? To get close to Josie? Is that how he knew she'd be here alone with Granny?

He tried to make sense of it.

The man he'd known as a child, a man who'd been his father's friend and co-worker at the barrel works, was a murderous drug-dealing, gun-running serial killer. A man known in the press as the Wolf River Killer. A man the feds just called the Wolf.

And he had Josie.

"Is that Bill's number on the refrigerator?"

Arlene looked at the number she'd written and nodded.

"Do you know where he lives?" Frankie asked.

"Yes, but he's not there," Arlene said, looking dazed. "I drove past his house just now to see him cause he hasn't returned my call. But his car wasn't there."

Frankie's phone suddenly buzzed in his pocket. He looked down to see an unfamiliar number.

"Where are you Frankie? I thought you'd be back by now."

He recognized Kade Mabry's voice.

"I'm at my Grandmother's house in Chesterville," Frankie said. "Tell me, was Bill Brewster one of Shipley's associates? Is he on your list of suspects?"

There was a momentary pause.

"Yes, he is," Kade said. "He's an associate of Shipley's

who worked with Dwight and frequents Rowdy's. He checks all the boxes. He doesn't have a record, but with Shipley watching his back, he can do pretty much what he likes."

"Well, he's got Josie," Frankie said.

"Are you sure?"

"Yes, I'm sure."

Frankie stared at the faint outline of a star still embedded in the rug.

"And I need to find him, now," Frankie added. "Can your guy track him like he tracked Shipley?"

"We'd need a good phone number for him," Kade said. "And I suspect he likely uses a burner phone like the others.

Frankie crossed to the refrigerator.

"If I gave you a number for him could you track it?"

Kade hesitated.

"It might take some time, but I could try...what is it?"

Frankie read off the number.

"Let me see what I can do," Kade said, "I'll keep in touch."

As the connection dropped, Frankie turned back to face his mother, who still stood in the middle of the kitchen as if frozen in place.

"Mom, if Bill isn't at his house...where would he go?" he asked. "Come on, you and Dad knew him for years."

Arlene shrugged helplessly, tears filling her eyes.

"Why do I always pick the wrong men?"

"We don't have time for that, Ma!" Frankie scolded. "Think! Where would Bill go to be alone with Josie?"

Shaking her head, Arlene hesitated, then pointed toward

the muddy rug.

"The other night when I teased him about his muddy boots, Bill said he was always tracking mud back from the property his grandfather had left him out by the river."

Frankie's heart jumped.

"Did he say where exactly?"

"Just that it was out past the Barrel Works."

Suddenly Frankie knew right where it was.

He and Dwight had passed a dirt road plenty of times on their way to work. There'd been a *No Trespassing* sign on the fence. One day he'd asked Dwight what was down there.

Dwight had told him that the property had belonged to old man Brewster, but he wasn't sure what had happened to it after he'd died.

"I gotta go, Ma," Frankie said. "Take Granny over to a friend's house or something. Just stay away from here until you hear from me. And keep your phone on."

Making sure his Glock was loaded, he grabbed Sherlock's leash and called to the dog.

"Come on, boy! Let's go find Josie!"

CHAPTER THIRTY-SIX

Sherlock sat in the passenger's seat next to Frankie, enjoying the view he had through the front windshield as the night air blew in through the window to ruffle his fur. He listened to the soft hum of the Interceptor's powerful motor as they turned onto Barrel Creek Trail.

Recognizing the road they'd driven earlier in the week on their way out to the barrel factory, Sherlock was surprised when Frankie pulled up and stopped beside a small dirt sideroad lined with a thick forest of trees.

The road was blocked off by a wooden gate with a large sign reading *No Trespassing.*

The Labrador looked past the gate, staring into the darkness beyond the headlights.

He barked as he saw the faint glow of a light ahead.

"You see that, too, don't you, pal?" Frankie said as he studied the gate with narrowed eyes.

Glancing over at Sherlock with a steely expression, Frankie put a protective arm in front of the dog.

"Hold on tight, partner, we're going in."

The dog barked with excitement as Frankie floored the

accelerator and the big SUV shot forward, barreling through the gate with an earsplitting crash.

Once past the gate, Frankie continued forward, sending the Interceptor bucking and bouncing down the pitted, dirt road as Sherlock crouched low in the seat, concentrating on maintaining his balance.

When they reach a clearing in the woods, Frankie brought the vehicle to a stop beside a small wooden building.

Too impatient to wait for Frankie to come around and open his door, Sherlock jumped through the open window, landing on a patch of thick green grass.

Lifting his nose to the sky, he inhaled the hated scent of the man who'd been in Granny's house, the man who'd taken Josie away, and let out a long, anguished howl.

He evaded Frankie's attempt to snap on his leash and ran forward, passing a black Bronco that was parked along the side of the building.

The scent of the man led him into the workshop.

Sniffing along the floor, he barked as he came to a stop in front of a collection of wooden barrels under the window.

Frankie examined the barrels, then grabbed a crowbar off a workbench and pried off the lid of the closest barrel, revealing a pile of bags packed with fine white powder.

"So, this is what they've been dealing in."

Moving on to the next barrel, he used the crowbar to reveal an assortment of guns and ammunition.

Suddenly Sherlock picked up another, more sinister scent.

Turning toward the smoky, acrid smell, he turned and ran back out of the workshop, following his nose to a section of the woods that had been cleared to make room for a fire pit.

He whined in his throat as he stared down at the ashes, then turned to bark for Frankie. He needed to warn him that the man had been here.

Death was nearby.

He barked again, then grew quiet as Frankie called out.

"Quiet, Sherlock!" he hissed. "You want to alert everyone in the neighborhood that we're...?"

Frankie's voice faded away as his eyes fell on the firepit.

He stared at the bits of charred bones littering the ash with stunned eyes, then bent forward with a shaky hand.

"It's cold," he said, sagging with relief. "That isn't Josie."

Something rustled in the bushes behind them.

Sherlock froze and listened.

Were those footsteps?

Lifting his snout into the air, he sniffed deeply, then barked out a warning.

As he began to run forward, he looked back to make sure Frankie was beside him. He hesitated for just a second as he picked up the sound of a car engine somewhere off the road.

Then a man's angry shout by the river drew his full attention. It had to be the man.

The man who smelled like blood and death.

Sherlock turned and ran, leading Frankie toward the river.

CHAPTER THIRTY-SEVEN

Bill Brewster shouted out as his boot caught on a gnarled root sticking out of the ground and he went down on one knee. Managing to get back to his feet, he struggled forward a few more steps, then dumped the girl into the wheelbarrow with a sigh of relief.

He was getting too old to be carrying bodies around. It wasn't good for his back. Bending down, he gripped the hardwood handles and hefted the back leg of the wheelbarrow off the muddy ground.

Fighting to balance his unwieldy cargo, he maneuvered the wheelbarrow down a well-worn path, watching out for large rocks and potholes, not stopping until he reached the wide, sloping bank of the Wolf River.

He dropped the handles and paused to catch his breath, cursing his own weakness. Looking down at Josie Atkins' limp body, he gave an angry shake of his head.

He was going to have to dump her too close to home.

He wouldn't have the time or opportunity to take her downriver, closer to the city. There were alligators down there that could help get rid of the evidence, but it was too late for that now.

The whole thing had been a mess from the start, although he'd had no choice but to silence her, otherwise, she might have told everyone in town who he was and what he'd done.

If he'd allowed that to happen, he would have gone from being known as the affable nightshift manager at Atkins Barrel Works to being the Wolf River Killer, the most hated man in the state.

Maybe even the country, thanks to Dusty Fontaine's articles.

Deciding his next victim just might be the pugnacious entertainment reporter turned crime writer, he sucked in a deep breath and wrenched the wheelbarrow to the side, tipping Josie out onto the riverbank.

She hit the muddy ground with a soft groan, then stirred.

Pushing herself into a sitting position, the girl opened her eyes and blinked up at him in confusion.

"Where am I?"

The high-pitched whisper escalated into a terrified scream as he pulled the gun from his jacket pocket and slid back the chamber to confirm it was loaded.

He didn't notice the dark figure moving through the trees lining the path until it burst out of the darkness, barking, and snarling at his feet.

Stumbling backward in panic, he slid the chamber shut and lifted his gun, but he knew as soon as the shot rang out that he'd missed his target.

He spun around, looking for the dog and the man he knew must be with him. Instead, he saw that the girl had already managed to stagger to her feet.

Lunging forward, he wrapped an arm around her neck and jerked her back against his chest, holding the gun to her head with a now-shaking hand.

"I know you're out there, Frankie!" he bellowed into the still night air. "Show yourself, or I swear to Christ I'll put a bullet in her head right now."

A tall, thin figure stepped halfway out of the shadows.

He knew from the shape that it was Frankie Dawson.

The P.I. was holding a gun, probably a Glock from the look of it, and it was aimed at Bill's head.

"Don't be a dumbass," Frankie called, his face still cloaked in darkness. "Think about it. You shoot her, and you'll be dead a second later. Be smart and we can negotiate."

Bill gritted his teeth in frustration, but he loosened his arm around Josie's throat, allowing her to suck in a breath.

He needed to convince Frankie he was reasonable. Even agreeable. He needed to persuade him to lower his guard. If he could distract him, he could get off a shot.

First, I'll shoot that skinny prick in the head. Then, I'll take out the dog. The three of them can go into the river together.

"I'm a businessman, Frankie," he said as he calculated the distance between them. "I'm always open to negotiation."

Inching forward, he aimed the gun squarely at the shaggy head outlined in the faint moonlight.

"What's your offer?" he asked, buying time as his finger tightened on the trigger.

Then Frankie's shadow was gone, shifting through the

trees, moving to his right.

"You let Josie go, and I'll let you walk away," Frankie called. "You might even make it out of state before they come looking for you. You could head for Mexico or even Canada."

Bill could hear the dog whining low in his throat nearby as Frankie spoke again.

"But there's one condition. Before you go, you tell me why you killed Dwight and Cheryl. And why you're trying to kill their daughter? I mean, what the fuck is wrong with you, anyway? I thought you were a decent guy."

Raising his voice, Frankie suddenly took several steps forward, his big feet cracking branches as he went, seemingly heedless of the girl trapped between them.

"Hold on!" Bill shouted. "Just give me a minute!"

He pulled Josie tighter against his chest, eliciting a high-pitched gasp, and swallowed hard, knowing he didn't have much time.

There were bound to be cops on the way. Or there soon would be once they found Shipley's body.

And Frankie was right.

If he shot the girl now, there would be nothing to stop the man from blowing his head off. Or worse, tackling him and taking him into custody.

Panic rose in his chest. Was this the end? The day of reckoning that he'd been expecting ever since he'd started packing guns and drugs into the barrels he'd helped build all these years?

He should have known Otto Shipley was bad news from

the start. The Vice detective had been too confident. Too sure that he would never get caught. But after he'd been promoted to chief of police, Bill thought Shipley might be unstoppable after all.

His mistake had been recruiting his employer's son. Dwight had joined their operation, driven by greed as the money had started rolling in, and then kept silent through fear when he'd started to get cold feet.

"Why'd you kill Dwight?" Frankie demanded.

It sounded as if he was moving forward. Getting closer.

"Tell me that, at least. Why kill your own friend?"

"He was going to snitch on me," Bill said. "I warned him. So many times, I warned him to stay quiet. But he didn't listen. He called you, and he planned to go to the police."

Frankie's voice seemed to be coming from a cypress tree at the water's edge. Had he really gotten that close?

"What about those women?" Frankie asked. "If you were just trying to save your ass, why kill those innocent women?"

Bill opened his mouth, then closed it, not sure he had an answer to give. At least not one that would satisfy a man like Frankie Dawson.

How could he explain that the money hadn't been enough to satiate the hunger inside him? That after he'd impulsively killed Georgia Treadwell, he'd developed a need for it?

"It was an urge...a craving," he finally managed. "After the first time...with Georgia Treadwell...I couldn't control it.

I was sick, I guess, which means it wasn't my fault."

"You're still sick," Frankie spit out, his voice raw. "And Franny? Is that why you killed Franny? Because you're sick?"

That was an easier question to answer.

"No, that was different. She was just in the wrong place at the wrong time," he admitted. "She saw me the night I took out Booker Boudreaux. It wasn't personal, but after that, I couldn't let her live."

"So, you killed Booker?" Frankie asked.

Bill nodded, although he wasn't sure Frankie could see him clearly in the moonlight.

"He saw me with Georgia Treadwell, and he threatened to tell the police. Eventually Dwight figured it out, too."

"And Dwight didn't tell anyone?"

The anger in Frankie's voice was palpable.

"I told Dwight to stay quiet if he wanted to live. If he didn't want his family to find out that he'd been smuggling drugs and guns. And he knew I had friends in the BCPD. Otto Shipley and Ike Ranger were dangerous enemies to have."

"So, Dwight stayed quiet while Lacey Emerson went to prison," Frankie said. "Just another life destroyed."

It was a fair statement.

"That's about the shape of it," Bill agreed. "But don't think too harshly of him. The man was caught between a rock and a hard place. And he felt guilty about it. He told me. He said he'd felt too guilty to go to your sister's funeral."

Bill chuckled at the memory.

"He sure was relieved when you moved away."

His amusement faded when he heard footsteps nearby. Someone was running through the trees by the river.

As Bill turned his head, Josie dropped straight down, slipping out of his grip. She hit the ground and then rolled to her right, kicking both legs out as hard as she could.

Her feet connected with Bill's shins, and he fell back, squeezing off a shot just as his hand hit the ground, sending the gun flying.

Expecting to feel the impact of a bullet in his chest at any minute, Bill looked up to see Josie's startled face, then dropped his eyes to the bloodstain blooming across her shirt.

With a final, breathless gasp, she tumbled backward into the river and disappeared beneath the dark, murky water.

CHAPTER THIRTY-EIGHT

Everything seemed to be moving in slow motion as Josie teetered on the edge of the riverbank and then fell backward with a breathless gasp. Frankie charged forward, pausing only to kick Bill Brewster's fallen Glock into the weeds, before plunging into the river after her.

Ignoring the cold slap of water against his face, he sputtered and grabbed for a tree root sticking into the river before realizing the water was only waist deep.

After gaining his feet, Frankie slogged to the spot where Josie had fallen in and felt around under the muddy water.

His hand settled over a limply floating arm, and he grabbed it, pulling Josie's water-logged body to the surface.

Relief flooded through him as she gasped in a breath of air and then choked out a mouthful of bloody water.

She'd been shot, but she was still alive.

Sliding one arm under her shoulders and one under her knees, Frankie lifted her small body to his chest and turned back toward the riverbank.

A series of sharp, frantic barks drew his attention to Sherlock, who was standing at the water's edge.

He looked past the agitated dog, his eyes searching the

darkly forested terrain for Bill, unsure where the man could be now that he'd been disarmed.

Did he run back to his workshop? Or maybe he took off for the border like I suggested.

The possibility that the man responsible for killing Franny might escape, that he could go on to seek revenge, or even to kill again, filled him with dread.

We need to end this now...tonight.

But as he rushed to get Josie out of the water, Frankie's foot slipped on the muddy bank, sending him back into the river with a splash just as a bullet zipped past his head.

Gaping back toward the riverbank, he saw Bill Brewster standing in the moonlight. The man was holding a small Ruger in his hand.

How did the bastard get another gun?

Before he could decide which way to move, another bullet sliced into the water, skimming Josie's fall of blonde hair, which trailed along in the water beside him.

The two gunshots had sent Sherlock scurrying back into the cover of the trees, but the Labrador continued to bark a frantic warning as Bill aimed his little gun at Frankie's head.

A wolfish grin spread across the man's grizzled face.

"You, or the girl, first?" he asked. "I'll give you a choice."

Before he could respond, Frankie saw the flutter of movement in the trees behind Bill.

A dark figure stepped out into the moonlight, and for a minute Frankie thought he must be hallucinating.

Is this a dream or have I finally gone crazy?

The graceful figure lifted an arm in his direction. A glint of metal was followed by the crack of a gunshot.

Bill Brewster's head jerked forward with a spray of blood and tissue, the force of the bullet sending him plunging face-first into the dark water. Frankie watched in horror as the Wolf River seemed to swallow him up.

"Frankie!"

Two figures ran toward him. As they drew closer, he recognized Ranger and Kinsey. Help had arrived, although he wasn't sure how they had found him.

"An ambulance is on the way," Kinsey called out. "They should be here any minute."

Splashing into the river, Ranger reached for Josie, helping Frankie carry her out of the water.

"She's alive," Frankie said between chattering teeth. "But we need to stop the blood...and we need to warm her up."

As they laid her gently on the riverbank, Frankie scanned the path for the shooter who'd saved his life.

Was it really her? Is she here?

His heart stopped when he saw Peyton standing behind Kinsey, her wide amber eyes luminous in the moonlight.

Sticking her Glock back in her holster, Peyton pulled off her jacket and draped it over Josie's wet, motionless body.

Without hesitation, she pulled her cardigan over her head and pressed it against Josie's wound.

"What are you doing here?" Frankie asked, staring down at the thin white t-shirt she'd worn under her sweater, still suspecting this was all just a dream.

I'll wake up any minute and she'll be gone, and I'll be back in the river with Bill Brewster's gun pointing at my head.

But when she reached out and touched him, her skin incredibly soft and warm on his cold, wet arm, he knew she was real, and that she'd come for him.

Despite everything that had happened, she'd come.

"How'd you find me?" Frankie asked as Sherlock appeared and settled down next to Josie, adding his warmth.

Peyton held up her phone with an embarrassed smile.

"I never stopped tracking your location," she said. "You know what they say. Old habits die hard."

CHAPTER THIRTY-NINE

Josie grimaced as Dr. Habersham's voice filtered through the thick fog of pain that enveloped her. She tried to open her eyes, but they were too heavy, so she focused on listening to the conversation being held beside her.

Where am I and why is Dr. Habersham here? Am I dying?

An image of a hard, cruel face flashed through her mind. A man had come to the house. He'd taken her...

A flash of panic knifed through her.

Granny Davis? Sherlock?

She tried to form the words. She needed to know if they were okay. But her mouth was bone dry, and her throat felt swollen and sore.

"She lost a lot of blood during surgery," Habersham said. "During the transfusion, we used four units which is considerable considering her age and size."

"But, you're sure she's going to be okay now?"

Recognizing Frankie's voice, Josie again tried to open her eyes. A painful flash of bright light caused her to squeeze them closed again.

"The surgeon managed to extract the bullet, which missed any organs but got lodged in her ribcage,"

Habersham said. "So, she has a good chance of making a full recovery."

He cleared his throat.

"And we found something unexpected, although I'm not sure it's relevant at this point."

Before he could continue, there was a knock on the door.

Josie's heart beat faster in her chest. The last time she'd heard a knock on the door, a killer had been on the other side.

Is he still out there somewhere? Has he come back for me?

She willed her legs to move, to prepare to run, but like the rest of her, they refused to respond.

"How's she doing?"

The softly spoken words quelled Josie's panic.

That's Detective Kinsey. She was there when they saved me.

Memories of the river, and the cold, murky water came back to her. Frankie had been there, as had Kinsey and Ranger. They'd hovered over her.

And a woman had taken off her jacket and covered her.

"I was just telling Mr. Dawson and his wife that Josie should make a full recovery," Habersham said. "But we did find something unexpected."

He hesitated, then sighed.

"As I was saying, I'm not sure it's relevant at this point, seeing that the girl's parents are both deceased, but I believe it's best she knows. It could be pertinent in future medical treatment. And as her guardian, I think you need-"

"Just say it," Frankie snapped. "What's wrong with her?"

Habersham cleared his throat again.

"Nothing's *wrong*. But when we were preparing her for the blood transfusion I saw that Josie's blood group is type O. Her father, whom as you know I recently treated for cancer, was AB negative, which is fairly rare."

"So, what does that mean?" Frankie asked.

Again, Dr. Habersham hesitated.

"It means Dwight Atkins isn't Josie's biological father."

The doctor's words echoed in Josie's ears as the room fell silent. No one spoke as a wave of dizziness washed over her.

Dr. Habersham must be lying. Or he must be wrong.

"I just thought someone should know," Habersham said. "Now, I need to move on to my next patient."

As the door clicked shut behind him, Kinsey spoke up in a quiet voice.

"It's true," she said. "I found Cheryl's journals in a trunk in the Atkins' attic earlier today. I scanned through most of them. She knew about Dwight's illegal activities with Shipley, although she didn't mention Bill Brewster."

"And there was something in there about Josie?" Frankie asked. "About her having a different father?"

A shuffling sound was followed by a ruffle of pages.

"It's all in here," she said. "I marked the page. It's best if you read it for yourself. I'm going to collect the bullet from the surgeon. He was supposed to save it for me."

Frankie didn't speak again until Kinsey was gone."

"Peyton, I don't think I can read this," Frankie said. "It's going to break Josie's heart. We should just tear up the page and pretend that idiot Habersham never told us."

"You mean destroy evidence?" Peyton said. "Even if you are willing to do that, isn't it better for her to find out now and deal with it than to find out later in some other way?"

Cursing under his breath, Frankie moved closer.

"Fine. I'll read it. But that doesn't mean I have to tell Josie what it says if I don't like it."

Unable to protest, or even shake her head in dissent, Josie tried to block out Frankie's voice as he began to read.

"The test was positive just as I suspected.

I'm pregnant. And if my dates are right, Dwight isn't the father.

I know I should tell him the truth, but that would break his heart and mine.

Despite everything, I want this child.

And if Dwight left me, I'd be a single mother on my own with a baby to raise.

No, I can't tell him about me and Frankie.

I have to pretend that night never happened.

And if I'm lucky, no one will ever find out."

CHAPTER FORTY

F rankie heard Peyton's soft gasp and looked up, thinking she must be as stunned by what Cheryl had written in the journal as he was. But she wasn't looking at him or at the journal in his hand. She was looking at Josie, who was lying motionless on the bed, her eyes open.

"You...and *my mom?*"

Josie forced the words out in a ragged whisper.

"It was just that once. The night of Franny's funeral."

Stepping up to the bed, Frankie took Josie's hand in his.

"I was a mess. My heart had been ripped out of my chest, and Dwight hadn't even bothered to come to the funeral. I know why he wasn't there now...but back then, it hurt."

Josie studied him with an unflinching gaze that reminded him of Franny, and his heart squeezed.

"After the funeral, I didn't know what to do. Didn't know where to go. So, I showed up at Dwight's place. I wanted to tell him just where he could shove all his bullshit about friendship. But he wasn't there."

Frankie remembered Cheryl standing in the doorway, her sad blue eyes full of compassion as she'd led him inside.

"I broke down. I just lost it."

He'd sobbed on her shoulder like a child while she'd held him and patted his back, telling him it was going to be okay.

"Your mother comforted me. She said Dwight had gone. That they'd argued and he'd stormed out. She didn't know if he was ever coming back."

Images of the long-ago night flashed through his mind. He'd been lost in his grief, and Cheryl had been the only thing to hold on to. He'd pulled her to him, not out of anger, or even desire, but with the desperate need to feel alive.

"I never meant to hurt Dwight. And afterward, I hated myself for betraying him."

He glanced toward Peyton, scared of the condemnation he might see in her eyes, but she was staring toward the window with an unreadable expression, so he turned back to Josie.

"I was a coward, I admit it. I couldn't face him."

Thinking back to those dark, chaotic days after the funeral, Frankie shook his head.

"And I couldn't face living in the same town without Franny. I thought I'd failed her. That she'd gotten into drugs and overdosed, and I'd let it happen. The shame and the guilt and the regret...it was too much."

"But now you know that Franny didn't overdose," Josie said. "Bill Brewster killed her while she was trying to help her friend. You didn't fail her. It wasn't your fault."

Frankie heard the truth in her words. It felt like a weight had been lifted off his chest for the first time in fifteen years.

Franny's death at Bill Brewster's hand had been a nightmare. It had been a tragedy. But it hadn't been his fault.

And the endless blame had ruined enough of his life.

"I know that now. But at the time, I was a mess. I left town a few days after Franny's funeral. I didn't know about you. I never knew I had a daughter. I just left and-"

"And now you're back," Josie added in a raspy whisper. "You came back when dad needed you. When I needed you."

Hope bloomed inside him at her words.

"Then, you don't hate me?"

Josie shook her head.

"No, I don't hate you. But that doesn't mean..."

She paused, swallowing hard and blinking away tears.

"That doesn't mean my dad isn't my dad anymore."

"Of course, Dwight's your dad," Frankie said, squeezing her hand. "He'll always be your dad, and he'll always be my friend. But I made a promise, and I intend to keep it."

As Josie looked up into Frankie's face, a tear escaped one blue eye and rolled down her cheek.

She tried to speak again, but only managed a cough.

Pouring a cup of water from the pitcher on the bedside table, Frankie held it to her lips, allowing her to take a sip.

"Dad never told you about your sister," she said. "That was wrong. He should have told you Franny's death wasn't an accident. But he was scared of what Bill Brewster would do. He was trying to protect *me*."

"I know," Frankie said, watching as Josie yawned and her eyes grew heavy. "And that's what I plan to do from now on. I'll stay here, and I'll protect you."

* * *

Frankie turned the Mustang onto Ironstone Way and drove to the end of the long, winding street. A big white van and a black Ford Interceptor were parked in front of the Atkins house, blocking the driveway.

Parking his car along the curb, he climbed out and stood at the end of the drive. He hadn't expected the evidence response team to still be there.

"Mr. Dawson?"

Special Agent Kade Mabry had appeared beside the van.

"I stopped by to pick up some clothes and stuff for Josie," Frankie said. "She's getting out of the hospital today."

"That's wonderful news," Kade said, leading Frankie toward the house. "We're almost done here anyway."

They waited as a crime scene technician in white coveralls carried a heavy box through the front door, then stepped inside the foyer.

Frankie looked down, picturing Cheryl's sprawled body, half-expecting to see her blood at his feet, but all evidence of the violence had been washed away.

He turned his eyes to the stairs and raised an eyebrow.

"Am I okay to go up there on my own to grab some clothes for Josie, or do I need an escort?" he asked.

"I'll go up with you," a voice said from behind him.

Turning around, he saw Nell Kinsey in the doorway.

"Does this mean she's ready to go home?"

Frankie nodded, feeling a sudden surge of gratitude toward the woman who'd discovered his connection to Josie.

"Yep, but she needs some clothes, and she wants her phone. You know how teenagers are."

Kinsey grinned at the comment.

"Sounds as if things are going well with you two?"

There was a conspiratorial gleam in her eyes, and Frankie was suddenly sure she hadn't told anyone else in the department that he was Josie's biological father as well as her new guardian.

The information might come out eventually, but he was confident it wouldn't come from Kinsey.

"It's as good as can be expected, considering," he replied. "How's it going with the investigation? Did you find enough evidence to prove Bill Brewster was your guy?"

Following him up the stairs, Kinsey began to fill him in on the progress they'd made.

As Frankie stuffed some jeans and t-shirts into a pink gym bag, she told him they'd found enough evidence, between Bill Brewster's place and Otto Shipley's home office, to arrest Officer Jackson as well as a recently retired BCPD detective, and two long-time employees at Atkins Barrel Works.

"Kade thought there'd be more people involved," she said. "But he figures Shipley was trying to shut down his illegal dealings before he reached retirement."

Kinsey opened a drawer and pulled out a stack of underwear and a few bras. She tucked them into the gym bag for him, then added a hair brush off the dresser.

"I think the chief was trying to contain Bill Brewster until he was ready to ride off into the sunset and disappear."

Reaching into the closet, Frankie picked up some flipflops and a pair of tennis shoes, then followed Kinsey back down to the first floor.

Ranger and Kade stood by the front door.

"I've got a question for you," Frankie said as he stopped in front of the men. "Do you think Shipley knew Bill Brewster was the Wolf River Killer? Do you think he just let him keep on killing anyway?"

Kade shrugged his wide shoulders.

"We can't be sure he knew Brewster was responsible for the bones," he said. "But he had to suspect he killed Dwight and Cheryl. Why else would he try to stop Josie from talking? Shipley knew if Brewster was caught, he'd likely go down with him."

The mention of Josie reminded Frankie why he was there.

"I've got to get to the hospital," he said, looking at his watch and moving toward the door. "Catch you all later."

He'd made it halfway to the Mustang when he heard Kinsey calling his name.

He turned around to see her running after him.

"One more thing," she said, lowering her voice. "We found some legal documents in there. Dwight and Cheryl both had wills. It looks like they've left everything in trust for Josie. The house and the business. And they've named you as her guardian until she's eighteen."

Kinsey paused as if expecting some sort of reaction, but Frankie just nodded, still trying to process the information.

"The feds will probably be done with the place in the next day or two if you were wanting to bring her back here."

Frankie studied the big house, looking up at the window where he first saw Josie's pale face in the moonlight.

"Oh, we'll be back here at some point," Frankie said. "But

for now, I better go. I don't want to keep my girls waiting."

* * *

Peyton was sitting next to Josie's hospital bed running a comb through the girl's fine, blonde hair when Frankie returned with the gym bag.

Once Josie had changed into faded jeans and a loose white t-shirt, Frankie gingerly lowered her into a waiting wheelchair and pushed her out to the car.

When they pulled up to the house on Monarch Avenue, Granny Davis was standing on the porch next to Sherlock, who barked an excited greeting and ran forward.

"Down, Sherlock!" Frankie called, scared the dog would hurt the girl's delicate ribs if he jumped up on her.

But Josie was thrilled to see the Lab, and she managed to scratch him behind the ears as Frankie helped her into the house and settled her onto the sofa.

"Peyton told me Sherlock's a private investigator, too. She said he's your partner," Josie said. "Is that true?"

"Of course, it's true," Frankie confirmed. "He's the one who tracked you down. Sherlock's a top-notch investigator."

Josie's smile turned into a giggle when Sherlock barked at the sound of his name and ran to the door.

"Looks like somebody's ready for a walk," Peyton said, plucking the leash off the hook by the door.

"Granny and I can make Josie something to eat while you take him out," Arlene offered. "Franny always loved my grilled cheese sandwiches. And I think we have carrot sticks."

Leaving his mother fussing over the girl, Frankie followed Peyton and Sherlock outside.

"I'm heading back to Willow Bay first thing in the morning," she said as they stepped onto the sidewalk. "I've missed too much work already."

"Tell them you quit."

Frankie stopped to take her hand in his.

"Move up here and stay with us."

She sighed but didn't pull her hand away.

That was a good sign. It gave him hope.

"Look, Frankie, we've been through this already," Peyton said, turning to face him. "Losing our baby...losing our chance to have a family...that changed everything."

"No," Frankie said, tugging her closer. "We have a family. We *are* a family. You, me...and now Josie. We've all been through hell, but somehow, we're standing here together. We've survived by holding on to each other."

He gripped her hands tighter.

"Please, don't let go now."

For the first time since she'd left him, Frankie saw a hint of uncertainty in Peyton's amber eyes.

"I don't know," she said with a sigh. "And we won't even be living in the same city anymore. Not if you stay here."

Frankie's hope faltered, but his voice remained firm.

"I can't leave Josie. And I can't take her away from her home, from everything she knows. She needs to feel safe."

He sighed.

"This is my chance to make up for the years I've missed and all the stupid mistakes I've made."

He shook his head, clearing away the bad memories.

"I ran from here when things got bad. You can see where that got me. I want to teach Josie better than that. No more running away. No more hiding from the past."

Peyton swallowed hard and smiled, but Frankie detected disappointment on her face. Had she wanted him to come back to Willow Bay with her, after all?

"You're going to make a great dad," she said, blinking back tears. "Whether that girl in there knows it or not."

"I'd be a hell of a lot better with you by my side," he said. "I'm going to need you. *We're* going to need you."

She wiped at her eyes and caught sight of Sherlock, who was sitting patiently on the sidewalk as if listening to their conversation.

"Don't you already have a partner?" she asked, flashing him a grin that made Frankie's chest swell with happiness.

"I think Sherlock would be willing to make room for you in the company," he said. "How about Dawson, Dawson & Bell Investigations?"

Rolling her eyes, Peyton shook her head.

"So, the dog comes before me?" she asked.

"He does have seniority," Frankie reminded her. "And besides, Sherlock is a canine prodigy."

The Labrador stood at the sound of his name and tugged Frankie toward the corner. As they walked toward the setting sun, Peyton allowed Frankie to hold on to her hand.

The End

If you enjoyed ***His Soul to Keep***,
you won't want to miss Melinda Woodhall's
Lessons in Evil: A Bridget Bishop FBI Mystery Thriller.

In the first book of the series, criminal psychologist and FBI Profiler Bridget Bishop tackles a chilling string of homicides which bear a startling resemblance to a series of murders committed by a man since convicted and executed for the crimes.
Read on for an excerpt from Lessons in Evil!

LESSONS IN EVIL

A Bridget Bishop Thriller: Book One

CHAPTER ONE

The needle on the gas gauge hovered on empty as Libby Palmer steered her mother's old Buick down the Wisteria Falls exit ramp. The heavy traffic on the interstate had added an extra hour to her drive back from D.C., and Libby had just decided she was going to run out of gas when the Gas & Go sign came into view.

Eyeing the gas station with relief, Libby turned into the parking lot, brought the car to a jerking halt beside an available pump, and shut off the engine with a resigned sigh.

Her trip into D.C. certainly hadn't turned out the way she'd hoped when she'd left home that morning. Despite her new clothes and valiant efforts to impress the hiring manager at the Smithsonian, she was still woefully unemployed.

So much for showing Mom once and for all that majoring in art history wasn't a colossal mistake.

A fat drop of rain plunked onto the windshield and slid down the glass as Libby opened the door and stepped out into the dusky twilight, credit card in hand.

A hand-written note had been taped over the card reader.

Machine broken. Pay inside.

Looking up at the darkening sky in irritation, Libby pulled the hood of her jacket over her dark curls and hurried toward the store. She hesitated as she saw the missing person flyer taped to the glass door.

It was the third time that day she'd seen one of the flyers with a picture of the pretty blonde girl who'd gone missing from her apartment near Dupont Circle the week before.

Brooke Nelson hadn't been seen since; foul play was suspected. The FBI had been asking anyone with information to call a dedicated tip line, and a slew of the flyers had been posted around Washington D.C. and the surrounding area.

"You going in or not?"

A man in a black jacket and faded jeans held the door open, waiting for Libby to pass through.

"Uh...yeah, sorry about that," she said, ducking her head as she stepped into the brightly lit building.

Wrinkling her nose against the pungent scent of stale coffee which hung in the air, Libby made her way to the counter and presented her credit card to the clerk.

"Twenty dollars on pump one," she said, hoping her card wasn't maxed out. "And can I get the key to the restroom?"

The clerk looked her up and down, taking in her disheveled curls and rain-spattered jacket as he handed her a receipt and a silver key on a red plastic keyring.

His eyes held a suspicious gleam.

"Restrooms are outside to the left." He held up her credit card. "You'll get this back when you return the key."

Libby nodded and stepped back, bumping into the solid figure of a man in line behind her.

"Sorry," she murmured, avoiding eye contact as she turned and headed outside.

Keeping her head down against the spitting rain, she hurried around the little building to the restroom, stuck the metal key in the lock, and found the tiny, tiled room surprisingly clean.

She stopped in front of the chipped mirror over the sink, wiping at the mascara smudged under her disappointed brown eyes.

"You didn't want to work at that stupid museum anyway, did you?" she asked her reflection. "I mean, who'd want to live in boring old Washington D.C. when they could live in exciting Wisteria Falls?"

Rain was falling in a steady downpour by the time Libby had returned the key to the clerk, retrieved her credit card, and pumped twenty dollars' worth of gas into the Buick's big tank.

Dropping back into the driver's seat, she started the engine and pulled back onto the highway, lowering the volume on the radio as she picked up speed, uninterested in the local weather and traffic report.

As she drove over Landsend Bridge, she glanced down toward the Shenandoah River but could see nothing of the dark water churning below the metal and concrete structure.

Always fearful the ancient truss bridge might suddenly give way beneath her, Libby drove cautiously, holding her breath until the Buick's wheels were back on solid ground before pressing her foot toward the floor, eager to get home.

She didn't see the girl standing on the side of the road until she rounded the sharp curve just past Beaufort Hollow.

Stomping on the brakes as the Buick's headlights lit up a pale face framed by sodden blonde hair, Libby brought the car to a sudden stop in the middle of the empty road.

Worried another car may round the curve behind her and plow into her rear bumper, she steered the Buick onto the shoulder and shut off the engine.

With a quick glance in the rearview mirror, she climbed out into the rain and ran toward the girl, who stood beside a black sedan. The car's trunk was wide open, and the emergency lights were blinking.

"Are you okay?" Libby called as she approached the car.

The girl's face was hidden in shadow, no longer illuminated by the Buick's headlights, but the jarring blink, blink, blink of the sedan's emergency lights revealed the outline of her bowed head and thin shoulders.

"Did your car break down?"

Libby's question was met with silence. She wondered if the girl had been in an accident. Perhaps a tire had blown.

Maybe she hit her head on the dashboard. Or maybe she...

The thought was interrupted by the girl's raspy whisper, but Libby couldn't make out what she was saying.

Stepping close enough to put her hand on the girl's thin

shoulder, she inhaled sharply.

"You're trembling," Libby said, impulsively pulling off her jacket and draping it over the girl's shoulders. "You must be hurt. Come with me to my car and..."

"Help...me."

As the girl lifted her head, the emergency blinkers lit up a heart-shaped face, which looked strangely familiar.

Libby stared into the girl's tormented blue eyes, her pulse quickening as she pictured the missing person flyer on the door at Gas & Go.

"You're that girl, aren't you? You're Brooke Nelson."

"I'm...sorry," the girl croaked and swayed on her feet as if she no longer had the strength to stand. "I'm so sorry."

The crack of a branch behind Libby sent her spinning around just as a dark figure loomed up in front of her.

A scream froze in her throat as she stared up, gaping in terror. The man's face was half-hidden by the hood of his jacket, but she recognized his cold stare.

Adrenaline shot through her as she saw the knife in his hand. Lunging toward the road in a desperate bid to get back to the safety of the old Buick, she slipped and fell to her knees.

An iron fist reached out and grabbed a handful of her hair.

Snapping her head back, the man pulled her to her feet and wrapped his free arm around her neck.

He tightened his hold until Libby could no longer breathe.

"Brooke and I were...waiting for you," he hissed, his breath coming in excited gasps. "The time...of reckoning is...here."

Waves of dizziness washed over Libby as she scratched and pried at the unyielding arm around her throat, and hot tears blurred the flashing lights around her.

"Stay still...or I'll break your neck."

His breath was hot in her ear as he dragged her toward the open trunk of the sedan, then forced her inside.

She opened her mouth to scream as she looked back and met Brook Nelson's anguished eyes but could only manage a raspy cry before the trunk slammed shut, throwing her into darkness.

* * *

Water trickled somewhere nearby as Libby struggled to open her eyes. Her throat burned, and it was hard to swallow as she blinked around the dimly lit room.

Where am I? What is this place?

Rough walls and a cracked wooden floor held a small metal-framed bed and a straight-backed chair. Rickety stairs led up to a small landing and a narrow door.

"You awake?"

She jumped at the man's voice.

"I thought maybe I'd squeezed too hard."

A dark figure stepped into view. The man who'd forced her into the trunk of his car stared down at her.

"It'd be a shame to go through all that trouble to snatch you only to kill you off so soon."

Studying her face, he reached out a hand to tuck a still soggy curl behind her ear.

Libby cringed in terror but found she couldn't pull away. Her hands were bound to the chair with bright blue duct tape, as were her ankles.

"Where am I?" she croaked, wincing at the pain in her throat. "Why are you doing this?"

He appeared not to have heard her questions as he moved toward the stairs. Propping a booted foot on the bottom step, he stopped and cocked his head as if listening.

"I know what to do," he finally said, giving a resolute nod. "I've read the handbook. I won't take any chances."

Libby looked around the room, confused.

Who's he talking to?

She suddenly remembered Brook Nelson's terrified eyes. The poor girl must have been abducted, too. Was she being held in the same place?

"Where's Brooke?" Libby wheezed out, ignoring the stabbing pain in her throat. "What have you done to her?"

Turning to face her, the man frowned.

"You're not gonna try anything stupid, are you?" he asked, shifting his weight on the creaking wooden floor. "My mentor warned me you'd cause trouble. He told me not to be fooled."

"Who warned you?" she asked, looking up the stairs toward the door. "Is someone else here?"

The man cocked his head.

"I guess you could say that. Now stop asking so many questions. I've got important work to do."

"Please," Libby called out as he turned away. "Tell me what you did to Brooke. Tell me where she is."

Looking over his shoulder, the man shrugged.

"She's served her purpose," he said softly. "As will you."

Continue Reading *Lessons in Evil* from The Bridget
Bishop FBI Mystery Thriller Series

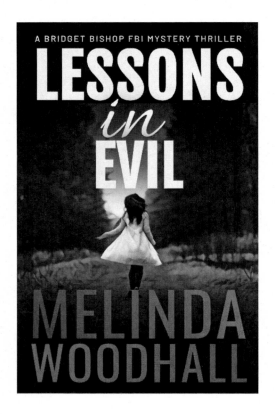

Want More Thrills?

Sign up for the Melinda Woodhall Thrillers Newsletter to
receive upcoming bonus scenes and exclusive insider details
at www.melindawoodhall.com/newsletter

ACKNOWLEDGEMENTS

IT WAS SO MUCH FUN TO PICK UP FRANKIE'S story again after leaving him in Willow Bay at the end of my Veronica Lee series, and I'm truly grateful to the readers who encouraged me to give Frankie his own series. Their positive feedback, along with the constant support of my family, inspired me to write this book.

I couldn't have finished this book on time and with a smile on my face without the loving patience of my husband, Giles, and the constant encouragement of my five fabulous children, Michael, Joey, Linda, Owen, and Juliet.

I also relied heavily on the support and love of my extended family, including Melissa Romero, Leopoldo Romero, Melanie Arvin Kutz, David Woodhall, and Tessa Woodhall.

The joy of writing a book and holding the finished product in my hand always reminds me how lucky I am to have been raised by my mother, an avid, passionate reader, who filled our home and my life with wonderful stories.

ABOUT THE AUTHOR

Melinda Woodhall is the author of heart-pounding, emotional thrillers with a twist, including the *Mercy Harbor Thriller Series*, the *Veronica Lee Thriller Series*, the *Detective Nessa Ainsley Novella Series*, and the new *Bridget Bishop FBI Mystery Thriller Series*.

When she's not writing, Melinda can be found reading, gardening, and playing in the back garden with her tortoise. Melinda is a native Floridian and the proud mother of five children. She lives with her family in Orlando.

Visit Melinda's website at www.melindawoodhall.com

Other Books by Melinda Woodhall

Her Last Summer	*Catch the Girl*
Her Final Fall	*Girls Who Lie*
Her Winter of Darkness	*Steal Her Breath*
Her Silent Spring	*Take Her Life*
Her Day to Die	*Make Her Pay*
Her Darkest Night	*Break Her Heart*
Her Fatal Hour	*Lessons in Evil*
Her Bitter End	*Taken By Evil*
The River Girls	*Where Evil Hides*
Girl Eight	*Road to Evil*